W9-COZ-836

LADY IN DISTRESS

Rosamund Hunter was stranded by the roadside in the beginning of a blizzard when Justin Halliday, the Earl of Wetherby, stopped his coach. There being no inn nearby, he offered to take her to the isolated manor where he was bound.

Rosamund could not question his kindness. She could only say, "I hope Mrs. Halliday will not be too vexed to see me."

The earl nodded to his coachman, who closed the door and climbed back to his perch. Only then did the earl remark, "There is no Mrs. Halliday. Indeed, there is no one else there but servants."

Lord Wetherby may have saved Rosamund from death. But would her fate in his hands be better or worse . . . ?

MARY BALOGH, who won the *Romantic Times* Award for Best New Regency Writer in 1985, has since become one of the genre's most popular and bestselling authors. She also won the Waldenbooks Award for Bestselling Short Historical in 1986 for *The First Snowdrop* and the *Romantic Times* Reviewer's Choice Award for Best Regency Author in 1988, the Waldenbooks Award for Bestselling Short Historical in 1989 for *The Obedient Bride* and a *Romantic Times* Lifetime Achievement Award in 1989.

Snow
Angel

Mary Balogh

A SIGNET BOOK

SIGNET
Published by the Penguin Group
Penguin Books USA Inc., 375 Hudson Street,
New York, New York, 10014, U.S.A.
Penguin Books Ltd, 27 Wrights Lane, London W8 5TZ, England
Penguin Books Australia Ltd, Ringwood, Victoria, Australia
Penguin Books Canada Ltd, 2801 John Street,
Markham, Ontario, Canada L3R 1B4
Penguin Books (N.Z.) Ltd, 182-190 Wairau Road,
Auckland 10, New Zealand

Penguin Books Ltd, Registered Offices:
Harmondsworth, Middlesex, England

First published by Signet, an imprint of New American Library,
a division of Penguin Books USA Inc.

First Printing, June, 1991

10 9 8 7 6 5 4 3 2 1

1

It's going to rain," Rosamund Hunter said, leaning toward the window of the carriage and looking up to the heavy gray sky.

"Snow," her brother said, glancing through the opposite window. "It's going to snow."

Rosamund looked across at him and laughed. "Even about the weather we must quarrel," she said. "It has not been a very relaxing journey, has it, Dennis? You will be sorry you came for me at all and did not leave me to rusticate in Lincolnshire."

"Snow is nothing to laugh at," Dennis Milford, Viscount March said. "It could seriously delay our journey. We have two more days to go even if the roads remain clear."

"I would not relish a few days snowbound at an inn, I must confess," Rosamund said. "We must hope that on this occasion I am right and those clouds shed rain rather than snow."

"Besides," her brother said, "I would not have left you in Lincolnshire, Rosa. Not once your year of mourning was decently at an end. And not when Lana and I had found someone else interested in you."

Rosamund tapped one gloved hand sharply on the window ledge, deciding whether she would take the bait or not. But she could not resist. It was not in the way of things—and never had been—for her and her brother to agree on much. And it had certainly never been their way to agree to disagree. Confrontation was the only way they had been able to approach each other.

"I thought we had said everything that was to be said on

that topic yesterday," she said, not even trying to hide the annoyance from her voice, "and the day before. And the day before that."

"The Reverend Tobias Strangelove is perfectly eligible," Lord March said, "and eager to meet you again when we go to Brookfield next month."

"Poor Toby," Rosamund said. "He has been at a disadvantage since the day of his birth with a name like that, hasn't he? I was moderately fond of him, Dennis, when we were growing up. But my feelings never went beyond fondness. Indeed, I always feel the urge to yawn whenever I think of him, which is not a kind thing to say at all, is it? I wish you had not encouraged him in the impression that I might be eager for his addresses. Just as if I were your daughter and not your sister."

"You must admit that he is closer to you in age than Hunter was," he said.

"Doubtless there are many thousands of other gentlemen closer to my age that Leonard was," she said. "It would be tedious to consider them all as prospective husbands, though."

"You cannot have had much of a life with him," Lord March said. "I always felt guilty for having allowed you to marry him."

"What nonsense," she said. "You had to give your consent, I suppose—I was only seventeen. But I chose Leonard, remember, not you. I do not recall being prepared to take no for an answer. And I had a very good life with him, I thank you." She spoke curtly. "I know it must be the common belief that I could not have been happy with a man thirty-two years my senior, and one who was portly and quite bald even when I married him. You were probably delighted for me when he released me by dying just eight years later."

"Not delighted, Rosa," he said. "How could I be delighted with my brother-in-law dead and you in mourning? Give me credit for some feelings."

"Well, I was happy with him," she said defiantly, tears of mingled anger and grief in her eyes. "He was the kindest man ever to live, and I wish he had lived to be ninety. Although even then I would not have been quite sixty." She sighed.

"Anyway," Dennis said briskly after reaching across the carriage to pat her on the hand, "it's time to forget him, Rosa. He has been dead for fifteen months. It's time to look about you for someone else."

"I shall do so," she said, "in my own time and my own way. I don't need your help, Dennis, thank you. I am your sister, even though I'm fifteen years younger than you. I am not your daughter. You can use all your energies on matchmaking for her, and have clearly been doing just that."

"My mother-in-law chose my daughter's husband nine years ago, and Lana and I approved even at that time," he said. "last year she was old enough for them to ask formally for her and I gave my consent. She is agreeable. Anna does not rebel merely because her parents and her grandparents have chosen an eligible husband for her, you see, Rosa. She trusts us to make a wise choice and to have her best interest at heart."

"That is very satisfactory for all of you," Rosamund said dismissively. She looked up to the sky again and shivered. She hoped they would not be stranded by snow at some wayside inn. Such a delay in returning to his wife and daughter would make Dennis a very disagreeable companion, and the two of them would doubtless spend every waking moment quarreling. She had almost forgotten what it was like to bicker. She and Leonard had never done so.

She looked across the carriage at her brother, who was staring moodily from his window. He was putting on weight about the middle and he had begun to comb his hair across the top of his head from a low side parting to hide his thinning fair hair. And yet he was still a good-looking man. And she was fond of him. She always had been, despite the constant quarrels before she had married and gone into Lincolnshire with her husband.

Had they quarreled so much before Papa died when she was ten years old? she wondered. It was hard to remember. Perhaps the antagonism had developed only from the awkward situation that had succeeded his death. Dennis had already been married to Lana and apparently very happy with her. It had been a brilliant match for him, Lana being the daughter of the Marquess of Gilmore and enormously wealthy in her own right. And they had already had an infant daughter. Rosamund had suddenly felt like a stranger in her own home, though Lana had always been kind to her and Dennis had done his best to be a father to her.

That had been the trouble, of course. He had not been content to be her brother. He had tried to take Papa's place. And she had resented that horribly—and he doubtless had resented having a rebellious young sister on his hands when he had his own family to concern himself with.

Rosamund sighed inwardly. She probably would not have married Leonard at the age of seventeen if life at home had not seemed so intolerable. But she had gone to Bath for a month with Dennis and Lana and Lord and Lady Gilmore, and at the end of the month she had been betrothed. A month later she had been married, five months before her eighteenth birthday.

She had never regretted her decision. She had known that her father had not been a wealthy man and that her dowry was small. She had quarreled loudly with Dennis on several occasions when he had expressed his intentions of adding to that dowry himself. She would not be beholden to him, though of course she could not dream of a brilliant match with her dowry. Sir Leonard Hunter had not been a wealthy man, but he had been well connected and the head of an old, respected family. More to the point, she had liked him, and she had married him.

She was not sorry. They had spent a happy eight years together despite appearances. She would not change her decision even if she could go back now and do so.

"Hunter might at least have left you a decent competence," Lord March said after they had been silent for a few minutes.

"The property had to be left to his nephew," she said. "There was not a great deal else. He left me as much as he could and trusted that Felix would provide me with a home and an allowance. He has done so for the past fifteen months."

"You don't need to live like a poor relation," Lord March said.

Rosamund clamped her teeth together hard and stared sightlessly from the window. She could feel fury boiling inside her, perhaps because her brother had hit on a raw nerve.

"Not when Tobias can be brought to the point with no effort at all," her brother added.

She turned to him, her eyes flashing. "So that is what this is all about," she said. "Finally we arrive at the full truth. You are afraid I am going to be a burden on you, a fading poor relation to be provided for for the rest of my days." She knew she was being unfair. But anger is not a rational emotion, and neither is hurt pride.

"Don't be ridiculous," he said, raking her with scornful eyes. "You a fading creature!" He clucked his tongue.

"I would not dream of imposing on your charity," she said with great dignity. "You need not fear it, Dennis. And you do not need to sell me to the first bidder, either. I will find my own husband, thank you kindly. And I will do it quickly to get myself off your hands."

"Don't be ridiculous," he repeated, and kept his eyes resolutely on the scenery beyond the carriage window.

"That is all I am to you, is it not?" she said. "I am ridiculous and a nuisance and a burden. And I must be treated like merchandise. Toby Strangelove, indeed! I should have stayed where I was. Felix did not need the house—he lives in London. And he never so much as hinted that I was unwelcome there."

"You are still a spitfire at the age of six-and-twenty," he said. "I thought you might have changed, Rosa. I thought perhaps Hunter would have tamed you."

"You probably imagined him taking a whip to me every day," she said. "He happened to love me, Dennis, difficult as that may be for you to comprehend. He was unfailingly courteous to me. He did not constantly bicker with me."

Lord March tossed a look at the roof of the carriage. "In the last few days," he said, "I have sometimes wished that I had left you where you were. Life has been peaceful for the past nine years. I begin to wonder why I came for you. You are obviously not grateful."

"Oh," she said. "Stop this carriage immediately. I am getting out."

Lord March favored the roof of the carriage with another look. "And walking back to Lincolnshire, doubtless," he said. "Be thankful I don't take you at your word, Rosa."

"I am getting out," she said, leaning forward before her brother realized what she was about and rapping sharply on the front panel for the coachman to stop. "I am sorry in my heart that I came, and I have no intention of riding another mile with you."

The carriage drew to a halt.

"Don't be ridiculous," Lord March said.

"I have every intention of being just that," she said coldly, "since that is what you clearly expect of me."

A footman opened the door and peered in.

"The steps, please," Rosamund said.

"Don't be ridiculous," Lord March said.

She buttoned her cloak at the chin and retied the strings of her bonnet. She grasped her reticule. "You may hand me out," she said to the footman.

"You expect me to beg you to stay, don't you?" Lord March said. "You expect me to grovel at your feet and apologize for every fancied insult. You may put up the steps," he said to the footman. "It would serve you right if I let you go, Rosa."

Rosamund held out an imperious hand to the footman. "You may hand me down," she said icily.

The servant looked uncertainly to his master.

"Well, go then," the viscount said irritably. "If you are determined to be so foolish, go ahead. I hope it does snow."

"Thank you," Rosamund said with exaggerated courtesy to the footman as he assisted her down onto the roadway. She looked up into the scowling face of her brother. "Do have a pleasant life, Dennis."

She turned and walked resolutely away along the road, in the direction from which they had come. She was walking into the teeth of an icy wind, she found. And there was already snow sifting down.

How ridiculously she was behaving, she thought as she listened to the horses clopping off into the distance. Dennis was quite right. She had forgotten about such childish rages. It was mortifying to know that she was still capable of them at the age of six-and-twenty.

She smiled as she drew her cloak more closely about her and shivered. For how long would Dennis punish her? She wondered. How long would it be before he had the carriage turned in order to come after her? And when he came up to her, should she accept the olive branch graciously and smile at him? Even laugh, perhaps? Or should she remain icily cold and pretend that she was surprised to see him, and not altogether pleased?

She shivered again. It would not be difficult to act icily cold. The wind paid no heed whatsoever to her heavy winter cloak but seemed to be penetrating to the very marrow of her bones. The snow was turning from sleet to thick white flakes.

Viscount March, inside the carriage, was mentally estimating how far two miles was. He would allow the carriage to continue for two miles before ordering it to turn back for Rosamund. It would serve her right if he went five—or ten. It would serve her right if he did not go back for her at all.

Accusing him of being mercenary, indeed. Accusing him of wanting to marry her off just because she would be a burden on him. All he wanted was to see her happily and respectably married. That was all he had ever wanted. It had fairly broken his heart nine years before when she had insisted on marrying Hunter, a baronet who had been close to fifty at the time and who had looked ten years older. And even that time she had done it because she had felt herself a burden on him and Lana and Anna.

Ridiculous woman. It would serve her right if he left her to freeze out on the road. Had they traveled two miles yet? It must be pretty close, perhaps even a little more. It was far enough, anyway. She must be chilled through to the bone, and sure enough, it was starting to snow in earnest. By the time he picked her up, turned around, and found the nearest inn, there was like to be snow on the road. He hoped it was just a passing shower.

Yes, this was far enough. He leaned forward to tap on the front panel. But before he could do so, the coach lurched alarmingly to one side and he was thrown forward and sideways to land painfully nose-first against the opposite seat.

The carriage had lost a wheel.

It was snowing—not just sleet but fluffy white flakes, the kind that stuck. And they were coming down faster and thicker every moment.

Well, the Earl of Wetherby thought, relaxing back against the comfortable cushions of his traveling carriage, he must be almost there now—*there* being Price's hunting box in Northamptonshire. He had been watching the clouds with an apprehensive eye ever since noon, afraid that they would empty their load before he could reach his destination. The very last thing he wanted to do was be forced to spend a day or two snowbound at a country inn.

But he must be almost there. The house could be no more than a few miles distant.

It would be entirely in keeping with this whole fiasco, of

course, if he were forced to put up at an inn. Indeed, it was amazing that the snow had not come down a few hours before. Even now, he noticed, sitting forward in his seat and looking out into the late-afternoon twilight, the snow had settled in a thin film on the road and hedgerows.

And what the devil was he doing in the middle of Northamptonshire headed toward a hunting box he had never seen before, quite alone? He might have been comfortable in his town house in London or in the reading room at White's or in Jude's boudoir.

No. He frowned. Not at Jude's—not with her sneezing and wheezing and barking all over him. Comfound it, he had planned things so carefully. He was to be officially betrothed to Annabelle in one month's time—if she accepted him, that was, and there seemed to be no reason why she would not. Certainly there was no way he could now avoid it, even though no public announcement had been made yet and even though his official offer had not been made to her yet. But he had finally bowed to the persuasions of his mother and his own sense of responsibility and spoken to the girl's father. And his mother was delighted, and his sisters.

Who was he, then, to be undelighted? No one had held a pistol to his temple and forced him to this turning point in his life. And there was no point in getting cold feet now when his decision had been made and voiced.

He was to be thirty years old in three months' time—a dangerous age for a man, it seemed, especially when that man happened to be a wealthy and landed member of the British aristocracy. It was perfectly acceptable to be twenty-nine and single. One was merely still sowing one's wild oats. It was not acceptable to be thirty and single. One was being selfish and endangering one's succession. It was time to set up one's nursery. And he had come to accept the inevitable, however reluctantly.

Lord Wetherby sighed and crossed his booted ankles on the seat opposite the one on which he sat. If the deed must be done, Annabelle was a perfectly good choice. She was rather lovely and seemed sensible enough. And he had known for several years that when he did get around to marrying, he would be expected to choose her as his bride. His mother had had her heart set on it for years. He had not fought her wishes, since he had no real objection to them and knew no other lady whom he preferred.

He would not think about it anymore. He would marry the girl and get on with the next phase of his life. He would be reasonably contented once he got used to it, he supposed, but he did resent the way things had turned out for this particular week. He resented it bitterly. He had one month of freedom left, and look what had happened to it.

He had an annoying belief in marital fidelity. Annoying, because it was not a belief shared by many of his peers. Many men of his acquaintance seemed to have perfectly satisfactory marriages and yet a cozy little love nest set up somewhere, too. And annoying because he was satisfied with Jude. She had been his mistress for almost a year, and she knew just how to please him. It was a comfortable relationship, and the thought of having to end it irritated him. The thing was that he could not even extend the liaison until the day of his wedding, whenever that was to be—doubtless he would find out soon enough. Oh, no, he knew that he would feel obliged to see the last of Jude as soon as his betrothal was an accomplished fact.

They were to have had a week together at Price's hunting box, with Price and his latest ladybird—a last hurrah to freedom. And then Price's aunt had decided to leave this world at a most untimely moment, the day before their planned departure, with the result that Price had had to stay for the funeral. He had been very decent about the whole thing, though. Wetherby and Jude must still go into North-amptonshire, he had insisted. He would send word to the two servants he kept there.

But on the morning of their departure, when he had driven up to the house where he kept Jude, a trunk full of new clothes and finery for her strapped to the back of his carriage, he had found her in bed with watering eyes and a hacking cough and a running nose and a raging fever. He had sent a servant to summon a physician, accepted her offer not to feel obliged to kiss her, and climbed back into his carriage.

To return home, defeated? No. Inexplicably, he had given his coachman the signal to begin the journey that had been planned for four passengers but instead had only one.

What was he doing? How was he to enjoy a final week of freedom all alone in the middle of nowhere? And doubtless he was going to be very much alone. He put his face close to the window and gazed along the road. It was all whiteness. And there seemed to be plenty more snow ready to fall. He was going to be incarcerated in that house for days. By the time he got out of there, he would probably be screaming for company—any company—to ease his loneliness.

He saw the figure by the roadside at the same moment as his coachman. Certainly the carriage lurched to a stop as Lord Wetherby was raising his hand to knock on the front panel. Whoever it was was hunched up, head down, trudging in the opposite direction from that being taken by the carriage. Making for some cottage? But he had noticed no habitation for the last several miles.

It was a woman, he saw as his coachman hailed her and she looked up. And no country girl, either. Her bonnet was fashionable and her cloak of good fabric, though both were liberally covered with snow. He opened the door and vaulted out into snow that was already ankle-deep.

"It is quite all right," she was telling the coachman. "My brother will be along for me in just a moment." Her teeth were chattering.

"Has your carriage met with some accident, ma'am?" the earl asked her.

Dark eyes were directed his way from a heart-shaped face with bright red cheeks, chin, and nose. "Oh, no," she said. "It is quite all right, I do assure you. I just got down to walk for a while, but Dennis will be back for me soon."

The earl peered ahead through the snow, but there was

neither sight nor sound of an approaching carriage. She had got down to walk? In a snowstorm?

"We quarreled, actually," she said in a rush by way of explanation. Her teeth chattered again.

"It looks as if you have been walking for some time, ma'am," the earl said. "And it is beginning to get dark. Do, please, allow me to take you up."

She looked somewhat wistfully up into the interior of the carriage. "Dennis will have a heart seizure if he does not find me," she said. "I had better keep walking, sir. But I thank you."

She tried to smile, but it seemed that her facial muscles would not quite obey her will.

"May I present myself?" he said. "Justin Halliday at your service, ma'am."

"I am pleased to meet you, Mr. Halliday," she said. "Rosamund Hunter."

"We will keep a watch out for your brother's approach from the carriage," he said, reaching out a hand for hers. "I cannot leave you here, Miss Hunter, and risk becoming a murderer." He smiled.

"Oh, perhaps I will, then," she said, putting one gloved hand in his. "I had no idea it was possible to be quite this cold." Her teeth clacked together as he released her hand, took her by the waist, and lifted her into his carriage before jumping in after her and closing the door.

"He said it would snow," she said as the earl took a heavy blanket from the opposite seat and spread it over her knees. "He will be pleased that he won that argument at least."

"Do you mean," he said, "that you have been walking since before the snow began, Miss Hunter? But that must be more than an hour?"

"Is that all?" she said. "It seems more like three. He must be very angry with me. And I am not a miss. I am a widow."

"I'm sorry," he said.

"Yes," she said, "so am I. If Leonard were only still alive, I would not have found myself on this road today arguing with Dennis."

"You're very cold," he said. "Pull the blanket up over your shoulders."

"I think I will," she said, clamping her teeth together to stop them from rattling. And she drew the blanket up to her chin. She regarded him candidly from her dark eyes and laughed. "How do I know that you are not a highwayman abducting me?"

"In a carriage?" he said. "With no pistols and no mask? Where would be the romance, ma'am?"

"I don't know about romance," she said, "but I do know that it would be dreadfully unpleasant to be on horseback with you at this moment if you really were a highwayman. Dennis is going to give me a thundering scold for allowing myself to be taken up like this. He likes to treat me as if I am a little child just because he is fifteen years older than I and was my guardian from the time our father died when I was ten until I married at the age of seventeen."

"Better that he be annoyed with you than grief-stricken to find your frozen body against a hedgerow," he said.

She laughed. "I daresay you are right," she said. "He must have been very angry. I thought he would have gone three miles at the farthest before turning back for me."

The carriage stopped again at that moment and the coachman opened the door after knocking on it.

"This is where we turn off, sir," he said. "Another two, three miles down this road if I have the rights of it. What about the lady?"

The earl turned to look at her.

"Another hour or less," the coachman said, "and the roads are going to be impassable."

"You had better come with me," the earl said to Rosamund.

"But Dennis will have an apoplexy," she said.

Lord Wetherby thought that Dennis probably deserved an apoplexy, but he did not say so.

"If I knew of an inn farther along the road," he said, "or if I knew this country at all, Mrs. Hunter, I would take you farther. But I might be taking you into greater danger. The house I am making for is close. I believe we have no choice but to go there. Your brother will surely realize that you have taken shelter somewhere.''

"Oh, dear," she said, "I should not have been so foolish, should I? He told me I was being ridiculous.''

"Shall we continue along this road for a while, then?" the earl asked.

She looked at him with sudden decision. "No, Mr. Halliday," she said, "I would not inconvenience you so. I will have to come with you and hope to find Dennis tomorrow. I hope Mrs. Halliday will not be too vexed to see me."

The earl nodded to his coachman, who closed the door and climbed back to his perch. The carriage was soon in motion again, turning sharply to the right.

"There is no Mrs. Halliday," Lord Wetherby said with a smile. "Indeed, there is no one else there except for two servants. I am borrowing a friend's hunting box for a week. There will be just you and I, Mrs. Hunter."

"Oh, dear," she said. "It sounds quite shockingly improper." She looked at him and laughed.

Despite the rosiness of her cheeks, nose, and chin, and the dampness of her dark hair beneath a bedraggled bonnet, she was really remarkably pretty, the Earl of Wetherby noticed for the first time.

2

The house was a hunting box? That was what her companion had said. But Rosamund, gazing out through the carriage window onto a predominantly white world, found herself looking at a quite imposing gray stone house. Obviously whoever had built it had intended to have large hunting parties. There must be at least eight bedchambers abovestairs and as many rooms below.

The snow was still whirling thickly down and had settled at an alarming speed. The coachman had to kick it aside before lowering the carriage steps outside the door of the house, and when her companion went down them in order to hand her out, his booted feet completely disappeared into the whiteness.

Dennis was going to be furious. And frantic. And what about him? Would he be hopelessly lost and stranded looking for her?

"Your brother will not take foolish risks," the earl said, guessing her thoughts as she put her hand in his and set her foot on the top step. "And he will guess that you have found shelter somewhere. There is really no alternative, ma'am, but to relax here until the storm has passed and the roads have cleared."

"Yes," she said, joining him in the snow, "you are quite right, sir."

A manservant opened the door of the house and ushered them into a tiled hallway from which a stairway rose straight to the floor above. He opened the door into a sitting room after assuring them that there was a fire in there.

"I shall tell Mrs. Reeves that you have arrived, sir," he said, "and have her bring you some refreshments."

"Ah, warmth," Rosamund said, crossing the room and holding her hands out to the fire. "Blessed warmth."

Lord Wetherby made his way to a sideboard on which were glasses and several decanters. "Brandy is what we both need," he said. "I hope you do not get a chill out of your ordeal."

"Oh, I never take chills," she said, but she took the glass from his outstretched hand. She frowned at the amber liquid. "I have never tasted it. Is it very strong?"

"Drink it in one gulp," he said. "It will warm you from the inside."

"A prospect not to be resisted," she said. She swirled the brandy around in the glass a few times the way she had seen Leonard do it, lifted it to her lips, and tossed back its contents. She swallowed . . . and clutched first her throat and then her stomach. She coughed and thrust the empty glass at her companion.

He laughed. "It will feel good once you have recovered from the shock," he said.

Rosamund continued to cough. "Poison," she said with a gasp. "I'm going to die."

"No," he said, "I assure you you are not."

She felt warmth spread inside her and managed to get the coughing under control. And she glanced at the man who was standing three feet in front of her, his own glass still in his hand. He was laughing at her, his eyes dancing with merriment. And she noticed suddenly and for the first time that he was a very handsome man.

His teeth were white and even and his eyes were very blue: a quite lethal combination, she decided. His hair was fair and wavy and rather too long—too long by fashionable standards, though not by any standards of attractiveness. He was half a head taller than she, slim, and yet not puny, either. Oh, no, definitely not puny. The slimness related to his waist and hips. He had muscles in all the right places.

Carriages were noisy things, Rosamund realized suddenly. Lack of conversation was not noticed in a carriage. Not that there had been any lack of conversation there. But the sitting room in which they stood seemed very quiet.

He was still smiling. "Have you decided to survive?" he asked.

"It was very unkind of you not to warn me," she said.

"Had I allowed you to sip at it," he said, "you would have grimaced after the first sip, as I have seen so many ladies do, and refused to take another drop. Don't you feel warmer now?"

Considerably warmer. "Yes, thank you," she said. "I do."

Fortunately for her poise and dignity the door opened at that moment to admit the woman who served as cook, housekeeper, and maid all in one. And Rosamund blessed her silently. She was clearly a garrulous soul.

"What a blessing it is that you arrived safe and sound," she said, bustling over to a table and setting down a large tray. "They won't come today, I told Reeves. Not in this weather they won't. But, then, it would have been such a shame to have had to spend goodness knows how many days at an inn. The linen is never aired or the food decent in inns, is it, madam? I have brought you some tea and cakes and bread and butter. The liquor is over there, sir. Oh, you have found it, I see. And a good thing, too. I'm sure you need warming. I'm Mrs. Reeves at your service. Mr. Price did not name the gentleman we were to expect."

"Halliday," the earl said quickly. "Justin Halliday. And Mrs. Hunter."

Mrs. Reeves looked assessingly at Rosamund and then at the earl. "Reeves has carried your trunks up to the main bedchamber, sir," she said. "There is a fire burning there and all the sheets have been properly aired, I do assure you, ma'am."

Rosamund was speechless at the implications.

"You will need to prepare another room, if you please, Mrs. Reeves," Lord Wetherby said. "Please move my things into it. Mrs. Hunter will occupy the main bedchamber."

"I shall see to it at once," Mrs. Reeves said. "Don't worry, sir, about the chills or damp sheets. I aired out the green room too until we heard yesterday that Mr. Price would not be coming."

"Thank you, Mrs. Reeves," the earl said dismissively.

"Oh, dear." Rosamund looked down at her plain woolen dress after the housekeeper had hurried from the room. "All my things are in Dennis' carriage."

"Well," Lord Wetherby said with a grin, "I shall not expect you to dress formally for dinner, Mrs. Hunter."

She gazed ruefully at her half-boots, which she still wore, and thought of comfortable slippers and warm nightgowns and hairbrushes and shawls in her trunk.

"I do have a trunk of ladies' clothes with me," the earl said. He smiled when Rosamund looked up at him in astonishment. "They belong to my, ah, sister. She was supposed to be accompanying me here but had to remain behind with a severe cold at the last moment. She is, I believe, almost your exact size."

Rosamund frowned. Why would Mr. Halliday's sister send her trunk with him if she was not coming herself?

"I took up her trunk the day before our departure," the earl said, "as she was not to be at home the night before. She, ah, stayed with her aunt. With *our* aunt, that is."

"I could not use her things," Rosamund said.

"I do assure you she will not mind at all," he said. "I will have Reeves take the trunks back into your bed-chamber."

"Thank you," she said. "I will not use much, you know. Mainly just a nightgown." She felt herself flushing and wished she could recall the words.

She was too busy with her own discomfort to notice the earl grimace and close his eyes briefly.

"Will you pour?" he asked, indicating the tray.

Rosamund jumped to her feet and crossed to the table, where she made a great to-do about pouring two cups of tea.

* * *

The Earl of Wetherby sat on in the sitting room after Mrs. Reeves had removed the tray and then returned to show Rosamund to her room. He wished he could have the last half-hour back again.

Mrs. Reeves would doubtless have been able to lend her a few things—slippers, a nightgown, whatever else were necessities for women. Had he had to open his mouth and offer her the trunk of clothes he had bought for Jude? He had wished to bite his tongue out just a few moments after the words had escaped him—as soon as she had mentioned a nightgown, in fact.

Oh, Lord, a nightgown. There were two in the trunk. If they could be called nightgowns, that was. And the other clothes, though not nearly as indecent as those nightgowns, were far more the type of garment one would buy for one's mistress than for one's sister.

Well, the damage was done now, he thought as he crossed the room to pour himself another glass of brandy. And he was not going to lose any sleep over it. She might think what she would. It really did not matter to him, except that he would not wish deliberately to embarrass her.

She was deuced pretty. About the same size as Jude, it was true, though not as curvaceous, perhaps. No less attractive, though. Slenderness could be just as alluring as more generous curves. There was no other similarity between the two women except height. Jude was auburn-haired and green-eyed. Mrs. Hunter had dark hair and dark eyes. Glossy hair and long. She wore it in coils at the back of her head.

She was not only pretty, but also animated, her face eager and mobile when she talked. Damnation! Why could she not look like a horse and bray when she laughed? He did not particularly want to be snowbound with a pretty, animated woman. Oh, correction: he did, he did. But not with a lady. He wanted Jude. The situation would have been perfect. No Price. No Price's ladybird. Snow outside to prevent them from either going out or receiving unexpected callers. Nothing to do all day and all night except make love.

The thing was that he had planned it all out to be a last fling of freedom—one last grand orgy of uninhibited sex and pleasure. And the weather had cooperated beautifully with those plans. Except that the plans had gone awry. He was stuck with the wrong lady—*lady* being the operative word.

Damn! If she weren't so deuced attractive.

Rosamund abovestairs in the main bedchamber, warmed by a roaring fire, unpacked the trunk carefully, examining each garment with curiosity. Mr. Halliday's sister liked bright colors, it seemed. And she favored silks and gauzes and muslins even though it was only the end of January. Fortunately there were a few warm shawls. The sister also favored low necklines. She must have a good bosom, Rosamund concluded.

The sister's feet were one size larger than her own, but that would be no major problem. Rosamund pulled off her boots thankfully and slipped her feet into a pair of soft blue kid slippers.

There were several jars of perfume, all with soft, seductive scents. Rosamund closed her eyes as she sniffed at one of them. Very feminine. Very alluring. Leonard would have liked it. Leonard had liked her to wear perfume. There was a diamond-studded bracelet in a velvet box in the middle of the trunk.

She felt almost as if she were prying—prying into someone else's life. Mr. Halliday's sister must be very lovely, she guessed, and very feminine. She must like to attract gentlemen . . . But, then, what woman did not?

Finally she drew out a nightgown and held it up in front of her. It would not do for winter, she thought as soon as she lifted it from the trunk. It was too light and flimsy. A moment later, when it was hanging straight in front of her, held at arms' length, she looked at it quite disbelievingly. It was sheer white lace, and she could see the bed and the wall opposite through it without any difficulty at all.

My goodness gracious me, she thought and felt herself

flush, it must be an overdress. There must be something to go underneath it. Goodness, one would not wish even one's maid to see one in that. Certainly not one's husband. But then Mr. Halliday's sister was doubtless not married.

She put the nightgown aside and refused to look back at it. But at the very bottom of the trunk she found another, one that made the white one look prim enough to belong to a spinster aunt. This one was of black lace and appeared to have no back and not a great deal of front, either. And when Rosamund held it against herself in some disbelief, she found that it reached barely to her knees.

Goodness gracious! Did Mr. Halliday know? she wondered. She folded both nightgowns and replaced them in the trunk. The other clothes she put away in drawers or hung in the wardrobe. The orange silk she would wear to dinner, she decided, with the paisley shawl and the white slippers. All the clothes, she noticed suddenly and frowned, appeared to be perfectly new.

She would be most interested to meet Miss Halliday. She wondered if Mr. Halliday had some trouble with the girl. Perhaps he was her guardian and had planned to bring her into the country to try to talk some sense into her. She hoped for his sake that the cold had not been a ruse and the girl now rushing all over London being indiscreet.

Poor Mr. Hallilday!

She just wished he were not quite so handsome. It would be very awkward to be trapped alone like this with any gentleman. But to be stuck with a handsome gentleman was embarrassing, to say the least. And a young gentleman, too. She was not used to young men. She felt uncomfortable with them. Most of Leonard's friends had been older gentlemen. She had felt at ease with them.

And she had felt comfortable with him. She felt a sudden longing to have him there with her, large and imposing, with his shining bald head and his double chin and his large hands framing her face and his dry smacking kiss and his kindly smile.

Oh, dear, she did miss him quite dreadfully at times.

The orange gown had been his favorite, the Earl of
Wetherby mused as he sat at dinner with Rosamund, making
polite conversation. He had pictured Jude in it when he
bought it, her large bosom bulging over the low décolletage,
her green eyes squinting at him as she leaned forward to say
something to him. Jude always leaned forward when she was
wearing a low-cut dress. She knew it raised his temperature
a few degrees. And he had imagined how the color would
look with her auburn hair.

And now Mrs. Hunter was wearing it, and with her dark
coloring, it looked quite magnificent. She did not lean toward
him, of course, as she talked, but he could see the beginnings
of a cleavage above the dress. And her breasts looked firm
and alluring against the silk. Her hair was coiled higher on
her head than it had been earlier in the day.

Jude would have looked like an expensive tart in the dress.
Mrs. Hunter looked like a lady. Jude, of course, would not
have worn the shawl. The girl had an endearing lack of
concern for her own comfort when she was bent on luring
him to bed. And she always had a flattering eagerness to get
him there, though he paid her a regular monthly allowance
regardless of the number of times she provided him with that
essential service.

"You look very lovely, Mrs. Hunter," he said, feeling
that her enthusiastic praise of the very ordinary meal before
them were becoming somewhat strained. "I trust you found
everything you needed?"

"Oh, yes, indeed," she assured him, her cheeks flushing
becomingly. "Except a nightgown." Her blush deepened.
"I shall ask Mrs. Reeves if she can lend me one."

"There was no nightgown?" he was unwise enough to ask,
twisting the stem of his wineglass between his fingers.

"Yes, there was," she said. "But not to my taste."

His eyes strayed to her throat and that part of her chest
visible above the gown. They were covered with red
blotches.

"I am sorry about that," he said.

"Is your sister a very young lady?" she asked.

"No," he said. "Both my sisters are older than I." Oh, foolish words. Foolish, foolish words.

"Oh," she said.

He smiled at her.

"Everything is new," she said. "They are not your sister's, are they?"

He twirled the wineglass, lifted it to his lips, and drank from it. She watched his every movement. It was most disconcerting. He wished there were a minstrel gallery with a full orchestra playing a gypsy dance. Or twenty guests sharing the table with them, all engaged in noisy argument.

"No, actually," he said, and smiled again.

"Your mistress's?" she asked.

He continued to smile. "Are you very shocked?" he asked.

She considered a moment. "No," she said. "Why should I be? I do not even know you, sir, and I was not invited here. It would be foolish indeed to sit in moral judgment on you. Was she the one with the cold?"

"Yes," he said.

"How sad for you," she said, "when you had spent so much money on new things for her and had found such a secluded love nest. The bracelet too was a gift?"

"A parting gift," he said. "I am getting married."

"Oh, are you?" she said. "And are dismissing your mistress before you do? I am glad."

What a strange conversation to be having with a lady whom he had met only a few hours before, the earl thought. She appeared to have forgotten her earlier embarrassment, a strange fact considering the turn their talk had taken. Her face had regained the animation he had noticed in his carriage. Her upper lip appeared to be a little fuller than the lower. It was slightly upturned—a most attractive feature. It made one want to reach out a finger to touch it or to lean forward to kiss it.

"And I am glad to meet with your approval," he said.

"The nightgowns," she said, leaning forward so that after

all he could see the tops of rounded breasts as well as the beginnings of cleavage. She was laughing. "Would she really have worn them?"

He leaned back in his chair, his hand still stretched out to twirl his wineglass. He was beginning to enjoy himself. "Perhaps for a few minutes," he said.

She looked at him uncomprehendingly for a moment before flushing again and resuming her upright position in her chair. "Oh," she said, "I see."

"Do you?" he said.

Her eyes danced into merriment and she laughed again. "They are shockingly naughty," she said.

"Yes, aren't they?" he said. "They were chosen with great care."

The earl was somewhat relieved when Mrs. Reeves bustled in at that moment with two dishes of steaming pudding on a tray. He really ought not to have encouraged this line of converstaion. Mrs. Hunter was a lady.

She seemed to feel the same way. She began on another topic when Mrs. Reeves withdrew.

"Are you marrying for love?" she asked.

He was amused. "Why do you ask?"

"Because if you are," she said, "it would seem to me that you would have wanted to break off with your mistress without bringing her here. And if you are not, I wonder that you are breaking off with her at all."

No, perhaps the topic of conversation had not been changed, after all.

"Love is a woman's invention," he said. "Or rather being in love is. Women do not like to admit that they are swayed by a man's looks and sexual appeal. It seems ungenteel to them to be taken with physical attraction. So they dress up their emotions prettily and call them being in love."

"How dreadfully cynical," she said, "and how wrong. My husband was in love with me. He adored me for the eight years of our marriage before he died. I was never in love with him."

Lord Wetherby raised his eyebrows.

"I used to call him silly," she said, "treating me as if I were a fragile doll and setting me on a pedestal as if I were not human at all but some sort of angel. I used to tease him about it, and he used to tell me that one day I would fall in love and I would understand him better."

The earl forgot about his pudding. He was intrigued. Who was the poor fool who had made such an ass of himself?

She leaned forward again, a little more than before, so that he swallowed and returned his attention hastily to his plate. "I loved him, of course," she said. "I loved him more than I ever loved anyone except perhaps Papa. I loved him dreadfully, though he always used to laugh at me when I told him so, and call me a foolish child and tell me I would know one day what it was like really to love."

Her face, Lord Wetherby saw when she straightened a little and he dared to look at her again, was flushed and eager, her dark eyes large and very direct.

"We knew for three years that he was going to die," she said. "I think he suspected even before that. He had a cancer."

"I'm sorry," he said. "That must have been unbearably distressing for a young man."

"He was fifty-seven years old when he died," she said. "But that is not old, is it? I wish he had lived another twenty or thirty years. I wish he had lived forever. I loved him, you see, though I was not in love with him at all."

He looked at her curiously. He would have put her age at no more than two- or three-and-twenty, but she had been married for eight years and her husband must have been dead for longer than a year—she did not wear mourning. She was clearly older then she looked. But even so at least thirty years younger than her husband.

"Do you love her?" she asked. "Even if you are not in love with her, do you love her? Or will you be able to grow to love her?" She spoke quite earnestly and looked at him very directly, as if the answer mattered to her.

"I do not know her well," he said, "though we have been acquainted for many years. But I do believe that marriage should be a total commitment, Mrs. Hunter. I will do my very best to come to care for her."

"Good," she said, picking up her spoon at last and tackling her pudding. "I am glad."

He watched her with amusement.

"How did you come to marry Mr. Hunter?" he asked. "Let me guess. He was very wealthy and your family thought he was a good catch." There was some cynicism in his voice.

"Wrong again," she said, looking up at him with that bright smile that he was finding increasingly attractive. "He was not very rich, though we were quite comfortably well off. And Dennis just about had a fit when I told him Leonard was going to come to offer for me."

The earl settled back in his chair, his wineglass in his hand, and regarded her with a half-smile.

"We were in Bath," she said, "which is reputed to be a town for elderly people these days. But there were some young men there and they acted very silly, the lot of them, and made me dread even going outdoors—always sighing and saying the most outrageous things. Leonard used to come to my rescue and walk me about the Pump Room and sit beside me at concerts. I could relax with him."

The earl was hard-put to it not to show open amusement. Most girls, he suspected, would have reacted in quite the opposite way.

"When he told me that one day I would welcome all the silliness of one of those young men or another like them, I told him I never would. I would rather marry him any day, I told him. He would not believe me at first. It took me several days to convince him. Dear Leonard. He did not want me to tie myself to an old man, he said. I am afraid I won him by trickery in the end." She smiled guiltily at her plate and peeped sideways at the earl.

"Oh?" he said. He had one hand over his mouth. He was

afraid that at any moment he would offend her by laughing out loud. She was a veritable delight.

"When he told me that he would be leaving Bath within a few days," she said, "I threw my arms about his neck and burst into tears and told him that Dennis would marry me to some horrid young man if he did not rescue me. He patted my back and told me he would marry me. And then he told me how he loved me. He never stopped telling me so for the next eight years."

"Very naughty of you," Lord Wetherby said.

"Yes," she said, smiling brightly at him again. "But, you see, it was not all trickery. I really was crying, and Dennis probably really would have married me to someone horrid— or tried, anyway. He is trying it again now."

"Is he?" he said. "Are not matchmaking relatives an abomination."

"Yes," she said, smiling at him. "Is that what has happened to you?"

"Yes, partly," he said.

They smiled at each other with mutual sympathy.

If he did not get out of that room soon, the earl thought, he was going to disgrace himself and terrify Mrs. Hunter out of her wits by leaning forward, taking her chin in his hand, and kissing that very alluring upper lip.

"Are you finished?" he asked, pushing back his chair and getting to his feet. "Shall we move to the sitting room?"

"Would you not rather stay for your port?" she asked.

"No," he said, "I will forgo the pleasure." Though if he were wise, he thought, he would sit over the port for the next two or three hours.

"Leonard never would, either, when we dined alone," she said with a laugh. "He used to say"—she lowered her voice in imitation of a man's tones—" 'Why should I sit alone with the port, dearest, when I can be in the drawing room drinking in the sight of you instead.' He was always being silly, as I said earlier."

Perhaps not so silly, the earl thought, taking her hand on

his arm to lead her from the dining room. Of course, the old codger had been free to take her off to bed with him after drinking of her kisses in the drawing room. As for him, he should have reserved his drinking for the port.

"Cards?" he said as they entered the sitting room. "Do you play?"

"Oh, yes," she said, turning her head to smile up at him. "But I must warn you that I am an expert. My husband was a very good teacher."

"I will not play the gentleman and allow you to win, then," he said. "If you are to win, you must do so by your own skill."

She laughed.

3

Rosamund was sitting on her bed, her knees drawn up against her, her arms encircling them. She felt quite snug and warm with a coal fire blazing in the hearth and one of Mrs. Reeves' voluminous nightgowns covering her from chin to toes.

He had planned to be here with his mistress. In this room. In this bed. She was to have worn one of those nightgowns—for a few minutes. Rosamund felt uncomfortably warm suddenly and plucked the linen away from her, shaking it to create a cool draft.

She wished for perhaps the hundredth time since her arrival that afternoon that he were not so handsome. Although he was very easy to talk to and she could forget herself when they were talking, there were occasional silences—and very uncomfortable they were, too.

They had played cards until nearly midnight—a half-hour before—and spoken scarcely a word, concentrating on the games. At least he had been concentrating. She had lost all but one hand quite ignominiously despite the boast she had made at the start.

She had been too busy being aware of him to be able to concentrate fully, particularly his long-fingered, well-manicured hands. She had kept imagining them stroking over that white lace—for a few minutes. And moving beneath that lace after a few minutes. The trouble was that she had not only seen them doing so in her mind, but had also felt them doing so.

It was hard to concentrate on cards when one was having such lascivious thoughts about one's opponent, unwilling though they had been.

And she was not the only one. Oh, he must have been concentrating harder than she to have won most of the games so handily. But he had not been indifferent to her presence either. His eyes had been on her almost every time she had found the courage to peep up at him—lazy, heavy-lidded, very blue.

It really was a very awkward situation she had found herself in, Rosamund thought, plucking at the nightgown again. And why was she sitting on the bed instead of lying in it at almost half-past midnight? She knew why. Was she going to do it? If so, she might as well get on with it. If not, she might as well blow out the candles and climb beneath the bedclothes and go to sleep. That was what she would do, in fact.

But when he stepped off the bed, she did not pull back the blankets and climb between the sheets as any virtuous and sensible young lady would have been. She crossed the room to the trunk and opened the lid. And drew out the white lace nightgown. She would just look at it.

But looking was not enough. She found herself one minute later undoing the buttons of the flannel nightgown with reluctant, hesitant fingers, drawing the garment off her shoulders and letting it fall in a heap at her feet. She fingered the white lace again, picked the garment up from the bed, and lifted it over her head.

It felt like gentle fingers sliding down her body. She looked down at herself, her face burning hot. She swallowed. She should not. She really should not. But of course she would. She stepped across to the other side of the room, where there was a full-length mirror.

She had always been embarrassed to look at herself naked. She never did so when she stepped out of the bathtub. She was not naked now, of course, but she could see herself clearly through the white lace. It clung to her breasts, half-covering them, narrow straps passing over her shoulders. It fell shimmering to the floor. Her hair, brushed loose down her back, looked very dark in contrast.

Rosamund swallowed again and turned sharply away. Two minutes later the nightgown was folded neatly in the trunk again, the flannel had been donned once again, the candles had been blown out, and Rosamund was in bed, the blankets drawn up about her ears.

She must not do that again.

It was a very naughty garment, she had told him at dinner, and he had agreed. He had chosen it with care, he had said. For how many minutes would his mistress have worn it? she wondered. And when he removed it, would it have been beneath the bedclothes or standing beside the bed? She really did not want to know the answer, she thought, pulling the blankets even higher.

What would it be like to be touched by Mr. Halliday? she found herself wondering a few moments later, totally unable to shut off her mind and address herself to sleep. To have those long, sensitive fingers on her shoulders and arms, in her hair? To be kissed by those well-formed lips? Held against that slim, firmly muscled body? Rosamund shivered ever though the fire still burned cheerfully.

She had begun to wonder about younger men several years before, and had always ruthlessly suppressed the thoughts. She had been too young when she had gone to Bath, and too naïve: she had never been beyond the neighborhood where she had grown up and to Brookfield, the Marquess of Gilmore's home. She had been frightened by the attentions of young men. And she had still been missing her father even though he had been dead for seven years. She was unhappy with Dennis, not because he had ever treated her badly or ever given any indication that she was not welcome in his home, but because he was not her father and had tried to act as if he were.

She had wanted a father, one of the right age and appearance and demeanor. She had chosen Leonard to be her father. Oh, she had not consciously done so, of course. She had taken him as a husband. But she had realized some time after their marriage, when she had grown up a little, that that was what she had done. And he had been a good father to her: kind, indulgent, always willing to listen to her and advise her, always loving.

Of course, he had been a husband, too. They had had a real marriage. He had come to her every Tuesday and Friday nights, when her monthly cycle would allow, and occasionally on Sundays, too. She had not minded. She had never found what he did to her distasteful or repulsive. But she had always been embarrassed by it, even after seven years—he had been too ill in the last year to come to her at all.

It had always seemed like the only shared activity in which they were not together, although it had been the most intimate of all. She had always felt as if he were a million miles away from her in mind. He had always breathed very heavily, sometimes grunting, until he was finished with her. Sometimes, during the seventh year, it had taken him a very long time to be finished.

She had never minded because he was her husband and she knew she gave him pleasure. But she had always been embarrassed. It had not seemed right. It had seemed almost incestuous.

She had begun to wonder about younger men—slimmer men, more-hard-muscled men, more virile men. Men like Mr. Halliday. She pulled the blankets all the way over her head.

Oh, dear, she ought not have gotten out of Dennis' carriage. What a very foolish and childish thing it was to have done. And what disastrous results it was having. She was stranded alone with a man who was supposed to be with his mistress. And she was having thoughts about him that were making her blush down to her toenails.

She hoped the snow would have stopped and the sun would be shining by morning.

The snow was falling thicker than ever the following morning.

"Lord love us," Mrs. Reeves said as she served breakfast,

"it's like as if we have to get a whole winter's worth of snow in two days. I was only saying to Reeves last week, I was, that it looked as if we weren't going to get any this winter, after all. And now look at it."

Lord Wetherby had spent a great deal of time looking at it from the window of his bedchamber that morning. It was impossible to tell where the driveway and the road were.

"It's a good thing you was planning to stay a week, sir," Mrs. Reeves added. "I don't know as how you would be able to get away even if you wanted."

The earl smiled at Rosamund when they were alone. "Are you still worried about your brother?" he asked. "Don't be. There were a coachman and a footman traveling with him, you say? Servants are invariably sensible people. They would not have risked their skins even if he was prepared to risk his. He is shut up inside some inn, fuming at the discomfort and the delay, you may be sure.

"And worrying his head off about me," she said. "Poor Dennis. I always gave him a great deal of grief. He must have been very relieved when Leonard took me off his hands. And now, as soon as he has resumed responsibility of me, I have caused him this monumental worry. I ought not to have got out of that carriage yesterday, should I?"

"We do not always behave rationally when angry," he said. "I'm sure that at the time it seemed the only possible thing to do."

"I have a bad temper, only with Dennis," she said. "I was never angry with Leonard. We never quarreled at all."

Silence fell at the table so that Lord Wetherby could hear himself crunching his toast.

"When do you think the—" she began.

"What do you like to do—" he said at the same moment. She smiled. "What do I like to do?" she asked.

"On snowy days," he said, finishing his sentence.

"Sit and watch it," she said. "Walk in it when it has stopped falling. Make snow angels. I love snow. It is so rarely that we have a good fall. It's ironic that we should have one of the best at this particular time, is it not? When do you think it will stop and begin to melt?''

"For your sake, I hope soon," he said. And for his own sake, too. After a night of restless tossing and turning, he had expected the morning to be easier. One's mind did not so readily turn to women and beddings in the early light of day, and the chances were that she would wear something less alluring than that orange gown of the evening before.

She was wearing her own pale-blue woolen dress, and her hair was dressed rather severely at the back of her head. But wool was a good fabric for a slender woman. It clung enticingly. And that particular shade of blue looked good with her coloring.

Perhaps even so he could have been reasonably comfortable with her if she had not chosen to wear one of the perfumes he had bought for Jude. It was the one he had chosen with the most care. He had even imagined, inhaling it, exactly where he would dab it on her body and exactly when. It did nothing for his peace of mind to find it wafting delicately across the breakfast table from Mrs. Hunter's person.

"I'm afraid there is not much in the house here with which to entertain a lady," he said, "except cards. We cannot play cards all day long, though, can we?"

She leaned across the table toward him as she had done a few times the evening before, her face eager. "What would you have done if your mistress had been here?" she asked, and instantly turned poppy-red.

He grinned at her. "I know just how it feels," he said, "to realize what you are saying only when the words are already escaping your mouth, Mrs. Hunter. I'm sure you have a good-enough imagination to know just how I would have spent this day with Jude. But you are not my mistress. I did say there was not much here to entertain a *lady*."

"That was the stuff of nightmares," she said. "I shall be waking up for the next several months shaking my head and grimacing over that one." She helped herself to another piece of toast and spooned a generous pile of lemon curd onto it.

The earl watched her in some amusement. Life must never be dull with Rosamund Hunter around.

"Now, if you were a gentleman," he said, taking mercy on her after watching her for several seconds as she spread and respread the lemon curd on her toast, "we could play billiards. But you are not, so we can't. Price did say there were some books here somewhere, though I have not yet found any."

She set her knife down and looked eagerly across at him. "Oh, but I do play billiards," she said. "I asked Leonard to teach me, and he did, though he laughed at me a good deal. I never could beat him, but then no one else could either, and I would never let him humor me and allow me to win. He was very good."

The earl raised his eyebrows. "Then billiards it will be for this morning," he said. "Perhaps the snow will have stopped falling by this afternoon and we can get some fresh air. You can make some snow angels for me."

She laughed. "Oh, but there are no children here," she said. "One can do that and build snowmen and throw snowballs only when there are children to entertain, or someone is sure to accuse one of being childish."

"I promise not to accuse you of that," he said, raising his right hand with mock solemnity. "And snowballs, did you say? I know a thing or two about snowballs."

She laughed.

She was a widow, one part of his mind was thinking. The young widow of an older man who had been dead for more than a year and of a man who had been ill for three years before that. An attractive widow. Perhaps she would not be averse . . .

He shook himself free of the thought and sipped on his second cup of coffee.

A little flirtation, perhaps? But under the present circumstances, a little flirtation would be impossible. If he once touched her and she did not slap his hand away, he would take her up to his bed and make of his life a hopelessly complicated business. She was a lady.

No, better to forget the whole thing before it took root in his mind.

"Shall we find the billiard room?" he asked when it became obvious that she was not going to eat the toast on her plate.

Billiards seemed safe enough. It was a masculine game, a slow and rather dull one. Something that could be made to last through the morning. And Mrs. Hunter obviously took it seriously. She concentrated on making her shots and really played quite well.

But the Earl of Wetherby discovered something new about billiards. It was perhaps the most erotic game invented by man. If he stood at the opposite side of the table as she readied her cue, his eyes were drawn to her breasts, brushing the table, one sometimes flattened against the rim. He was only thankful that the neckline of her dress was high. If he stood behind her, he could not keep his eyes from a rounded and very feminine derriere as she leaned over the table and the wool of her dress clung to her.

Before the morning was half over, he had to resist the urge to tear at his cravat and rush out into the falling snow to cool himself off. He would find those books before luncheon, he swore to himself, and they would spend the afternoon in the sitting room, one at either side of the fire, reading, like an elderly and comfortable married couple.

"I win," she said, turning to him with a bright smile.

"So you do," he said. "You had a good teacher, I see. Did we decide on a prize?"

"No," she said, laughing. "It was always a kiss with Leonard and me. But since we kissed each other whoever won—though it was always him, of course—it was rather silly, as I used to tell him." She suddenly turned that poppy-red shade again.

"Well, then," he said, hearing his words even before they came from his mouth but quite unable to change them, "a kiss it will be."

She looked up at him in shock and embarrassment and caught her lower lip between her teeth. Her upper lip gave more than ever the impression of being upturned.

He took her face between his hands, watched her release her lower lip, and lowered his mouth to hers. He did not part his lips, but kissed her lightly, feeling the softness of her, the warmth, the moistness of her lower lip. He did not hurry. His nostrils were teased by that seductive scent.

"Mm," he said, raising his head and looking down into a pair of large dark eyes, "your husband was a very sensible man. Having to give such prizes would console any man for losing a game."

She swallowed awkwardly. "It was just nonsense," she said, "as I always used to tell him."

If he just touched her once, he had thought at breakfast. He still had her face cupped between his hands.

"May I call you Rosamund?" he asked. And he certainly had not planned those words in advance.

"Yes," she said, turning sharply away and fishing a couple of balls out of a side pocket of the table, "if you wish."

"Will you call me Justin?" he asked.

"Yes," she said again, moving around the table to another pocket, "if you wish."

He strolled to the window and tried to persuade his heart to slow down. "I do believe the snow is easing a little," he said. "I could use some fresh air after luncheon, couldn't you?"

"Oh, yes," she said, sounding as eager for cool air and open spaces as he was feeling.

If the snow had not eased off enough for them to go outside, Rosamund thought later when she was upstairs pulling on boots and gloves and fastening her cloak warmly about her throat, she would have had to go outside anyway. If she had to remain inside the house for one more hour, she would surely burst.

The air had positively pulsed between them all morning and through both meals. And surely it could not be all one-

sided. She could not be so overpoweringly aware of him
while he felt nothing. Surely he felt as she did.

A most disconcerting thought!

Leonard had always said she had a positive gift for opening
her mouth and ramming her foot inside. He had found that
gift quite endearing and had always hugged her and kissed
her smackingly and laughed heartily when it happened. But
it was one thing to say alarmingly embarrassing things when
there was just Leonard to hear her, and quite another to say
them in front of Mr. Halliday . . . Justin.

She must close her mind to the morning's examples, she
thought, turning resolutely to the door of her room, or she
would lose the courage to go back downstairs to face him
again. But her hand paused on the knob and she closed her
eyes.

Asking him what he would have done with his mistress
today, indeed! She had had sudden and vivid images of a
girl spread on her bed clad only in the black nightgown and
of him about to remove it. On top of the covers and not
beneath them. Oh, it was most mortifying. Women of her
class were not even supposed to know about such creatures
as mistresses.

And then telling him that a kiss had always been the prize
claimed by Leonard when they had played billiards. How
could she have! Rosamund shuddered. Just as if she were
issuing an open invitation.

That kiss! She still felt a tightening of her breasts and a
weakening in her womb and her knees when she thought of
it. Why, oh, why, had she got out of Dennis' carriage the
day before?

She opened the door resolutely, and went downstairs,
pulling up her hood over her hair as she did so.

"The snow is very deep," the earl said. "Will your boots
keep it out?"

"For a little while," she said, looking down at her half-
boots. He was surely wearing the same topboots and the same
caped greatcoat that he had been wearing the day before.

She had not really noticed then how very large and virile they made him look. She noticed now.

But this is foolish, she thought, giving herself a mental shake and striding toward the front door.

A world of white magic greeted them outside. The sky was still gray and heavy and promised more snow later on, and there was a chill breeze to whip up air that was already very cold. But it was a magical world anyway. The trees were hung with snow, and the ground beneath them was an unbroken white carpet. Rosamund stood on the steps, the only area that Reeves had swept off, and drew in a deep breath.

"Oh, beautiful," she said. "Isn't it beautiful?" She turned to the man who was standing silently beside her.

"Magical," he said, echoing her thoughts. He went down the steps and into snow that reached almost to the top of his boots. "Are you coming down here, Rosamund, or is snow only to be looked at?"

She laughed. "It is so deep," she said, taking his hand and stepping down into it. "I have never seen snow so deep. Oh, Justin, isn't it lovely? What I would not have given to have had snow like this when I was a child."

"There is a child in all of us," he said as they waded slowly along what they thought to be the driveway. "If you want to shriek and frolic, don't hold back on my account. I may even join you."

"I would have made a whole army of snowmen," she said, "and been begging Cook for a whole bag of carrots for their noses. But alas, I am not a child any longer." She smiled at him. "It would be lovely to have children, wouldn't it?"

And there, she had done it again, she thought as she bent to pick up a handful of snow to mold into a ball in her hands. How embarrassing!

"I must admit I have never felt the urge," he said, sounding amused. "You never had children?"

"No," she said. "Leonard's first wife did not have any either. We would have liked one."

"Well," he said, "there is lots of time. You are young yet. In the meanwhile, what about that angel?"

"Oh, no," she said, dropping the ball she had molded. "I would feel remarkably foolish."

"A pity," he said. "How about a snowball fight?"

She looked at him warily. "A fight?" she said. "You and me? Oh, no."

"You're afraid of losing," he said.

"I am not," she said.

"Yes you are," he said. "Or afraid of getting snow in your face or losing some of your dignity. You are a coward."

"Oh, I am not," she said indignantly, bending quickly and grabbing up a handful of snow to take him off his guard. But when she whirled on him, a shower of snow hit her squarely on the nose and his laughter mingled with her sputtering gasp.

"You might as well throw it, since you have it," he said. But he ducked as soon as she released as snowball and it sailed harmlessly over his shoulder. "The first round goes to me."

A breathless, laughing, giggling snowball fight occupied the next five minutes as they stood twenty feet apart recklessly hurling the soft snow at each other. Justin Halliday had a far surer aim than she had, Rosamund decided almost immediately. Her hood had blown off her head, and snow was dripping down her face and inside her collar. And she could not seem to stop giggling.

"Are you prepared to hoist the white flag?" he asked a moment before releasing a snowball directly at her right cheek and hitting his mark dead on.

"Never," she said breathlessly, but as she moved to scoop up more snow, her feet skidded awkwardly and she sprawled sideways right into the thick of it.

He was laughing when he came over to help her up. "Poor Rosamund," he said, hauling her to her feet with a firm hand. "You look rather like an angel, you know—all white. Except that angels are not supposed to spit snow and mutter

expletives that are on the verge of being unladylike. Do you
admit defeat now?''

"I had better," she said, "since I believe I have as much
snow inside my clothes as outside. You win, Justin.''

"I'll give you a rematch tomorrow," he said. "What is
my prize to be?''

"Not a kiss," she said hastily.

"And glad I am to hear it," he said. "It would be a
somewhat icy kiss, I fear. You can pour tea for me after you
have changed. How does that sound?''

"Fair enough," she said.

Altogether, she thought, cheerful despite her cold and
discomfort as they made their way back to the house, the
hour outdoors had lightened the tension between them considerably. She would be able to handle the rest of the day with
ease.

Good sense and sanity had been restored.

"I shall pour your tea as soon as I have changed and
warmed up," she said to him when they were on their way
upstairs. "Perhaps even two cups, if you are very good.''

"Really?" he said. "And what constitutes being very
good, Rosamund?''

He was smiling when she looked across at him, just as
he had been all the time they were outside. His face was
reddened by the cold. His blue eyes were twinkling.

But her tongue delayed just a moment too long over a glib
reply. And his smile faded just a little, and his words hung
in the space between them, and his eyes dropped for just a
moment to her lips.

"Drinking the first cup without spilling a drop," she said.
But she said it too late.

Oh, dear, she thought a minute later, standing with her
back against the closed door of her bedchamber. Oh, dear.
Dennis should have chained her to the seat of his carriage
the day before. He really should have.

4

Books had been found—nine of them. Very clearly, the Earl of Wetherby thought, they had not been contributed to the house by Price, or if they had, they had been intended as decorations or as doorstops or paperweights. Their subject matter did not seem quite in Price's line—or in his either, for that matter.

Despite the unsuitability of the books, he and Rosamund Hunter were each reading one, seated silently engrossed at either side of the fireplace.

Engrossed! He would not have been surprised, he thought, focusing his eyes on the book before him for a moment, to find that it was upside down in his hands. It was time to turn a page. He turned one just as Rosamund did the same thing with her book. He looked up and met her eyes for a fleeting moment.

It was deuced uncomfortable. He had suggested the books after dinner rather than cards because there had been far too much awareness and tension between them the evening before. She had agreed with an eagerness that had suggested she was having similar thoughts.

They had conversed with great animation over dinner. She had told him about the neighbors with whom she had associated for the nine years since her marriage, revealing a wit and a keen observation of human nature that had kept him laughing much of the time. And he had told her something of his boyhood, when he had been made much of, a son at last after two daughters and a full seven years after the second of those. He had grown up surrounded by doting females.

"It took me quite by surprise," he had told her, "when I went out into the world and discovered that there were some women who actually disputed my claim to be God's great gift to the female branch of the human race."

She had laughed.

Anyone coming in upon them during dinner would have thought them the heartiest of good friends. And in a way they were. It was very easy both to talk and to listen to Rosamund Hunter. It was the silences that were the trouble. Silences between friends were supposed to be relaxed and easy affairs. Obviously he and the lady were not friends.

"Is your book interesting?" he asked now, and thought as he was saying it that if he had spent time trying to compose the most inane question imaginable, he could hardly have done better.

"Yes, very," she said brightly. "I have always admired poetry."

Well, he thought, consoling himself, her answer lacked something in profundity, too.

"Is yours interesting?" she asked.

"Yes, indeed," he said. "Sermons are always good for provoking thought."

So much for that line of conversation, he thought, returning his eyes but not his mind to his book and remembering to turn another page.

It was snowing again. Not as heavily as before, but enough to keep them housebound. Without a doubt, even if the snow stopped during the night and the sun shone the next day, Mrs. Hunter was not going to be able to leave until at least the day after. And no one would be able to come in search of her, either.

That meant that they were facing the rest of this night together, all the next day, and the next night at the very least. He did not think he would be able to do it. He might have to take a blanket and pillow out to the stables to sleep with the horses.

She was wearing a pale-lemon satin, one he had thought

would look good with Jude's coloring. With Rosamund's dark hair and eyes it looked nothing short of stunning. She wore the paisley shawl about her almost bare shoulders again. Her hair was looped down over her ears and coiled simply at the back. Her eyelashes were thick and long, he noticed, glancing up at her as she looked down at her book.

She had good skin, creamy and soft. It would be good to touch her. It had been good to touch her that morning, though in reality he had barely kissed her at all, knowing that if he had deepened the kiss by even one fraction he would have ended up making an idiot of himself.

But why so? She felt the same way. She was as aware of him as he was of her. She was a woman, not a girl. She was no virgin. She was a widow. Perhaps she would not be unwilling. Perhaps they could put this tension to rest by doing what they had both been thinking of doing and wanting to do since some time yesterday afternoon.

But would she crumble afterward and be tortured by guilt and remorse? Would he? He had never bedded any but women whose profession it was to sell their favors. He had never slept with a lady. And in one month's time he was to betroth himself to Annabelle.

But he was not betrothed yet. He had one month left of freedom before pledging himself to a lifetime of fidelity to one woman.

He wanted Rosamund Hunter. He wanted her badly. But if he could just force his mind onto this one sermon, if he could just concentrate long enough to read it through from beginning to end, then perhaps he would be able to resist temptation. He turned back three pages to the beginning.

He had read two sentences when Rosamund got abruptly to her feet.

"It's too warm by the fire," she said, and crossed the room to seat herself on a stool close to the window, her back to him. She opened her book and gave it her attention again.

Now where was he? the earl thought. He had been quite engrossed for those two sentences.

* * *

What she should have done, Rosamund was thinking, was to plead a headache. She could have taken herself off to her room and been safe for another night. Why, oh, why, had she not thought of that? But having pleaded the heat of the fire in order to remove herself from such closeness to him in order to set him behind her, out of the line of her vision, she must now stay for a while and continue to read her book—or not to read her book.

She felt like jumping to her feet again and screaming. She felt like having a major fit of hysterics. She turned a page.

There would not be anything so very wrong in it, would there? She had heard that many married ladies took lovers, though the idea had always shocked her. How could they, she had always thought, when their husbands had exclusive rights to their bodies? Just as women had exclusive rights to their husbands' bodies. It had always made her furious to know that many married men kept mistresses.

She had also heard that widows very frequently took lovers. She had not felt any great moral shock at the idea, but she had always been convinced that it was something she could not possibly do. She could never give that outside marriage. It was such a very intimate and physical and embarrassing thing.

And yet these were no ordinary circumstances—not by any means. And it would be just for a day or two. It would end this tension between them and it would satisfy her curiosity about younger men. How vulgar that sounded! She turned another page.

And she became aware suddenly, though there had been hardly any sound, that he had put down his book and stood up. And that after a few moments of standing quite still he was coming up behind her. She kept her eyes on her book and felt that her heart was beating right up into her throat.

His hands came beneath her arms and cupped her breasts. His thumbs found her nipples. Rosamund closed her eyes and swallowed. She felt warm breath on the side of her neck a moment before he kissed her in the hollow between her neck and her shoulder.

"I want to make love to you, Rosamund," he said. His voice was low and husky, almost unrecognizable.

She kept her eyes tightly closed for a moment and then she turned slowly on the stool. His hands moved up to her shoulders. His eyes, gazing down into hers, were intensely blue.

"Yes," she said. "I want that too."

His mouth on hers was as light as it had been that morning, but his lips were parted, she noted with some shock, so that she felt heat and moistness and his tongue moving lightly across the seam of her own lips. She clutched her closed book to her bosom.

He raised his head and stooped down on his haunches in front of her. "One thing must be clear," he said, touching one of her cheeks with his fingertips. "I am to be betrothed soon, Rosamund. I am committed to that. I don't want to hurt you or give any wrong impression."

"Just tonight and perhaps tomorrow night," she said. "I understand, Justin. I want no more. But this is a time out of time, isn't it? And I want it to happen—just a very brief affair."

"Yes," he said. "Just very brief." He hesitated. "I need to know. Am I like to get you with child?"

She felt her cheeks grow warm. She was the one who should have thought of that. It had not crossed her mind. She had grown unaccustomed to thinking of it. After the first year of her marriage she had forced herself to stop expecting that it would happen. There had been no point in getting herself upset month after month. She had almost forgotten that conception could be the result of intercourse. She made some quick mental calculations.

"No," she said, "it is the wrong time."

"Good." He continued to look at her and stroke her cheek.

What now? Was the next move supposed to be hers? She tried smiling. She was not at all sure she had succeeded.

"Go on upstairs," he said. "I'll come to you in twenty minutes' time."

"All right," she said, standing up and setting her book down on a small table. She smiled at him once more and left the room. It all felt so ordinary, she thought, so matter-of-fact. As if they had just made some agreement about . . . about what they would have served for breakfast, or something like that.

She had not expected to be alone like this, with time to think. Twenty minutes, in fact. And time to prepare. What had she expected? To be swept off her feet, she supposed, taken right there in the sitting room, with the chance only to feel and not to think at all.

What had she said? What had she agreed to? What was she about to do? Oh, goodness gracious, it did not bear thinking of. What was she going to do now? Undress? But what should she wear? The choice was between the ridiculously large and shapeless flannel gown and the white or the black lace. Well, the laces were quite out of the question. But would she not look ridiculous in the flannel?

Perhaps she should remain dressed. But he had sent her upstairs on the tacit understanding that she would get ready. And should she lie down in the bed, or remain standing or sitting in the chair by the fire? She had always been in bed for Leonard, but then that had been a different matter altogether. She would die of mortification if Justin walked into her room when she was in bed.

But then she would die of mortification anyway.

Oh, her treacherous mouth. This time she had not stuffed just one foot inside it but both. She wished she could relive the last five minutes so that she could show the proper outrage at both his actions and his words.

Rosamund shivered as she unpinned her hair and began to brush it. No, she was not sorry for her decision. She wanted this to happen. She was not sorry at all. She just wished that he had not let them be separated for twenty minutes. She would positively die when he walked through the door.

He was not at all sure that it had been the right thing to do to leave her to get ready, Lord Wetherby thought as he stood outside the door of her room later, his hand raised to knock. It would doubtless have been better not to have broken the tension of the moment but to have taken her by the hand and led her to the bedchamber and undressed her himself. He just did not know what was proper procedure with a lady.

The thought made him smile. There was no proper procedure with a lady, was there? He knocked lightly at the door and opened it.

She was standing at the opposite side of the room, her back to the fire, her dark hair smooth and straight to her waist, her eyes enormous and fixed on him. She was swathed from the chin to the toes in a very large and shapeless flannel nightgown. Strangely, she looked very enticing. He was glad she had not worn one of the lace creations. He smiled and closed the door behind him.

He was wearing a dark-blue brocade dressing gown, Rosamund noticed immediately. She had not thought of that—of his being undressed, that was. Foolish of her. Her eyes strayed to the neck of the dressing gown. There was no sign of a nightshirt beneath. He looked unnervingly attractive. Her heart was beating into her throat again. She tried to smile and failed miserably.

"You look beautiful," he said, coming across the room toward her and taking her face in his hands as he had done that morning in the billiard room.

"It belongs to Mrs. Reeves," she said. "The nightgown, I mean."

"I didn't t hink it was one of the ones I had bought," he said.

He had a strange trick with his eyes: he could make them smile even when the rest of his face was serious. She had noticed it before. At such close quarters she was almost mesmerized by it. She closed her eyes.

She was very tense. He could tell that. She did not cooperate at all in his kiss, but stood quite still and kept her lips firmly closed. She did not angle her head to meet his mouth comfortably. He widened his mouth over hers and prodded at her lips with his tongue. He moved his hands down to caress her shoulders and arms, to wrap his arms about her.

"You're as stiff as a board," he said. "Are you nervous?"

"Yes," she said.

"Are you having second thoughts?" he asked.

"No," she said. "Forty-second." Her teeth began to chatter and she clamped them firmly together.

"Do even numbers mean no or yes?" he asked.

She looked at him blankly.

"Do you want me to go away?" he asked. "I will if you want." Though it would mean one hell of a sleepless night.

"No," she said. "I want you to make love to me."

She said it rather as if she were asking him to draw one of her teeth.

"Let's sit down for a while, then," he said, suiting actions to words and seating himself in the large chair beside the fire. He drew her down onto his lap and set one arm about her, coaxing her head onto his shoulder. "Just relax, Rosamund. There's no hurry at all, is there? You aren't a virgin by any chance, are you?"

"No," she said hastily. "Of course not."

"I'm glad to hear it," he said. And he began to unbutton her nightgown down the front.

It was strange to be sitting there talking, she thought, when she had expected business to begin without further delay. She closed her eyes and tried to ignore what his hand was doing. But when it reached inside the nightgown and moved lightly over one of her breasts, she turned her face in to his neck.

"Just relax," he said quietly into her ear. "You're very beautiful. Did your husband ever tell you that?"

"Yes," she said.

His thumb stroked over the tip of her breast. She thought

it felt slightly rough. It sent a strange ache up into her throat. Unexpectedly she felt herself relaxing, though it was not exactly relaxation either. But she was no longer frightened or even particularly embarrassed. She should have been—Leonard had never touched her there.

She was exquisite. He had always thought he liked large-breasted women—like Jude. Rosamund's breasts were small and firm and shapely and petal-smooth. Her nipples hardened to his touch. She had relaxed. She was no longer stiff and unyielding. He lowered his head to kiss her cheek, and she turned her head until their mouths met.

Her lips were still closed, but they were yielding. She parted them tentatively to the probing of his tongue and he explored lightly the warm, moist flesh behind. She opened her mouth and her tongue trembled over his as he pushed it inside. He could feel himself becoming aroused. She was quite as alluring as he had expected her to be. Perhaps more so. She seemed strangely inexperienced. But then she had not had numerous bedfellows to teach her the tricks of the trade.

He slid the flannel nightown off one shoulder and down her arm and lowered his head to kiss her throat, her shoulder, and her breast. She was warm, smooth, inviting. She smelled faintly of the perfume she had worn that morning. He lifted his head to look into her eyes.

"Shall we resume this conversation in bed?" he asked her.

"Yes," she said, sitting up and drawing the nightgown back up onto her shoulder.

Her heart began to thump again as she got to her feet. This was it, then. There could be no going back now without making an utter fool of herself. Not that there had been any going back for the last several minutes, of course. But she did not want to go back. She wanted more of his kisses, more of his hands.

He stopped her at the side of the bed and turned her toward him, his hands on her shoulders. He bent his head and kissed her briefly.

"Do you want the candles out?" he asked.

There would still be light from the fire. But not enough. She had chosen her course, and doubtless she would live with the guilt of it for months to come. But since she had chosen it and could feel no regret yet, she wanted to taste the whole of it.

"No," she said.

He smiled, lifted the flannel back from her shoulders, and let the whole garment fall in a heap at her feet. He put his arms about her and drew her against him before she could die of embarrassment.

"This has never happened to you before, has it?" he said against her hair.

"No," she said.

"It will be beautiful, I promise you," he said. "You are beautiful. You have nothing to be ashamed of or embarrassed about."

She lay on the bed a moment later as he untied the sash of his dressing gown and shrugged out of it. As she had suspected, he was naked beneath it. And magnificent. And frightening. She caught her lower lip between her teeth.

It was strange, he thought a little later as he lay beside her on the bed, how making love to an innocent could be a far more wildly erotic experience than making love with the most experienced courtesan. And Rosamund Hunter was an innocent, even if she had been married for eight years. Her husband must have exercised his conjugal rights—she had said she was not a virgin—but she knew nothing.

But she responded to the touch of his hands and his mouth. And he found that he was in no hurry. He was fully aroused, but he was used to waiting for his pleasure so that it would be all the sweeter for the delay. And he liked to touch her, to feel her growing response, to hear her involuntary gasps, to feel her trembling hands on him.

He had set her hands against his chest, and she had left them there for a while, spread against rough hairs, afraid to move them. She could feel his naked thighs against hers,

his hands on her, knowingly seeking out unerringly places
that had her all but moaning out her pleasure and desire, his
mouth at her throat, on her breasts, sucking at her nipples,
on her mouth. And she could see him, his longish fair hair
rumpled, his blue eyes heavy-lidded with passion.

After a while her hands began to move tentatively,
curiously, wonderingly. Firm flesh, powerful muscles,
narrow hips, small firm buttocks. She did not have the
courage to move her hands forward. But she wanted him.
Ah, she wanted him.

"Make love to me."

His face was above hers. He was smiling down at her.
"That is what I am doing."

"I want more."

"You want me here?" he asked her, feathering kisses
along her nose and across her mouth. "Is this where you
want me, Rosamund?" His fingers were touching her,
parting her, stroking. One pushed a little way inside her.

"Yes," she said, inhaling sharply.

He smiled again. "In a moment," he said. "Does that feel
good?"

"Yes," she said, arching to him, biting down on her lower
lip. "Too good. Justin!"

"Mm," he said, kissing her more deeply. "Impatient, are
you?"

"Yes."

She closed her eyes when he lifted himself over her and
brought his whole length down on top of her. His legs pushed
hers wide.

She was all slim and supple grace and heat. He would have
to be careful not to explode as soon as he was inside her.
He wanted to be inside her for a good long while. Her eyes
were wide again when he looked down into her face.

"I'll just have to give you what you want, then, won't I?"
he said, and watched her eyes as he found her and pushed
himself slowly and deeply inside. They widened ever farther.
Soft and warm and moist heat.

"God, you're beautiful," he said, shaken by the power of his own reaction to her. Her eyes rolled upward and closed when he withdrew as slowly as he had entered and pushed back inside her.

She had not expected this. Oh, she had not expected this. If she had only known what it was to be like, she would have thrown an armour about herself, she would have gone trudging off into the snow as soon as it stopped falling that afternoon. This was going to be no momentary fling.

She had not expected this—this complete knowing, this totally being known. Every inch of his body and her own—known. This close naked embrace, his body pressing hers into the mattress, his firm and slender hips clasped between her thighs, his manhood buried deep in her, knowing her with firm and steady rhythm . . .

This was to be no fleeting affair, this opening of her body and baring of her soul. Her body was being unfolded, like layers being stripped away carefully, one at a time, from a parcel. He was going to reach the very innermost core of her, the part of her that was her and no one else on this earth. She could feel that he was going to reach there. She had not known that a man could reach a woman that deeply.

"Justin!"

"Sh," he said against her mouth. And a moment later, "Don't fight me. I'm going to wait for you even if it takes all night."

"Justin!"

He could feel the tightening of all her muscles. He could feel her climax coming. And he knew that she was terrified of it and fighting it. He slowed and deepened his rhythm.

"Come with me," he said, raising his head and looking down into her eyes. "Let's go together. We'll hold each other and go together. Come with me?"

He was as terrified as she, if only she knew it. God, what had he got himself into? It was not just pleasure and his seed he was about to release into her. It was himself. A foolish, fanciful thought at such a moment.

"Yes," she said.

And she kept her eyes on his as he pushed into her and nudged at her until he felt the inner tremors that would soon have her whole body shuddering. He withdrew once more and released all of his tension, all of himself into her in one final plunge.

She lifted her head to press her forehead against his neck, and she clung to him with arms and legs as she lost herself completely. When she returned to herself, she was lying against the pillow again, his cheek pressed to the side of her head, her arms about him, his whole weight pressing down on her. He was still buried inside her. She was throbbing with the aftermath of passion.

Well, she had wondered about younger men, she thought with the first rational and practical thought to come to her for many minutes. And now she knew.

Oh, dear God, now she knew!

5

It was not a night for sleep. If Rosamund had expected him to return to his own bedchamber once it was finished, she was soon to learn differently. The candles gradually burned themselves out and the fire died down. He drew the blankets up around them and held her snugly in his arms.

They talked . . . about nothing in particular. She could never remember afterward what they had talked of that could have filled so many hours. And they kissed warmly, lazily, between times, and smiled at each other while there was light to smile by, and even after that.

"I have never lived through such an uncomfortable day as today," he told her. "Or do I mean yesterday?"

"Me neither," she said.

"I learned something, anyway, which I thought I had always known," he said. "Billiards is not a game for women."

"But I won," she said. "Don't you like losing, Justin?"

"No more than anyone else, I suppose," he said. "But it is not that. It has something to do with the female body bending over a billiard table."

"Oh," she said.

"Yes, precisely," he said. "Oh."

"What are you going to do with your life, Rosamund?" he asked her somewhat later. "Are you going to marry again?"

"I suppose so," she said with a sigh. "Leonard left me as much as he could, but it is not enough for a total independence. And I hate the thought of living as a dependent on either his nephew or Dennis."

"Do you have anyone in mind?" he asked.

"No," she said. "I was only seventeen when I married, and I have been living in the country ever since. Dennis has someone in mind, though."

"You do not sound pleased," he said.

"I knew him when I was growing up," she said, "and he used to pay me silly, flowery compliments even then. Now he is ordained and has an influential patron—though he is wealthy in his own right—and has expressed a renewed interest in me. Dennis thinks it would be a good match."

"Perhaps it would, too," he said, stroking his fingers through her hair. "You have not seen him for how many years? Nine? Ten? Doubtless he has grown up just as you have."

"Yes, probably," she said.

"But you must not marry him just because you think you ought," he said. "You will have many offers, Rosamund Hunter."

"Is that a compliment?" she asked, smiling. "Thank you."

"It is the simple truth," he said.

They made love four more times in the course of the night. And Rosamund, who had thought the first time that she had been touched in every way it was possible to be touched, learned that it was not so, that sensual pleasures were as many as the stars in the sky.

By the time they drowsed at some time before the late dawn, it already seemed to her that one more day and one more night were precious little time. But she would not think of it, she decided. She would feel now and think later.

The Earl of Wetherby was having much the same thought as he dressed in his own room later that morning. One more day—already cut short by their sleeping late—and one more night were very little time, indeed.

He rather thought his good-bye to freedom was going to be more reluctant than he had expected. A week of lusty beddings with Jude was what he had planned and then a simple good-bye when they returned to London. She knew that this was to be the end. There would have been no tears—not from Jude. She had already chosen his successor and had talked to him quite freely and cheerfully about the man.

He would have been rather sad at knowing that one phase of his life was at an end, but he was resigned to the fact. He had always known that one day he would settle down to respectability and one woman.

But now things were going to be a little more difficult. Perhaps if he could have had Rosamund for a full week instead of just two nights and one day . . . But, no. That was not it at all.

Not at all. It must be because she was a lady and something of an innocent. It must be because she had given herself so sweetly and so totally, even though she had been almost as ignorant and every bit as frightened as a virgin.

It must be something!

All he did know for sure was that bedding her had not been simply a matter of taking and giving sexual pleasure, as it always had been with him. He could not quite explain to himself what else it had been, but it definitely had been something else.

Perhaps a continuation of the tension of the day before would have been better, he thought. At least then he would have been looking forward to the following day with some eagerness. He would have been relieved beyond words to see her on her way. But now? He preferred not to think of the next day. And the next day it would be, he thought with a glance toward the window. It was cloudy outside, but the clouds were high. There would be no more snow.

Mrs. Reeves would probably be wondering why they were both so late for breakfast, he thought, striding resolutely across to the door of his room. Or perhaps she would guess. Indeed, she would have to be unusually obtuse not to guess.

There was a strange breathless nervousness about sitting

at the breakfast table, watching him enter the room and stride across to take her hand and lift it to his lips and smile at her and bid her good morning. And a strange formality, too. But then Mrs. Reeves was in the room.

And there was wonder in the knowledge that this man, dressed so impeccably in his well-fitting green superfine coat and white linen, and form-fitting biscuit-colored pantaloons and black Hessians, that this man with his longish fair hair and blue-eyed smile was the man she had lain with all night, the man whose body held no secrets from her and who knew her far more intimately after just one night than Leonard had in eight years.

She felt like a bride the morning after her wedding night. Except that the comparison was quite inappropriate. She was merely his makeshift mistress. And it was a self-chosen role. She was quite happy with it.

"What do we have left to talk about?" he asked with a smile after Mrs. Reeves had left the room. "Have we exhausted every possible topic?"

They had sat in silence for a couple of minutes. But unlike the day before, it had not been an uncomfortable silence.

"Leonard took me to Scotland for a month four years ago," she said. "Did I tell you that?"

"No," he said. "You have been keeping secrets from me, Rosamund. Tell all."

He laughed through much of her lengthy account of her travels. Leonard had always laughed at her too when she had launched into speech. And he had always hugged her hard and called her the delight of his life.

"Rosamund," the earl said, "I wonder if the people who meet you realize how closely you are observing all their little foibles. It makes me shudder to think of how you will describe me later. Though your observations are never malicious, I must confess."

"I will never talk about you," she said.

His expression sobered and he reached out a hand for one of hers and squeezed it before releasing it again.

"I went to Europe last year," he said. "A sort of belated Grand Tour once the Continent was safe again."

"Italy?" she asked eagerly. "Did you go to Rome?"

"How could I go to Europe and not go to Rome?" he said.

"Tell me all about it," she said. "Oh, I do envy you. Leonard was going to take me traveling, but he was already failing in health when the Battle of Waterloo was fought."

He told her about Paris and Vienna and Florence and Venice and Rome while she sat gazing at him, her chin in her hand, her second cup of coffee growing cold.

"How I envy you," she said again when he had finished.

"Perhaps the Reverend So-and-so will take you abroad on your wedding trip," he said, grinning at her.

But she looked down at the tablecloth and reached for her cup. She put it down again when she found that the coffee was cold.

"How are we going to spend the day?" he asked briskly, getting to his feet and reaching out a hand for hers.

She flushed for no reason that she could fathom.

He laughed. "We can't do that all day as well as all last night and all tonight," he said. "We would suffer total exhaustion, Rosamund."

"Oh," she said, feeling herself blush more hotly. "How horrid you are. I was not thinking of that at all."

"Liar," he said.

"You are no gentleman, sir," she said, on her dignity.

He laughed again and drew her across the room to the window. "Ah," he said, "drips from the eaves. There should be enough melting today to allow travel tomorrow."

"Yes," she said.

He set an arm about her shoulders and drew her to his side. His free hand reached across to lift her chin so that he could kiss her mouth. "We will have to make the most of today, then, won't we?" he said.

"Yes," she said.

"Any regrets, Rosamund?" he asked.

She shook her head and rested it on his shoulder.

"Shall we go outside?" he asked. "Shall we see if I can beat you again at snowballs?"

"Yes, let's go out," she said. "But no snowballs, please. I have always had lamentably poor aim, whereas you are despicably accurate."

"You don't like losing?" he asked.

"No more than you," she said. "I will not insist on billiards today if you will not insist on snowballs."

"Agreed," he said, "though it would be worth all the humiliation of losing just to see you concentrating over the billiard table, Rosamund."

She straightened up. "You are no gentleman, sir," she said again. But this time she laughed with him.

The snow was somewhat crisper than it had been the day before. By the afternoon it would probably be quite wet and heavy.

"It is perfect for building snowmen," the earl said. "Shall we be unabashed children today, Rosamund? Shall we see who can build the larger snowman?"

"What is the prize to be?" she asked.

"The usual," he said.

"The loser pours the tea?"

He looked sidelong at her. "No," he said, "the other usual."

"Ah," she said, "an incentive, indeed." And she stooped down and set to the building of her snowman with a will.

Hers was tall and thin so that by the time she was molding its shoulders she had to stand on tiptoe. His was squat and very fat with a squat, fat head. He was finished and standing with folded arms watching her as she rolled the head into the shape she wanted.

"Oh, dear," she said, looking back to her snowman.

"I was wondering when it would strike you," he said.

"I wonder," she said after frowning and thinking for a few moments. "A chair from the house, do you think?"

"No," he said. "The legs would skid in the snow and you would break your neck. I could take you up on my shoulder."

"Yes," she said, "that might work. Why are you laughing?"

"I will wager another kiss that you cannot even lift that head," he said, "let alone balance on my shoulder with it and lift it into place."

"Oh, dear," she said.

"Do you concede defeat?"

"Not by any means," she said. "With the head on, mine would be larger than yours."

"But mine makes up in girth for what yours has in height," he said.

"If you were a gentleman," she said accusingly, "you would lift the head into place for me."

He laughed. "I might ruin my back for all time," he said, stooping and hoisting the large ball of snow into his arms and up to rest on the high shoulders. "Now if we turn our backs very quickly, we may not see it roll off again."

"It will not do so," she said with dignity. "I hollowed out the shoulders so that it would not fall."

"Ah," he said.

"Do you admit I have won?" she asked, looking brightly up at him.

He looked assessingly at both snowmen. "I will never hear the end of it if I don't, I suppose," he said. "Come and get your prize, then."

She came.

More than a minute later he caught at her wrist as she smiled and drew away.

"You owe me," he said. "You could not lift that head, remember?"

"And so I couldn't," she said.

"Very well, then," he said, drawing her back into his arms. "This is my reward and can be done my way. Right?"

"Right," she said warily.

And this time he plunged his tongue into her mouth and took full value for his winnings.

"They look rather naked, don't they, poor snowmen?" he said when it was over. "Wait here."

He was back a couple of minutes later with two carrots and several small pieces of coal. Soon both snowmen had orange noses, black eyes, and an array of black buttons. Lord Wetherby and Rosamund stood together, hand in hand, laughing and admiring their handiwork.

"The Reeveses and your coachman will think we are mad," Rosamund said.

"Aren't we?" he said. "And there aren't any angels yet. I want you to make me one."

"No sooner said than done," she said, and she fell backward into the snow, swished her arms and legs carefully out to the sides, and got up slowly. "You see? A perfect white angel. Let's see if you can make one too."

"I don't think I'm angel material," he said.

"Are you afraid of losing a little of your dignity?" she asked.

He looked at her sidelong again and threw himself back into the snow. He copied her movements.

"But you are not supposed to whip up a blizzard," she said, laughing. "Gently!"

She was standing close to his feet. He reached out with one booted foot suddenly, and before she realized what he was about to do, he caught her behind one knee with it. She toppled with a shriek on top of him.

"You weren't by any chance making fun of me, were you?" he asked, his arms going about her.

She looked down into his face and giggled. "Never," she said.

"Or taunting my clumsiness?"

"What clumsiness?"

"Or asking to be punished?"

"What is the punishment?"

"A thorough kissing."

"Oh," she said, still laughing. "Perhaps I am a little guilty then, Justin."

"The jury agrees with you," he said. "The judge has passed sentence. Two minutes at least."

"Oh."

"As soon as you have stopped giggling."

She giggled.

"Three if you won't stop," he said. "Contempt of court."

She giggled.

And was forced to serve the full sentence.

"Rosamund," he said, looking up into her face, which he held above his with both hands. They were both serious and gazing into each other's eyes. "You aren't sorry, are you?"

"About making fun of you?" she said. "No, not at all."

He smiled fleetingly. "About this," he said. "About this time out of time."

She shook her head.

"I'm glad," he said. "I would hate you to leave here convinced that you had done something unforgivably immoral or something like that."

"No," she said. "I won't. I will always remember with pleasure, Justin."

"And I," he said.

They smiled at each other.

"I must say it's deuced cold lying here," he said. "I could think of far cozier places in which to be making love to you without even having to tax my brain."

"It was your idea to make angels," she said.

"And yours to make fun of me," he said, rolling her to one side and dumping her into the snow. He got to his feet, brushed himself off quickly, and reached down a hand for hers. "Let's go and see if luncheon is ready, shall we?"

"That's the best idea you have had yet today," she said, turning as he slapped the snow from her cloak.

"I promise to come up with a better one after luncheon," he said. "Far better, in fact."

She was lying asleep in the crook of his arm. They were snug in his bed with a cheerful fire crackling in the hearth and the sun streaming through the window. The clouds had finally moved right off an hour before.

He was feeling pleasantly drowsy, too. He would sleep soon and make up a little for two almost sleepless nights—and prepare for the one ahead. He turned his head and smiled down at Rosamund's sleeping face. She had fallen asleep even before he had lifted himself off her. She had merely made sleepy protests when he had done so.

He hoped she had been telling the truth about the unlikelihood of becoming pregnant. God, he hoped he was not getting her with child. Not that he would ever know, of course. She would do the suffering all alone. But he cared too much to be concerned about only his own good name.

He cared too damned much. He should have instructed his coachman to keep on going two days before. Her brother would probably have found her. Or someone else would have taken her up. Or she would have found some other habitation. Or having taken her up and brought her here, he should have fought his baser instincts much harder than he had. He should have brought that book of sermons to this room and locked himself in.

But what had happened in the last day that was so earth-shattering? Nothing really. They had become lovers, to the mutual satisfaction of both. He was a man looking for a last fling before settling down to a respectable betrothal. She was a widow looking for a brief interlude of excitement. They had found what they wanted in each other.

They had shared six thoroughly satisfactory beddings and were likely to share as many more before she left the next day. Thoroughly satisfactory. She had shouted out his name a few minutes before so that he had been afraid for one moment that Reeves would come rushing upstairs to see if he were murdering her.

In two nights and one day he was having far more pleasure than he would have had in a week with Jude. But by tomorrow he would be exhausted. It would be time for her to go even if she did not have to do so.

He would have thoroughly pleasant memories of her—as she would of him, she had said outside that morning. Thoroughly pleasant. It was a great good-bye to youth and freedom.

He tipped his head sideways and rubbed his cheek across her soft dark hair.

Except that he cared too damned much. He felt something like panic when he thought of the next day.

"Was I sleeping?" She turned over onto her side suddenly and smiled drowsily up at him.

"Mhm," he said. "Very wise of you, and very flattering."

"Flattering?"

"I believe it was my lovemaking that put you to sleep," he said.

"Do you?" She closed her eyes and smiled. "The fact that I scarcely slept last night would not have anything to do with it?"

"What stopped you from sleeping last night?" he asked.

Her smile broadened. "Your lovemaking," she said.

"Precisely," he said, kissing her nose and then her mouth. "Go back to sleep."

"Is that an order?" she asked.

"Very definitely," he said. "I am going to sleep too. I intend to give you another sleepless night tonight."

"Mm," she said.

"Does that express approval or disapproval?" he asked.

"Sh," she said. "I am obeying orders."

He kissed her nose again.

The tension of the evening before had disappeared. But a new tension had taken its place—a tension of some desperation. All they had left, Rosamund thought as they played a hand of cards after dinner, was this evening and the night ahead. Reeves and Justin's coachman had already given it as their opinion that it would be possible to travel by late the following morning.

So little time. It was really just as well, of course. If she stayed much longer, he would grow tired of her . . . and she would fall in love with him. She had already conceded that it would be altogether possible to do so. But it was just because he was the first man to show her that physical love could be more—far more—than the wifely duty she had performed quite cheerfully for seven years.

She wondered fleetingly if Leonard had known. Perhaps he did but considered such behavior inappropriate with a wife. But he had had no mistresses. She knew because she had asked him after a few months of marriage and he had laughed at her and told her she should not talk of such things. But he had said that he would be a greedy man indeed if a lovely young wife like her did not satisfy him. No, he had told her, he had no mistress and never would have. She had believed him.

Perhaps Leonard had not known.

"Are you going to play a card, Rosamund, or are you going to continue staring through them?" the earl asked.

"What?" She looked up at him vacantly.

He smiled and laid down his cards, faceup. "I can see that I am going to win handily, anyway," he said. "Why prolong the agony? Do you want to play?"

She shook her head.

"Let's sit by the fire, then," he said.

He took the chair he had sat in the evening before, but he caught her by the wrist when she made for the chair opposite, and drew her down to sit on his lap. She curled up gratefully there and laid her head on his shoulder.

And somehow—she did not know how the topic got started—she found herself telling him about that last painful year with Leonard, when she had watched him lose weight and hide his pain behind smiles. When she had sat on a stool at his feet many times and held his hand and talked and talked endlessly on any topic that came into her head. When she had lain beside him on top of the covers of his bed countless times, his head sometimes on her arm, very still because she had learned that even her hand smoothing over his head could cause him distress. And talking and talking.

"What did I ever do to deserve you, dearest?" he had asked her once. And he had told her that when he was dead he wanted her to marry again as soon as possible. "For love, dearest. And for children. I want you to think of having children and being happy."

"I am happy with you," she had told him. "I'm happy with you, Leonard."

"Incredibly, I think you are," he had said. "But you will find a greater happiness, dearest, and a greater love. A different kind of love. You will know one day."

She believed, though she had never questioned him, that he and his first wife had shared a very special kind of love. Sometimes she had even felt a little jealous of the long-dead Dorothy.

"Sometimes," he had told her once, only a week or so before his death, "I think you are the daughter we never had, dearest. You have been the delight of my life." He had been very weak, lying with closed eyes, pale and gaunt against his pillows. He had mentioned his first wife by name for the only time in their eight-year relationship. She did not believe he had really known what he said. "Dorothy would have loved you, too."

"He fell asleep," she said, "and he never woke up. He died three days later. And during those days, I sat by him, willing him to wake up because there was so much I still wanted to say to him and had left too late."

"He knew," Lord Wetherby said. Somehow the pins had been removed from her hair and it was loose about her shoulders. "He knew, Rosamund. You loved him dearly, didn't you?"

"I don't think I loved even Papa more," she said.

"He knew," he said. "He was well-blessed, your husband. To have had his Dorothy first and then you. No, don't hold back."

"I feel so stupid," she said. "It was more than a year ago."

"But you were married to him for eight years," he said, "and loved him dearly. Grief does not end when mourning is put off."

And so she hid her face against his shoulder, took the handkerchief he put into her hand, and cried and cried as she had not done since the day of the funeral. She cried until her ribs hurt.

"He was a well-blessed man," the earl said against the side of her face, "to have had a woman like you, Rosamund."

"I'm sorry," she said, sitting up on his lap and blowing her nose loudly and resolutely into his handkerchief, "to subject you to this."

"Don't be," he said. "I feel privileged."

"There," she said more brightly, looking about her and setting the handkerchief down on a side table, "the sad story of my life. It was about this time last evening I moved over to that stool, wasn't it?"

"Yes." He smiled.

"I must look frightful," she said.

"A little red about the eyes and nose," he admitted, studying her. "Rather beautiful, actually. Do you want me to repeat what I said last night?"

She nodded.

"I want to make love to you, Rosamund," he said.

She looked back at him, unsmiling. "Yes," she said. "I want that, too, Justin."

He put one side of her hair back behind her ear. "I'll come up with you tonight," he said. "I want to undress you. May I?"

She nodded and got to her feet and reached out a hand for his.

6

The Earl of Wetherby wondered if he had felt anything like this with any of his mistresses over the years. He deliberately thought back to his partings with some of them. But, no, of course there was no similarity. Always he had ended the liaisons himself, because for varying reasons, he had grown tired of the woman. That was the difference, he supposed. This parting from Rosamund was an enforced thing, an experience he was quite unused to.

He had just woken up and had no idea of the time, but the embers of the fire were only a dim glow in the hearth. There was a chill in the room, though not beneath the covers. She was asleep in his arms, her naked body turned into his. He was memorizing the feel of her, the smell of her, knowing that for days to come, perhaps weeks, he would be reliving these few days in his memory.

Yes, it was just that he was not in full control of this affair. If he could keep her until he had had his fill of her, he would part from her as thankfully as he had parted from every other woman who had ever shared his bed. The trouble was that he had not had nearly his fill of her. And he had only a few more hours with her. Hence this feeling of near desperation.

She was fun to be with, he thought. It was not just that she was a most satisfactory bedfellow, though she was very certainly that. He really could not imagine that Jude would have enjoyed making snowmen and snow angels. She would have been horrified at the mere idea of poking her nose out of doors. The woman spent her whole life in a boudoir.

And Rosamund was so easy to talk to. It was absurd after little more than two days, but he felt that he knew her well.

For she had the gift of talking not just of surface matters but from her inner self. He knew her even after such a short time as a woman who had been devoted as both a wife and a daughter to her older husband and who had loved him dearly, but who nevertheless was now waking to the realization that much of life was still ahead of her. She was a warm, vibrant, and passionate woman.

The hand that was spread on his chest stirred.

"What time is it?" she asked him sleepily.

Oh, yes, it was a night when time mattered. "I have no idea," he said, covering her hand with his own.

She lay very still, listening. But there were no sounds. "It's not morning, is it?" she said.

"Not yet," he said, lifting her hand and kissing the palm.

"I thought perhaps I had slept the night away," she said.

"No." He found her mouth in the darkness with his own. "There is still time left."

What would he do, he wondered many minutes later as he lay on his back, her body cradled on top of him, her head pillowed on his shoulder, if it were not for Annabelle and his obligation to her? Would it make a difference? Would he go with Rosamund in the morning? Or get her brother's name and direction so that he could follow her later?

Would he marry her? And that would be the only option, he realized. Despite the torrid affair they were indulging in, there would be no question of making her his mistress. Would he marry her? He was in love with her—there was no doubt about that. But he had never believed in romantic love and did not trust it now. The intensity of these feelings could not last beyond a few days or weeks at the most.

If he were free to pay court to her, he would be quickly disillusioned. On the whole, he thought very sensibly before following her into sleep, it was as well that he was in no position to pursue her acquaintance beyond the next morning. It would be better to have these few but treasured memories of her.

"Justin," she said sleepily, turning her head and kissing the underside of his jaw.

* * *

It was still dark. Perhaps it was still night. But there were faint and indefinable noises coming from belowstairs. Mrs. Reeves must be in the kitchen already. The night must be over.

Rosamund closed her eyes again and felt a raw ache spread upward from her chest into her throat and behind her nose. The night was over. She was still lying on top of Justin, his arms and the blankets warm about her. Her legs were spread comfortably on either side of his. They were still joined from their last act of love.

She did not want it to be morning. She did not want the night at an end.

"Are you awake?" she whispered.

"Mm? Now I am," he said, lowering his head and kissing her nose. "Uncomfortable?"

"No," she said. "It's morning, Justin."

"Is it?" he said. "Even though it's not light yet?"

"There is someone downstairs in the kitchen," she said.

"Ah," he said. One of his hands was lightly massaging the back of her head.

"Should we get up?"

"Yes," he said. "You will be eager to be on the road."

"Yes," she said.

"You're sure you don't want me to go with you?" he asked.

"No," she said. "I would not inconvenience you. And I would rather Dennis did not see you."

"As you wish, then," he said.

"Shall we get up, then?" she asked. But she pressed her face into his shoulder. She could feel him growing inside her again.

He lifted her away from him and turned her onto her back. And he came after her and thrust deeply into her. He laced his fingers with hers and set their hands on either side of her head. He buried his face in her hair and began to move slowly in her.

She was quite unaroused. There had been no foreplay at

all. But she did not want to be aroused. She wanted to feel
every moment of this last loving with a rational mind. She
wanted to remember him, his physical person, with her body.
She wanted to be able to lie down that night somewhere,
probably at some inn, and remember what he had felt like.
She closed her eyes and lay still, ignoring the tears that welled
beneath her eyelids.

It was a long and slow and silent loving, and despite herself
she surged to meet his passion at the end so that their hands
gripped bruisingly against the mattress. And then he kissed
her and smiled at her in the growing light, got out of the
bed and drew on his dressing gown, and left her room without
a word.

That was it, she thought. The end of an affair. One that
had devastated her emotions far more than she cared to admit.
One that she had doubtless been wrong and foolish to indulge
in. But one that she would not erase from her past or her
memory for all the inducements in the world.

And one not to be dwelt on and brooded on that morning,
she thought, pushing back the bedclothes resolutely despite
the chilliness of the room and stepping out onto the carpet.
Otherwise, she would be a watering pot when they were
saying good-bye and he would think her very foolish. He
would think that she had fallen in love with him or something stupid like that. The very thought of his thinking any
such thing made her shudder.

Though it would be no more than the simple truth, she
thought ruefully. And he would be very right to think her
foolish. She was twenty-six years old and could not even
indulge in a brief affair with a handsome gentleman without
losing her heart to him.

How very gauche and naïve of her.

The arrangement was that the earl's carriage would take
Rosamund back to the main highway and along in the
direction Dennis had been traveling, to the nearest inn. In
all likelihood she would find him there if they had not already

encountered him searching for her on the road. If by any chance there was no sign of him at the inn and no one had either seen or heard of him, then she would continue on her way, asking at each succeeding inn.

"But what if I do not find him at all?" she had asked. "It will take two days to reach home, even if the roads are perfectly clear."

"Then I will wait until my carriage returns," he had said with a shrug. "I came here for a week to be quiet. It does not matter if I am here a day or two longer than planned. No one will send out search parties for me."

She left early after a breakfast she could not stomach and a conversation that was bright and cheerful and quite without depth. She could not afford to be late and perhaps miss Dennis on the road. Reeves and the earl's coachman had cleared the driveway of snow. The road looked passable. The coachman said it would be no trouble at all.

"Well," Rosamund said, standing at the open front door and extending her right hand foolishly to the earl, "this is good-bye. Thank you so much for taking me up and giving me a safe place to stay, Justin."

He ignored the hand and the formal little speech. He drew her into his arms and held her against him so that it felt as if every breath of air would be squeezed from her. She did not even notice the discomfort. He rocked her and then kissed her once fiercely on the lips.

"You are beautiful, Rosamund," he said. "I will always remember you with pleasure."

"Me too," she said, forcing a smile to her lips.

He looked searchingly into her eyes. "Are you quite sure there is no chance I have impregnated you?" he asked. "Shall I give you an address where I may be reached in the event that you will need me?"

She shook her head. "There is no chance," she said. "But I would not send to you anyway, Justin."

He hugged her to him once more. "Good-bye, then," he said.

"Good-bye." She smiled brightly up at him, touched his cheek briefly with one gloved hand, and ran lightly down the steps, where he followed her and handed her into the carriage without another word. He closed the door and stood back.

The delay seemed endless, Rosamund thought, before the carriage lurched slightly into motion. Her smile felt quite frozen in place. She raised one hand in a final farewell and then the carriage turned to make its way down the driveway. Finally, blessedly, she could see him no more.

And she could not afford to indulge in tears, either, she thought, biting hard on her upper lip. Perhaps they would meet Dennis quite soon. That ache she had felt before dawn returned, except that this time it was many times more painful.

And the feeling of emptiness was quite frightening.

She leaned toward the window to watch the road carefully even though there was no chance of seeing Dennis until they rejoined the main highway.

Although he was not wearing his greatcoat, Lord Wetherby did not go inside immediately. He watched his carriage for as long as it was in sight, and then he wandered over to where they had built their snowmen the day before. The figures were still visible, though there had been some melting. Despite her contention that she had hollowed out the shoulders of hers so that the head would not roll off, it was lying in the snow behind the body, its carrot nose and coal eyes still in place.

The earl smiled and turned to see the marks of her snow angel, still visible, and the marks of his, not so distinct. But of course they had blurred its outlines when he had toppled her onto him and spent several minutes kissing her.

Lord Wetherby realized in sudden surprise that he felt very much like crying. She was gone, and all that was left were these frozen and fast-melting mementos of fun and laughter and mutual attraction.

His snow angel! Melting into air.

She was gone and he knew nothing of her except her name and her brother's first name and the fact that she had lived in Lincolnshire with her husband. He would not be able to find her even if he wanted to, unless his carriage was forced to take her all the way to her brother's house, a two-day journey.

He must hope that she would find her brother and would be lost to him beyond trace. He would not wish to have the temptation of knowing where she might be reached. He was not free. In a month's time he would no longer be free to so much as to look with desire at any woman but Annabelle.

It was cold, he realized, shuddering suddenly. Deuced cold. And she was gone. She would no longer be there to warm his body or his bed.

Or his heart.

It was really absurdly easy, Rosamund found. When she had finally swallowed her tears and concentrated her attention on the road, she had been afraid, as she had been at the back of her mind for the past few days, that she had lost Dennis completely, that he had gone astray searching for her, that perhaps he had even hurt himself—she would not put her fears more strongly than that in her mind.

But it was so easy. Mr. Halliday's carriage turned onto the main highway and had proceeded for no longer than five minutes when it slowed at the approach of another carriage. And Rosamund, pressing her nose to the window, saw that it was Dennis' and rapped frantically on the front panel.

She did not wait for the coachman to descend from his perch to put down the steps and help her out. She thrust the door open and jumped down into the roadway, skidding rather inelegantly on its slushy surface. Dennis, peering from his window, soon did likewise.

"You're safe," they both said together, and fell into each other's arms.

"I'm so relieved that you did not perish searching for me,"

she said after they had hugged each other wordlessly for several moments, looking eagerly up into his familiar face.

"Where the devil were you?" he asked. "Why did you not come back when it started to snow? Do you realize that I have been out of my mind with worry?"

"And where were you?" she asked. "Why did you not turn back to fetch me? You knew that I would not be the first to give in."

"I was sitting at the side of the road staring at a carriage with only three wheels," he said. The volume of his voice was rising. "You would risk your life just because you would not be the one to give in? You have not grown up at all, Rosa. Why do I always have to be the one to give in? And who the devil does that carriage belong to?"

"Perhaps it would be wiser to quarrel when we are alone inside your carriage," Rosamund suggested. "The carriage belongs to a Mr. and Mrs. Reeves with whom I have been staying since the snow began. I have been very comfortable, I do assure you."

"I had better go back with you and thank them," he said.

"There is really no need, Dennis," she said. "I am of age, you know, and made quite adequate thanks of my own."

"Well, then," he said, and he nodded to the earl's coachman and handed him some coins before helping Rosamund into his carriage and climbing in beside her. "Do you realize that we have already lost more than two days, Rosa, and have had to waste this whole morning, too? We might have been well on the way home by now."

"Look at it this way, Dennis," she said. "I could have been dead and frozen in a hedgerow. How would you feel then? At least I am alive and well for you to scold."

"And I had to stay at one devil of an inn while you were comfortable with that Reeves family," he said. "I really don't think it fair, Rosa."

"But at least you had a peaceful few days," she said, "even if you were worrying about me. Imagine how many times we would have quarreled if I had been at that inn with you."

"Well, anyway," he said, "don't ever do anything like that again. It was a devilish childish thing to do. What caused it, anyway?"

"You wanted to marry me off to Toby," she said, "so that I would not be a burden on you."

He made an impatient sound.

"Tobias is a good catch," he said. "He will doubtless be a bishop one day. But it is only advice I was giving you, Rosa. You should know that I would never try to force your hand. Did I refuse my consent to your marrying Hunter, even though I disapproved? Did I?"

"No," she admitted, "though you grumbled and frowned a great deal and made me feel your displeasure. Are you forcing Annabelle into marriage?"

"Forcing her?" he said. "Anna? What utter nonsense, Rosa. One does not have to force a daughter into marrying an earl. And Wetherby is a young and a personable man as well as a very wealthy one. Of course I am not forcing her. Anna is a very biddable girl."

"Unlike me, your tone says," she said with a smile. "Very well, Dennis, I will grant that Annabelle is being obedient of her own free will."

"She is ever eager to do her duty," he said, "and to bring lasting joy to her mama and papa. And besides, the ultimate choice is to be hers. We are not going to use any coercion."

Rosamund sighed. "I never brought you joy, did I, Dennis?" she said. "But you were a good brother to me, I must confess. And still are. It was kind of you to come all the way to Lincolnshire in the dead of winter just to bring me home and ensure that I would be part of the family celebrations next month. I shall try to behave myself, I promise. I will even be polite to Toby."

"And consider marrying him?" he asked hopefully. "Really and truly, Rosa, you could hardly do better for yourself."

She clucked her tongue impatiently. "I said I would be polite to him," she said. "Who knows? Perhaps in nine years he has been transformed into a charming and an interesting

gentleman. I certainly am not promising to marry him.
Perhaps I will find someone else to my taste at Lord Gilmore's house party. Perhaps I will even run away with the
earl myself before he can offer for Annabelle.''

Dennis frowned. ''That joke was not in very good taste,''
he said.

''No.'' She sighed. ''It wasn't, was it? I'm sorry, Dennis.
I am so very tired. Aren't you? I really would not mind
having a little sleep.''

''Put your feet up on the other seat, then,'' he said, and
he picked up a blanket and settled it snugly about her. ''I
really was almost worried to death about you, you know,
Rosa. I'm glad you are safe, though I daresay you had as
dull a time of it as I did.''

''Yes,'' she said, smiling at him. ''Thank you, Dennis.
Thank you for everything.''

And she closed her eyes and saw Justin, his blue eyes
smiling at her. And felt his arms warm about her and the
rough hairs of his chest against her palms. And smelled his
cologne. She would never see him again. Even if she ever
wanted to communicate with him—even if by some unhappy
fate she was with child—she would not be able to do so
because she knew only his name, nothing else at all about
him. Much as they had talked, she realized, as close as they
had grown, he had told her almost nothing about himself.

She would never see him again. Never.

The ache was back in her throat. She rested her head
against the squabs, her eyes closed, fighting her tears.

Rosamund found herself over the next few weeks looking
forward to the house party at Brookfield, the Marquess of
Gilmore's country home. It was something to focus her mind
on when it wished to dwell on other matters. As Dennis'
sister and ward, she had gone there several times as a girl
and had always been made welcome by the marquess and
marchioness and indeed by the rest of the family too. She
had been treated very much like one of them.

Rosamund looked forward to a few weeks during which she hoped there would be enough company and enough entertainment to keep her from brooding. And she looked forward to renewing her acquaintance with people she had not seen for many years, not since she had been a very young girl, in fact. It was hard sometimes to realize that she had been only seventeen years old when she married. Just a child. Younger than Annabelle was now.

And at the house party they were to celebrate Annabelle's betrothal to the Earl of Wetherby, although that betrothal was not by any means official yet. The earl still had his proposal to make to Annabelle, and she still had to give her free consent. It seemed that Dennis and Lana were indeed not putting any great pressure on her. The reason for the gathering at Brookfield was the marquess's seventieth birthday.

"Grandmama and his lordship's mother dreamed of the match years ago," Annabelle explained to her aunt one afternoon as they were strolling in the bare rose arbor. "I met him at that time, though he was a grown man and I was just a child. We met again last spring when Mama and Papa took me to town for the Season. He danced with me a few times and escorted me to the theater once and took me driving in the park. He made an offer to Papa for me before we came home, and Papa encouraged his suit, though he thought I was still too young at the time to receive a formal offer. He asked his lordship to wait until we went to Grandpapa's."

Annabelle had told the story with the grave manner that had been customary with her whenever Rosamund had seen her during her marriage, though she remembered the girl as a sunny-natured child. She was rather lovely with her oval face, large gray eyes, and smooth dark-blond hair looped down over her ears. But she seemed almost too mature for an eighteen-year-old—too accepting of an arranged marriage. She would be screeching her protests if it were she, Rosamund thought.

"Mama and Papa were delighted by the offer," Annabelle said. "So were Grandmama and Grandpapa."

"And you?" Rosamund asked. "Are you pleased? Is he a handsome man? I have heard that he is. And is he interesting? Kind? Does he have that certain something? Are you in love with him?"

"He is an earl and well-connected," Annabelle said. "And everyone approves of him, Aunt Rosa. I trust their judgment."

The girl was going to accept the offer without question, Rosamund realized, although she had been given apparent freedom of choice. Rosamund wondered how her niece could be so different from herself. She would have bristled and threatened mutiny if a grandparent or parent had even suggested a match for her. Though perhaps not. Perhaps if Papa had lived, she would have listened to his advice. But, then, perhaps he would have advised her against marrying Leonard and she would hate not to have lived through that marriage.

As far as the Earl of Wetherby was concerned, she would just have to wait and see for herself what he was like. He sounded like a paragon from all Lana and Dennis said of him. Perhaps once she saw him she would understand very well why Annabelle was putting up no fight against an arranged marriage.

Yes, she looked forward to the house party. She needed some diversion. She found herself fighting an almost daily battle against depression, and she was not one to suffer such moods. It was all very well to think of him at night. She always did so quite deliberately, reliving his touch, his words, his lovemaking. But not by day. Then she thought of him unwillingly. By day there was only heartache in such thoughts.

For it had been only a temporary liaison, thoroughly satisfactory to them both, something to be remembered with pleasure on occasion but something to be allowed to slip very quickly from constant memory. She spoiled the sweetness of it by dwelling on it and making of it a painful thing.

Moreover, she annoyed herself. She had never thought to

find herself lovesick over a man who was unattainable. Gracious heaven, she had even felt a twinge of disappointment when she had discovered that she was not with child.

She must find someone to flirt with at the house party. Even Toby Strangelove if necessary. Though Josh and Ferdie and Robin were likely to be there too.

She was going to forget Justin Halliday—or if not forget him, at least relegate him to a far corner of her memory where he belonged. How foolish of her to be reliving every day and every night what he had probably forgotten within a day or two.

7

It was something of a relief to be approaching Brookfield, country home of the Marquess of Gilmore, at last. The Earl of Wetherby looked with some interest at the large, imposing stone gateposts with the iron gates and the square stone lodge beside it. An elm-lined driveway stretched beyond. The house was not yet in sight.

It was a relief—the point of no return, at last. Not that there had ever been any returning, not since the previous spring when he had met Annabelle again and given in to his mother's persuasions and to his own acceptance of the fact that he really must settle down soon and marry and start a family. But for almost a month, since his return from Price's hunting box, in fact, his mind had been considering all sorts of devious schemes for escape, all of them dishonorable in the extreme.

Well, there was no going back now. The porter was swinging back the gates so that the carriage might proceed along the driveway and was smiling and bowing and touching his forelock.

"Do you remember it, Justin?" his mother asked from the seat beside him. "It is all of nine years since you were here last. It has not changed, has it?"

"I have not forgotten," the earl said. "I was twenty years old at the time, Mama. I came on the visit with you, if you recall, because Papa was indisposed."

Lady Wetherby sighed. "He never did recover," she said. "But let us not think morbid thoughts on such an occasion. Annabelle was a very pretty child. Do you remember?"

"Yes," he said. "And I recall my horror when you and

Lady Gilmore conceived the notion that an alliance between our two families would be a desirable future goal.''

"Well," she said, laughing and patting his hand, "and so it was, too. And you must admit that it is all turning out well, Justin. She is a remarkably pretty young lady and very nicely behaved, too."

"Yes," he said, "she is."

"And so," she said, "after nine years Eugenia and I move one step closer to realizing our dream. When are you planning to make your formal offer to the girl, Justin? And I do hope you press for a spring wedding in London. You know my thoughts on that."

Yes, he did. It was strange how one became one's family's property more than one's own person once one had expressed the merest interest in marrying, he thought. If there was still the faintest possibility of escape on his own account—though there was not—he was certainly tied hand and foot by the knowledge of his mother's happiness for him and the knowledge that Marion, the younger of his two sisters, was also to attend this house party, mainly to witness the happy moment of her brother's betrothal. His mother, of course, visited her close friend the marchioness with some frequency.

Sometimes one felt very out of control of one's own destiny.

"I shall have to speak with Lord March," he said. "I'm sure we can arrange everything to everyone's mutual satisfaction."

To everyone's satisfaction, yes. His own included. He was very thankful that the moment had come, the point of no return. Perhaps after this day he would no longer dream of being free again, free to set out in search of . . . He pushed the thought ruthlessly from his mind—again. The house had come into view around a bend in the driveway.

Yes, he remembered it. It was a large Palladian mansion of yellow-brown stone, fronted by extensive formal gardens and a marble fountain. It was the place where he had spent an unspeakably dreary month nine years before, his only companions being his mother, the marquess and marchioness, and Annabelle Milford, their nine-year-old granddaughter, who had been spending a few weeks with them. He had been expected by a doting mother and the marchioness to converse with the child and entertain her—at a time in his life when his interest in women had run almost exclusively to buxom barmaids.

And now she was eighteen years old and he was returning to make his offer to her. And it was not, indeed, a bad match. He had been quite taken with her the previous spring. If he had not been, all of his mother's persuasions could not have made him offer for her.

"Ah," the countess said, peering through the carriage window as it rounded the formal gardens and approached the main doors across a cobbled courtyard, "we have been seen. There is a reception committee."

That was another thing, Wetherby thought, looking through the window at the six people gathered on the steps outside the house and in the courtyard below it. He was quite well acquainted with most of the members of Annabelle's family. It would not be easy to cry off even if he wished to do so—and of course he was not seriously considering any such thing.

The Marquess and Marchioness of Gilmore did not leave their estate very often, and when they did, it was to go to Bath rather than London. Lord Wetherby had not seen them for nine years. Even so, they looked familiar, both tall and slim and of proud bearing. Both had thick, silver-white hair; the marquess had the additon of a large mustache. Both were warm and gracious in manner. The earl had rarely known a couple who seemed so well suited to each other.

Viscount March was with them, as were Lady Newton, the marquess's niece, Lord Carver, his grandson by his elder daughter, and Lord Beresford, his great-nephew and heir.

Lord March helped Lady Wetherby descend from the carriage and bowed over her hand. The other gentlemen bowed to her too, and the marchioness and Lady Newton took her into their care.

"Laura, my dear," Lady Newton said, "you must be hagged. I do hate carriage travel, don't you? Every time I make a journey I swear it will be my last. I shall take root in my town house, I always say, and anyone who wishes to see me may come there. But I daresay I will never do it. Uncle issues a royal summons to attend a family do, and I come running—or bouncing along in a carriage, to be more accurate."

"Do come and have some tea, Laura," the marchioness said, kissing her friend on the cheek. "The housekeeper can show you to your room afterward."

"That sounds quite delightful, Eugenia," the countess said. "And, yes, Claudette, it is good to be on firm ground again. Though Justin always keeps a well-sprung carriage."

The earl shook hands with the marquess and Lord March and kissed the marchioness on the cheek before she disappeared inside the house with his mother.

"Your sister and her husband arrived an hour ago," the marquess said. "So you are the young sprig who had to kick his heels here all those years ago while my wife and your mama were laying plans for your future. You have grown up. I would hardly have recognized you." He chuckled and stroked his white mustache.

"We arrived only half an hour ago, Wetherby," Lord March said. "The ladies are still upstairs. But you will meet them at tea. You will be wanting to freshen up before then."

"Joshua and Ferdinand will see you to your room," the marquess said. "It's good to have you here, Wetherby. I hope we can make your stay a pleasant one."

The earl bowed and made a suitable reply.

"Well, Justin," Joshua Ridley, Lord Beresford, said, grinning and extending his right hand as the two older men moved away. "You have come as the proverbial lamb to the slaughter, have you?"

The earl shook his head. "I am approaching my thirtieth birthday," he said. "It's time, Josh. How old are you? Twenty-six? Seven? And heir to a marquess and to this?" He gestured toward the house and the land about it. "Your time will come soon enough and then we will see how broadly you grin.''

Ferdinand Handsforth, Lord Carver, laughed rather more loudly than the joke seemed to merit. "He has you there, Josh, you must admit," he said. "You tell him, Wetherby. Josh always likes to have the last word."

"You won't be immune, either, Ferdie, my lad," Lord Beresford said, "being the grandson of a marquess and a baron since your father's passing. Not that Ferdie will have to be coerced, of course, Justin. Even at the grand age of twenty-four he is a bachelor much against his will. But what woman would ever have him with that carrot top?"

"Oh, I say," Lord Carver said as the other two had a good laugh at his expense. "A low blow, Josh. It tempts one to make remarks about your limp."

Lord Beresford grinned. "Acquired at Waterloo in service of my country, Ferdie," he said. "The ladies find it quite irresistible. You will have to try again. Here is your room, Justin. You will doubtless be delighted to have one final half-hour of quiet and privacy. The place is fairly crawling with family members—most of them ours and only a few of your own."

"You are surrounded by us," Lord Carver said cheerfully. "We are making it impossible for you to cry off, you see, Wetherby."

"Ah," the earl said, "I see. But what if I am here entirely by personal inclination?"

"It would not be surprising," Lord Beresford said, grinning and slapping him on the back. "Annabelle is a pretty young thing. And talking of pretty young things, she has brought her aunt with her. Very fetching indeed, Justin. Too bad you won't be able to compete with me for her favors." He winked.

The earl found himself smiling as he closed the door of his bedchamber behind him. Henri, his valet, was already busy in his dressing room, he could see. It was good to be among friends again. Good to have plenty of people with whom to distract his mind.

He was looking forward to seeing Annabelle again, to getting to know her better in the relaxed atmosphere of a country home. He was going to make every effort to develop a friendship with her and a fondness for her over the next two weeks. Finally the past was permanently and irrevocably behind him. This was his present and his future. He was going to start it with a willingness and an eagerness to make a happy life for both himself and Annabelle.

There was no sense in brooding. He was going to stop doing it that very day. He strode across the bedchamber to the dressing room to see what clothes Henri had set out for him to change into.

Lana and Annabelle had already gone downstairs to tea without her, Rosamund discovered in some annoyance when she knocked on their doors. It was all the fault of the maid who had been sent to help her. She had told the girl that she did not like her hair styled elaborately, but the maid had made of it a marvelous creation, anyway. Rosamund had ordered her take it down and start all over again.

And now she was going to have to make a grand entrance all alone. Bother, she thought. It was so long since she had been at Brookfield and met all the family members that she felt almost shy. It was very silly, since she was not by nature a shy person. But having spent nine years in the confined neighborhood of Leonard's home in Lincolnshire, she had grown staid, she supposed. On their arrival she had seen only the marquess and marchioness. And she had glimpsed two young gentlemen from a distance, but she had not been able to identify them.

Oh, well, she thought, squaring her shoulders and making for the staircase, she could now cower in her room for the rest of the day. And she did know most of these people, after all, and had always liked them. The only ones she did not know were the Earl of Wetherby and his family members. But then their attention woud be focused all on Annabelle, anyway. She was not going to start giving in to shyness at her advanced age.

Fortunately, when she stepped inside the drawing room, she was immediately taken to the ample bosom of Lady Newton and had to make no effort at all to break into a group.

"Rosamund," Lady Newton said, hugging her and kissing her on the cheek, "how very fine you look, my dear. I hope you had not too unpleasant a journey. I was so very sorry to hear of the passing of your husband."

"Thank you," Rosamund said. "Goodness." She looked at the two young ladies with Lady Newton. "Eva and Pamela? But you were just children the last time I saw you. Of course, I must have been only fifteen or sixteen myself." She looked around for the eldest Newton sister. "Is Valerie here?"

"With her betrothed," Lady Newton said, indicating her eldest daughter, who was sitting behind the tea tray across the room, a thin young man at her side.

"I must pay my respects to her," Rosamund said.

But a touch on her arm delayed her and she found herself looking up into the long, narrow, heavy-browed face of the Reverend Tobias Strangelove, great-nephew of the marchioness. The first thing she noticed was that he was quite as abnormally tall as she remembered and that he had grown a great deal balder.

"Lady Hunter?" he said, and he took her hand in his and raised it to his lips. "May I say how gratified I am that you have seen fit to grace my great-uncle's house party with your lovely presence?"

"Toby," she said, "how lovely to see you again. But you are the Reverend Strangelove now, aren't you? Perhaps I should call you by your title or Tobias at the very least." She smiled.

"I do usually deplore familiarity to men of the cloth," he said, "since a person addressing a clergyman is really addressing the Church with all its solemn traditions. Indeed, it could even be said that he is addressing the almighty, since clergymen are his representatives on earth. But on your lips, my dear Lady Hunter, Toby sounds quite unexceptionable."

No, Toby had not changed one little bit apart from the hair. "Then you must call me Rosamund, as you used to do," she said lightly.

"It would be too presumptuous, you being the respectable widow of a respected baronet, Lady Hunter," he said. "But I will treasure in my heart your great condescension in offering such a mark of friendship and personal favor. Have you met his lordship?"

"The Earl of Wetherby?" she said. "No, never. Is he here?"

"He is conversing with your dear niece," the Reverend Strangelove said. "A very elegant and amiable gentleman, as I am sure you will agree. It is a tribute to your brother's good sense and diplomatic skills that he has been netted for Annabelle."

"Yes," Rosamund said, gazing in some curiosity across the room to where the earl stood, his back to her, talking with Annabelle and Lana. Yes, he was extremely elegant in a blue coat that looked as if it had been molded to his frame. And a broad-shouldered and muscular frame it was, too, she thought, though his waist and hips were slender enough. His pantaloons did nothing to hide well-muscled legs. His Hessian boots looked shiny enough to serve as mirrors. His hair was thick and fair and wavy.

He reminded her . . . Oh, he reminded her. But she pushed the thought from her mind. She must not begin seeing him in every young and well-favored gentleman she would ever meet.

"If you will take my arm, Lady Hunter," the Reverend Strangelove said, "I will do myself the honor of presenting you to his lordship."

Rosamund would have preferred to be presented by someone who would not deliver a long and involved and formal speech as he did so, but she was curious to meet Annabelle's suitor. She placed her hand on the sleeve that was extended to her.

The Reverend Strangelove cleared his throat when they

came up behind the earl. "Lana?" he said, bowing to her from the waist. "Annabelle?" He bowed again. "I had the pleasure of greeting you several minutes ago when you came downstairs, and I satisfied myself on that occasion that you felt refreshed after your journey, having spent a quiet half-hour abovestairs. Your sister-in-law, Lana, and your aunt, Annabelle, has now joined the company, and I have taken upon myself the honor of presenting her to his lordship." He bowed to the earl.

He continued at great length. But Rosamund heard not a word. The Earl of Wetherby had turned his head as soon as Toby cleared his throat, his blue eyes smiling with warm courtesy. And their eyes had met.

How long did Toby drone on? Did they stare at each other for the whole of that time? Did their smiles remain frozen to their faces, or did they fade? Rosamund could never afterward answer any of those questions.

Toby stopped talking finally.

"Mrs. Hunter," the earl said, making her an elegant bow.

"My lord," she said, curtsying.

"Ah, I did say," the Reverend Strangelove said, "though it may have been lost in the noise of convivial conversation going on about us in the rest of the room, *Lady* Hunter, my lord. Lady Hunter is the widow of Sir Leonard Hunter of Lincolnshire."

"Lady Hunter," the earl said. "I beg your pardon, ma'am."

"I hope you did not mind us coming down ahead of you, Rosa," Lady March said, "but Dennis brought word that Lord and Lady Wetherby had arrived."

"Not at all," Rosamund said.

"Rosamund." Beatrice Handsforth, Lady Carver, Lana's elder sister, laid a hand on Rosamund's arm and peered around into her face. "It *is* you. Goodness, how you have grown up. You were a mere girl the last time I saw you—the year before your marriage, I believe. Ferdie told me you had come with Dennis and Lana. Do come and talk to Christobel—my daughter, you remember? Ferdie's sister?

But of course you must remember—you were quite like one of the family for several years. She is all grown up now too and about to take the *ton* by storm as soon as the Season begins. But you do not have a cup of tea, dear. How remiss someone has been. I shall take Rosamund to the tea tray, Lana.''

Rosamund allowed herself to be borne off by Lana's sister without a backward glance. She fought to regain control, to find some semblance of normalcy in the scene about her. It was not real. It could not be real. She would wake up soon. Or else she had mistaken. She had only imagined that it was he. She had been struck with the similarity as soon as she had seen his back, and so her imagination had transformed his face, too.

A very foolish thought. A ridiculous thought, she realized when she glanced hastily back over her shoulder and met a pair of familiar blue eyes before jerking her head back again.

He had said he was to be betrothed in one month's time. Oh God, he had said it. Why had she not made the connection? But why should she have? Only the most bizarre of coincidences could have arranged this turn of events.

She needed air. She needed it now before she disgraced herself and fell to the floor in a swoon.

''Here we are,'' Lady Carver said. ''Valerie will pour for you, won't you, Valerie, dear? Do you two recognize each other? You were both just girls when you used to be such friends.''

''Rosamund,'' Valerie Newton said. ''I thought it was you when I saw you talking to Mama and the girls a few minutes ago. How lovely it is to see you again.''

No, she would not disgrace herself. She certainly would not. How unspeakably embarrasssing that would be—everyone fussing over her and he knowing very well what had caused her swoon. No, she would not.

''Hello, Valerie,'' Rosamund said. ''I hear you are engaged.'' She smiled brightly and determinedly.

* * *

The Earl of Wetherby continued to talk with Annabelle and Lady March. He continued to smile. He exchanged kisses with his sister Marion when she crossed the room to his side, and pleasantries with Lord Sitwell, his brother-in-law.

He did all that was right and proper by sheer instinct. He could never afterward remember what he had said or what had been said to him.

She was there—in that very room. For a month he had called himself all kinds of a fool for letting her go without finding out where he might communicate with her. For a month he had wondered if he would ever set eyes on her again, wondered if she would ever come to London or if they would ever be at one of the spas at the same time.

For a month he had told himself and told himself that it was better so. And just an hour before he had put her finally behind him, firmly in his past, to remain there forever. And yet here she was, at the same house party, in the same room as he. And that was not even the whole of it. She was Annabelle's aunt. The Dennis she had spoken of, the brother with whom she had quarreled before leaving his carriage, was Lord March, Annabelle's father. If he had gone with her that morning to find him, he would have discovered the truth.

God! He glanced across the room, half-expecting to find that he had mistaken the matter, that in reality she was a woman who merely resembled Rosamund. But when his eyes met hers for one painful moment, he knew the absurdity of that hope.

"I think we can slip away to the library and have that talk you asked for, Wetherby," Lord March said after what seemed like interminable minutes or hours of being sociable. He had laid a hand on the earl's shoulder.

Wetherby followed him thankfully from the room, though Rosamund had left a few minutes before. But the library was not empty, he found with surprise. Lady March was there as well as the marquess and marchioness.

"We will have the poor young man blushing and stammering and shaking in his shoes," the marchioness said, directing him to a seat. "If you wish, Lord Wetherby—may I call you Justin?—Lana and I will leave without more ado. But we are all such interested parties, you see, and we all wish to have our say in your plans."

The earl smiled. "Please, don't leave," he said. "I shall try my best to hold my own even against such odds."

The marchioness laughed. "Do offer Justin some brandy, William," she said to her husband. "He looks just like a young man who is about to lose his freedom."

"I hope that is a quite accurate description, ma'am," he said. He looked at Lord March. "I had your approval of my suit last year, sir. I assume that you have not changed your mind?"

God, he thought, looking at his future father-in-law, just a month before he had spent two full days and three nights with the man's sister. He had made love to her—how many times? And now he was renewing his request for the daughter.

"Absolutely not," Lord March said. "And Annabelle is looking forward to renewing her acquaintance with you."

"But how could she not?" the marchioness said. "She met you several times last spring, Justin? I don't wonder at all that she has been looking forward with pleasure to meeting you again here."

The marquess coughed.

"Oh, William," she said, "you know I am an incurable romantic. Why else would I have married you?"

The marquess chuckled.

"My reason for asking to speak with you, sir," Lord Wetherby said, turning back to Lord March, "was to ask if I may speak with Annabelle without delay. Or would you prefer that I waited?"

"I can't see any reason for delay," Lord March said, "since word seems to be out anyway and everyone is expecting the betrothal."

"It seems that my dear wife thought my seventieth birthday a momentous enough occasion to invite all these people here," Lord Gilmore said. "There is to be a grand ball for the occasion one week from today. It would be a grand idea to announce the betrothal on the same evening."

"What a splendid idea, William," the marchioness said. "Are you in love with my granddaughter, Justin?"

Lord Wetherby looked at them all in some discomfort. "I have not had a very lengthy acquaintance with her," he said. "I would hope that we can develop an affection for each other."

"Naturally," Lord March said.

"But it is as I thought," Lady Gilmore said. "Justin and Annabelle have had no chance to grow comfortable with each other. They met when she was just a child and he a very young man—you did look rather comical together on that occasion, Justin, dear, and I know that you wished your mama and me at the very bottom of the ocean. And then they met under all the formality of a London Season last year. They need time to get to know each other."

"But the announcement should be made, Mama," Lady March said. "Lord Wetherby has accompanied his mother here expressly for that purpose."

"Well, of course the announcement will be made, Lana," her mother said. "On Papa's birthday, as he has suggested. But I would suggest that the offer be made on that day, too, so that it will not be a stammering affair, but an agreement between two young people who have had a week to grow comfortable with each other. What do you say, Justin?" She smiled at him.

"I am agreeable to whatever is suggested, ma'am," he said.

Lord March coughed. "You understand, of course, Wetherby," he said, "that though Lana and I are delighted at the prospect of the match and Annabelle seems pleased by it, we have left the final decision to her. It would be a great embarrassment if she refuses you, but we will not try to force her."

"I certainly would expect nothing else," Lord Wetherby

said. "I will hope that during the coming week I can make myself irresistible to your daughter."

He could also make himself very resistible, he thought, temptation flashing into his mind. He had not thought there was any real question of Annabelle's refusing him.

"But of course," Lady March said hastily, "she is very ready to accept you, my lord."

"She would be a very strange young lady if she were not," Lady Gilmore said with a smile. "All the other young ladies in London will doubtless go into mourning."

They all laughed. The earl wondered idly what Rosamund had told her brother and sister-in-law about those days of the snowstorm. Doubtless she had not mentioned Justin Halliday—they would have known the name. He wondered what March would do if he knew that the man he had accepted for Annabelle had spent those days—and nights—tumbling his sister, and the weeks since dreaming of her.

"That would seem to be satisfactory to everyone, then," Lord March said. "You will speak with Annabelle on my father-in-law's birthday, then, Wetherby, and he will announce your betrothal during the ball in the evening?"

Lord Wetherby raised his glass. "Agreed," he said.

The marchioness clasped her hands to her bosom. "How splendid," she said. "I do love romance and betrothals and weddings. Who else can we match during these two weeks?"

Lord Gilmore laughed and set an arm about her shoulders. "No one," he said. "Everyone is either married already or is related to everyone else."

"Oh, the situation is not quite so desperate," she said. "Toby and Robin are the grandsons of my stepbrother and so only remotely connected to our other relatives. It is high time Joshua started to think of marriage. He is your heir, William. I have always thought I should try to match him with Christobel since she is the daughter of our elder girl and only his second cousin. But I cannot quite think her capable of coping with his wit. And then of course there is Lady Hunter, who is unrelated to anyone except Dennis, and is very eligible and quite lovely. It really should be possible to find her a husband.''

"Perhaps she would prefer to choose her own, Eugenia," the marquess said with a chuckle. "A remarkably handsome young lady, by the way, Dennis."

"Yes," Lord March said. "As stubborn as she ever was, though. Tobias is interested in her, but when I mentioned the fact on our way home from Lincolnshire, she was so irate that she got out of the carriage and I did not see her for three days. I thought she was lost in a snowstorm."

The marchioness laughed merrily. "I don't blame the girl at all," she said. "Tobias, Dennis! I am dearly fond of the boy and proud of him too, but he is no lady's dream of romance, you know."

"But it really was not funny, Mama," Lady March said. "Unspeakable things might have happened to Rosa during those three days. I am very glad I did not know of it until she was safely found again."

Unspeakable things, the earl thought. That was precisely what had happened to Rosamund Hunter—Lady Hunter. She had not mentioned the fact that her husband was a baronet. But then he has not been quite open about his identity, either. Would that he had been. If only they had known right from the start, they could doubtless have guarded against what had happened.

"Little Rosamund," the marquess said with a chuckle. "She was always into mischief when she was here, if I remember correctly. Usually egged on by Joshua, am I not right, Eugenia? With Tobias making lengthy excuses for her when she was in trouble with you, Dennis."

Lord March laughed too. "The trouble was," he said, "that by the time Tobias came to the end of his speech, I had usually forgotten the reason for my wrath."

"We will be boring you," Lady March said to the earl. "And you will be thinking my sister-in-law very lacking in conduct. I do assure you she is the dearest girl. You will be wanting to have some rest before dinner."

She got to her feet and they all followed suit.

So the Reverend Strangelove was the new suitor her brother had picked out for her, Lord Wetherby thought as he ascended the stairs to his room. And he had been her champion in times past. As Josh had been her fellow conspirator.

It was not at all difficult to imagine Rosamund involved in all sorts of mischief as a girl. He doubted she had changed a great deal.

He had flashing memories of her trudging along a road already covered with snow, shivering, her teeth chattering, too stubborn to turn back to meet her brother. And of her helpless with laughter as he pelted her with snowballs, her own flying quite wide of the mark nine times out of ten. And of her frowning with chagrin when she realized that she would not be able to lift the head of her snowman onto its shoulders. And of her lying full-length in the snow, quite unselfconsciously making a snow angel.

And he had a vivid image of her standing in front of the fire in her bedchamber, all but lost in the folds of Mrs. Reeves' flannel nightgown, rigid with terror, but telling him that she did not want him to go away. She wanted him to make love to her.

He stood against the inside of his closed bedchamber door, his eyes tightly closed, his teeth clamped together.

Damnation! He had arrived with such firm resolve and such high hopes for putting behind him what could not be recaptured. He had been so determined to get on with the rest of his life and to make of it as positive and as pleasant an experience as he possibly could.

Hell and damnation!

What the devil was he going to do?

8

"Well, Justin . . ." Lord Beresford was straddling a chair in the earl's dressing room, his arms stretched over the back of it. He was watching his friend get ready for dinner. "You look fine enough to take a whole army of ladies by storm. You have so much lace at the cuff you will have to be careful not to dip some of it in the gravy."

"Jealousy, jealousy," Lord Wetherby said, brushing with his hands at the sleeves of his maroon velvet evening coat. He had had so little time to himself. Why could Beresford not be like any normal gentleman and take his time over changing into his evening finery?

"Is the announcement to be made at dinner?" his friend asked. "Are there to be champagne and speeches and everyone kissing everyone else and slapping everyone else's back and all laughing their heads off? If so, I had better offer my condolences now."

"No, not tonight," the earl said. "Next week on the marquess's birthday—if it takes place at all, that is. Annabelle has not said yes yet."

"Ah," the other said. "But she will, of course. She would have to have windmills in the head to reject the grand prize of the London marriage mart, now, wouldn't she? You should have had your valet do that, you know, before he left. You'll never get it in the center."

Lord Wetherby was attaching a diamond pin to his neckcloth. He had wanted to be alone just for a short while to collect his thoughts. That was why he had dismissed his valet early. But as Henri had left the room, so Beresford had entered it.

Somehow he had to collect himself before going down to

dinner. He could not simply gape at her as he had done at teatime. Lord! He could not have imagined a worse scenario if he had set his mind to it. He had turned around to greet yet another family member, and found himself smiling straight into the dark eyes that had haunted his dreams for a month. She was March's sister. Had he known that March's given name was Dennis? But then there must be thousands of Dennises in England. He could not have been expected to guess.

"I suppose I'm fortunate that there is Annabelle to be fussed over and married off and to occupy everyone's thoughts for the next few months," Lord Beresford said. "At any moment now eyes are going to begin turning my way— you reminded me of it this afternoon. Here I am twenty-six years old, heir to the marquess, and free as a bird. I am mortally afraid I am going to be paired off with Christobel."

"Handsforth?" the earl said. "Carver's sister?"

"The very one." Lord Beresford said. "Red hair and freckles and all. It stands to reason that it would be a desirable match, doesn't it? The marquess has no son, but only two brothers, both deceased, one nephew, also deceased, and a great-nephew—me, the sole survivor and heir. What could make more sense than to marry me off to one of the grand-daughters? And since Christobel belongs to the elder daughter, she is the obvious choice. I would not have minded Annabelle so much, though someone ought to teach the chit to smile. But not Christobel."

"You don't like red hair?" the earl asked.

"It's not that," his friend said. "She giggles . . . and bounces. And one sometimes wonders uncharitably what she has inside her head to keep her ears apart. Anyway, I seem to be safe for the moment, though I may not remain so for the next moment. I don't trust these house parties. One never knows what is in store."

"Chin up," the earl said. "You escaped from old Boney with only a limp. Perhaps you will escape from the marchioness, too."

"Yes," Beresford said dryly. "With a wife. Did you meet Rosamund Hunter at tea?"

"March's sister?" Lord Wetherby stood back from the mirror and decided that the pin was not centered but was close enough not to matter.

"I haven't seen her for years," Lord Beresford said. "March forced her to marry an old man when she was scarce out of the schoolroom."

"She was not forced," the earl said. He met his friend's eyes in the mirror. "At least, that is what I have heard."

"She used to come here as a girl," Lord Beresford said. "She was always good fun—just one of the fellows, in fact. She used to climb trees and chase sheep and sled down the steepest hills. She has grown into a regular beauty, I must say."

"Yes," Lord Wetherby said, turning from the mirror and indicating his readiness to go downstairs. "I was presented to her at teatime."

"I rather fancy her," his friend said, getting to his feet. "She might liven up a potentially dull couple of weeks, don't you think?"

The earl opened the door without answering.

"A widow and all that," Lord Beresford said, winking at the earl. "Did you notice her figure, Justin? Or do you have eyes for no one but Annabelle these days?"

The earl's thoughts tingled with memories of Rosamund Hunter's figure. "Good, is it?" he asked, indicating that his friend should precede him through the door and resisting the urge to plant him a facer as he passed.

Lord Beresford made a shape with his hands that did not fit at all well with the earl's memories of her slenderness. "Quite good enough," he said, walking out onto the upstairs landing. "Quite good enough, my friend."

A good firm hand at his back would send him shooting over the banister and toppling to the tiled hallway two stories below, the earl thought uncharitably as he quietly closed the door of his dressing room.

Lady March, Annabelle, and Rosamund were approaching

the staircase at the same moment, the earl saw with a sinking of the heart. The two gentlemen bowed, exchanged pleasantries with the ladies, and allowed them to go first down the stairs. Beresford turned to the earl, raised his eyebrows, and made a whistling gesture with his mouth. Rosamund was dressed in an emerald-green long-sleeved gown that emphasized her slender curves. Her hair was piled high as it had been that first evening when she had worn the orange silk dress.

It was only as they reached the next floor and entered the drawing room that the Earl of Wetherby realized that he had not noticed at all what Annabelle was wearing. He approached her, complimented her on her appearance, which was decidedly good, he discovered when he focused his attention on her, and offered to fetch her a drink.

"Of course I remember you, my lord," Rosamund said with a smile.

Lord Beresford grimaced. "Does this mean I must call you Lady Hunter?" he asked. "It used to be Josh and Rosamund."

"But that was before you became so grand," she said. "It seems presumptuous to call a marquess's heir Josh."

The Earl of Wetherby was taking Annabelle across the room toward an older lady and a younger couple, who had been pointed out to Rosamund as his mother and Lord and Lady Sitwell, his sister and brother-in-law. She felt that she could relax for at least the moment with her former comrade-in-arms.

"It does, doesn't it?" he said with a grin. "You may call me my lord, then, and touch the ground with your nose as you curtsy each time you address me. Will that make you feel better?"

He had been a thin and wiry boy, always untidy, always laughing, always into some mischief, always ready to fight anyone who dared tease him about the dimple in his right cheek. He was no longer thin, though he was not particularly tall or muscular. His gray eyes looked as if they still laughed much of the time. His thick dark hair was quite as unruly as it had ever been, though it had clearly been combed fairly recently. The dimple was still there. He walked with a limp, she had noticed upstairs.

"I think I will settle for Josh," she said, laughing.

"If you feel you are being overfamiliar at any time," he said, "you can always extend it to Joshua. How old were you and I when we last met?"

"Fifteen, I believe," she said. "That was the year you fell into the stream and then splashed me with water for laughing at you."

"So it was," he said. "Tell me, Rosamund, were you always a beauty?"

"I believe the very first words my mother spoke when I was born were to the effect that I was the loveliest child ever to see the light of day," she said.

"Ah," he said. "I suppose fifteen-year-old boys are blind to such matters. Did you not have pigtails?"

"Yes," she said. "I did not win the battle to be rid of them until I was almost sixteen. What happened, Josh?" She glanced down at his leg.

"Battle of Waterloo," he said. "I was lucky the old sawbones who tended it did not hack it off. I believe I informed him—at least, I have been told I did; I was not quite rational at the time—that my great-uncle the Marquess of Gilmore would have his license and his head, not necessarily in that order, if he did not put that saw down and practice responsible medicine. Apparently I roared loudly enough to draw a faint cheer from the other men lying around." He grinned.

"I didn't know you had fought," she said.

"Cavalry officer," he said. "Scarlet regimentals and the whole paraphernalia. You should have seen me then, Rosamund. You would have been swooning with admiration."

"Oh, dear," she said. "Would I?"

The butler was announcing dinner.

"May I?" he said, extending an arm to her. "I want to

hear all about this gothic marriage of yours. Is it true you married the esteemed Sir Leonard on his eightieth birthday?''

"No," she said, laughing. "How absurd. You made that up on the spot. Josh. You never heard any such thing.''

"I was trying to be tactful," he said. "It was his ninetieth, wasn't it? Come on, I will seat you next to Justin, and we will see if we can worm the truth out of you between us.''

Rosamund had thrown herself wholeheartedly into the light, bantering conversation with Lord Beresford. She had focused her whole mind on him, determinedly ignoring Justin's presence in the room. She had been hoping that she could secure a place at quite the opposite end of the dining table from him. But she had no choice in the matter. Annabelle was seated to the marquess's left at the head of the table, the earl next to her. The countess, his mother, sat at the marquess's right. And her companion had steered her in their direction.

"Justin," Lord Beresford said, "your assistance, please. Rosamund is being very secretive about the age of her husband on their wedding day. It is somewhere between eighty and ninety. See if you can get the truth out of her.''

She sat down and turned her head unwillingly to meet those blue eyes, so familiar, so close.

"Well, Lady Hunter," he said, "you had better tell the truth, you know. We earls have dungeons in our castles with all sorts of atrocious instruments of torture. I daresay marquesses do, too, and will lend them out for a fee.''

What was the question? She stared at him. His tone was light. He was smiling. Someone was settling into the seat at her other side—she could not even remember who for one stupid moment. She was supposed to say something so that both of them could turn away and escape this embarrassment.

"What was the question?" she asked.

Lord Beresford chuckled at her other side. Josh, of course. He had always got her into more trouble than she ever needed. "The dumb-female act," he said. "I didn't expect ever to hear you use that tactic, Rosamund.''

"He was forty-nine," she said. She smiled brightly and

turned back to her dinner companion. "He had not even reached his fiftieth birthday, you see, Josh."

"Thank you, Justin," he said solemnly, looking past her. "I shall send her to you again and next time she proves troublesome. Obviously she stands in great awe of you."

Rosamund never afterward knew how she succeeded in eating anything during that meal or how she managed to converse and laugh with Lord Beresford beside her and with Lord and Lady Sitwell opposite. But somehow she did all of those things and managed completely to ignore the man at her other side.

No, not completely. Her right arm felt warmer, more sensitized than the left. And she kept it rigidly disciplined lest it brush accidentally against his sleeve. And her right eye kept seeing his hands as they held his knife and fork, the long fingers that had touched her.

She turned away to laugh at something Lord Beresford had said.

And then Eva Newton, at his other side, asked for the sugar bowl to be passed and Rosamund reached out a hand to it at the same moment as the earl, and their hands touched—and sprang away as if the sugar bowl had been standing on a hot stove.

"I beg your pardon," he said, his eyes on her hand as it reached for the bowl again.

Lord Beresford took her by the wrist and passed the sugar bowl on to Eva. "Ah, long fingernails," he said. "Did you scratch my friend with them, Rosamund? For shame." Then he grinned suddenly and looked up into her face. "Didn't you chase after me with these fingernails once upon a time?"

"Yes," she said, "when you stole the boat and would not let me row out onto the lake with you because I was merely a puny girl, as you put it."

"Was I ever so ungallant?" he said. "Did you catch me? I can't remember, though I don't believe I have any facial scars."

"No," she said.

"Did I take you in the boat?"

"No."

"Ah," he said, "a discourtesy to be rectified without further delay. I shall row you on the lake tomorrow or the day after if the weather is kind and if my great-aunt does not have other plans for the whole gathering. Annabelle and Justin must come with us to chaperon. You don't like the sound of that? Neither do I, actually, but the proprieties must be observed. Is that not right, Lady Sitwell?"

"Absolutely," she said. "In fact, David and I will come too, won't we, David? I love early spring."

"Very early," her husband said. "March is barely here."

It was inevitable, Rosamund supposed. When one was at a house party, it was almost impossible to avoid one other guest entirely. But it did seem a little unfair that on the very first day she should find herself seated next to him at dinner with plans being made for a boating party of six the next day, of which number they were to make two. But it was inevitable. If she had hoped to avoid him for two whole weeks, she was clearly doomed to disappointment.

Two weeks! She would remain acquainted with him for a lifetime if he was to be married to her niece. He was to be her nephew-in-law, if there were such a relationship. How absurd! How laughable! He would be able to call her Aunt Rosamund. She felt very close to the edge of hysteria. But she was saved for the time at least by Lady Gilmore's getting to her feet and signaling that it was time for the ladies to leave the gentlemen to their port.

He did not wish to stay to drink port, he had told her once. He had preferred to leave the dining room with her to play cards.

It was not to be thought of. Somehow through the night ahead she was going to have to do some long and serious thinking. She was going to have to adjust her mind to the fact that Justin was not after all lost to her sight forever, but was to be in her sight daily for the coming two weeks and in her life forever after.

Would it were not so! If only she had never seen him again. Parting forever had seemed cruel at the time. Now being forever acquainted with him seemed many times more cruel.

"Rosamund," the marchioness said, linking her arm through Rosamund's, "have I mentioned to you how very lovely you have grown? I do believe you were a handsome child, but you always had a torn dress or a smudged face or a braid that had come unbraided. It is amazing that Dennis' hair is not as white as mine."

"I'm afraid I was rather a trial to him," Rosamund said.

"But, then, he did put rather too tight a rein on you," Lady Gilmore said. "Now, do tell me how Sir Leonard treated you. At a guess I would say he indulged you quite shamefully. At least, during my short acquaintance with him at Bath it seemed to me that he doted on you."

He had thought her lovely when they were in Northamptonshire. But there he had had no one with whom to compare her. Now he knew her lovely indeed. She drew the eyes like a magnet and somehow made all the other ladies present look pale and insignificant. He was biased, of course. Had he met her for the first time that day, as he was supposed to have done, perhaps he would not have noticed her so particularly. But then, perhaps it would snow in July, too.

Besides, he was not the only one. Josh fancied her and had eyes for no one else. And the Reverend Strangelove was regarding her with a proprietary air. Even the marquess was watching her appreciatively. She was seated at the pianoforte in the drawing room, playing while Pamela Newton sang.

The Earl of Wetherby conversed determinedly with Lady Newton and her husband, Sir Patrick, and with Lord and Lady March. But only half his attention—not even that—was focused on the conversation. Somehow he was going to have to find time alone—that night, perhaps—to adjust his mind to this new turn of events, to bring his mind and his emotions and reactions under control. He and Annabelle were to go rowing with her and Josh, Marion, and David the next day.

Devil take Beresford!

Pamela moved away with Strangelove's younger brother. Rosamund stayed at the pianoforte and played something by Mozart, quite brilliantly. The Reverend Strangelove stood at her shoulder, talking constantly. Doubtless he was commending her on her performance. The earl wanted to set his hands at the man's neck and twist.

"Don't you agree, my lord?" Lady March asked.

Lord Wetherby jerked his mind back to the conversation in which he was supposed to be participating. "I do beg your pardon, ma'am," he said. "My attention was distracted by Lady Hunter's playing. She is very good."

"Yes, isn't she?" Lord March said with evident pride. "She always was, but Hunter paid for an expensive music master for her. He liked to hear her play."

This was ridiculous, the earl thought. Downright ridiculous. They had been lovers for two nights and a day—a very brief affair, as she had put it. They had been good together—damned good. He would have liked to have had longer with her. A week longer. That would probably have been enough.

As it was, they had not had quite long enough, not for him, anyway. And so he found himself looking on her now with desire unfulfilled. That was all it was. It was nothing so very earth-shattering. He wanted to bed her. He forced himself to look at her as she played and put into bald words in his mind exactly what he felt. She was very lovely. He had had her already and knew just how well she performed in bed and how well she satisfied him. And he would have liked to repeat those performances.

There. It was all very simple really. He lusted after the woman. And she was forbidden to him, partly because he was about to become betrothed and was forbidden to any woman other than Annabelle and partly because she was Annabelle's aunt.

It was all very simple—the eternal attraction of forbidden fruit. If he had been free a month before to pursue the acquaintance, he would probably have done so. And by now he would have tired of her, and she of him, he supposed.

"You look to be in a brown study, Wetherby," Lord Carver said from beside him.

"Just enjoying Mozart," the earl said.

"Played by the delectable Lady Hunter," the other said. "Who do you think is going to have her, Wetherby? Toby or Josh?"

"I would guess neither one is going to 'have' her, as you so crudely put it, Carver," the earl said, "unless she wishes to be had."

"My wager is on Toby," Lord Carver said. "He needs a wife and it will suit his consequence to have a beautiful one. At least she will never have trouble sleeping at night. He will bore her to sleep." He laughed heartily at his own joke.

"An admirable compliment," Lord Wetherby said, watching Rosamund play and Strangelove talk.

"Josh means only dalliance," Lord Carver said. "He is a shocking rake, you know, but you doubtless do. I don't think Lady Hunter would be interested in dalliance."

"You are probably right," the earl said.

He was not going to wait for the night and the privacy of his own room, after all, he decided suddenly, walking away from Lord Carver without another word and making his way toward the pianoforte. By God, he was going to settle this thing now. He could think of a dozen men if he tried who were on perfectly comfortable terms with former mistresses. This embarrassment was ridiculous.

"Lady Carver was looking for you, I believe, Strangelove," he said, interrupting a monologue.

"Most obliging of her," the Reverend Strangelove said with a bow. "And how condescending of you, my lord, to be the bearer of such a flattering summons. It seems ill-mannered to hurry away, but—"

"But we will excuse you," the earl said. "I shall give Lady Hunter my company."

The Reverend Strangelove hurried away after delivering another monologue of thanks on Rosamund's behalf.

"I know the piece of music, Rosamund," Lord Wetherby said from behind her. "It came to an end several measures ago. You do Mozart a disservice by improvising."

Her hands fell still on the keys.

"Neither of us could have forseen this," he said, "and neither of us would have wished for it. But it has happened. We are going to have to make the best of it."

"Yes," she said.

"Unfortunately," he said, "you have never had an affair with another man, and I am unaccustomed to liaisons with ladies of our own class. If we had just had a little more experience, I daresay we would be feeling far less embarrassment at the moment."

"Yes," she said.

He sat down on the stool beside her and thumbed through a piece of music, which he took from the top of the pianoforte. The narrowness of the stool brought his arm against hers. The warmth of her seeped through his sleeve. She was wearing a perfume as enticing as any of the ones that had been in Jude's trunk.

"Can we be sensible and adult about this?" he asked. "We were thrown together under circumstances that made it almost inevitable that we become lovers. We drew mutual enjoyment from that liaison. We said good-bye. It's over. Can we now put it behind us and treat each other like friendly acquaintances?"

"Yes," she said.

"You were not a lady of single syllables when I last knew you," he said. "Far from it."

"What am I supposed to say, Justin?" She rubbed at a spot on one of the keys. "What you say makes perfect sense, and I am glad you have said it. Perhaps now we will be able to look at each other without wishing to die and talk to each other without stammering and accustom ourselves to the new relationship that is about to develop between us."

"The aunt-nephew relationship?" he said.

"Yes, that." She polished a black key with the pad of one finger.

"Yes," he said, "we can accustom ourselves to it."

There was a silence that neither of them broke for several moments.

"Are you with child?" he asked quietly.

"No."

"I'm glad I have had a chance to know that at least," he said. "I was concerned."

"What were you concerned about?" The marquess, who had come up behind them unseen, clapped a hand on the earl's shoulder. Fortunately the question seemed to be rhetorical. He continued. "I have been waiting for you to start playing again, Rosamund. Can Wetherby not find you anything else suitable? Try this." He rummaged through the pile and drew out a piece of music by Bach. He opened it on the music rest, one arm over each of Rosamund's shoulders. "You have a fine touch, my dear. It is a pleasure to listen to you."

The earl stood up again and watched her play for a while before wandering away to find Annabelle. He must spend what remained of the evening with her. He had one week in which to develop a friendship and an affection for her strong enough to make both of them feel good about the formal offer that was to be made on the marquess's birthday.

He was not sure that anything had been solved as far as Rosamund was concerned.

9

The marchioness thought the idea of a boat ride on the lake a quite splendid one.

"I would not have thought of it so early in the year," she said. "Though I don't know why not. It is a beautiful day, and it is not as if you are planning to swim. At least, I hope you are not planning to swim." She looked at Lord Beresford.

He grinned. "Someone might be pitched in headfirst if he misbehaves," he said. "But no, Aunt, we are not planning to swim."

"Anyway, Joshua," she said, "it is good of you and Rosamund to agree to go along to chaperon Annabelle and Justin."

He laughed. "It is the other way around, actually, Aunt," he said. "They are to chaperon us."

"Then they have my sincerest sympathy," the marchioness said. "They never used to arrive home, Justin, without a couple of torn sleeves or hems between the two of them and an assortment of cuts and bruises and some guilty confession to make. Once they had chased a poor sheep into a hedge and could not get it out again."

"I suffered a great deal more pain than the sheep," Lord Beresford said, "when my father got hold of me. I remember quarreling with Rosamund because all she got from March was a scolding."

"But I would not have dreamed of tormenting the poor creature without you to egg me on, Josh," Rosamund said, batting her eyelids at him.

"Oh, no," he said, "never. I hear you are a candidate for instant angelhood when you die, Rosamund."

"From the same source as you heard of Leonard's age, I suppose," she said.

It was decided at the breakfast table that Valerie Newton and her fiancé, Mr. Michael Weaver, would go boating too so that they could take two boats instead of loading down the one.

Annabelle did not really want to go, Rosamund discovered when they went upstairs to get ready. The girl wandered into Rosamund's bedchamber when the maid was still dressing the latter's hair.

"It is far too early in the year to go boating," she said.

"But it is a lovely day, Annabelle," Rosamund said, "and quite calm."

"There is a walk of a whole mile to the lake," Annabelle said.

Rosamund laughed. "I think I can drag my aged bones that far," she said. "I'm sure you can too."

"I have never really enjoyed boats," the girl said.

Rosamund dismissed the maid and turned around on the stool to look at her niece. She frowned. "For a girl who is to be betrothed in less than a week's time," she said, "you do not seem very happy, Annabelle."

"Because I do not want to go boating?" Annabelle said. "How silly."

"He is a very handsome man," Rosamund said, "and very amiable. You do like him, don't you?"

"Lord Wetherby?" Annabelle said. "Of course I do, Aunt Rosa. And even if I did not, I trust the judgment of Mama and Papa and Grandmama and Grandpapa."

Rosamund did not pursue the point. She drew on a warm pelisse and a bonnet and led the way downstairs. It was just Annabelle's nature, she supposed, to show very little enthusiasm. She had scarcely seen the girl smile since her return from Lincolnshire.

And yet she was to marry Justin. How could she not smile every moment of every day? But it was not a thought to be pursued.

Valerie linked her arm through Rosamund's as they left

the house. "Do walk with me, Rosamund," she said, "and tell me what you have been doing for the last eight or nine years. Goodness, is it really that long? I'm a veritable old maid, aren't I? It's a good thing that Michael did not realize that."

The sky was a clear blue. The grass had lost its winter lack of luster and was a fresh green. Trees were budding into the bright green of early spring. The sun gave warmth, tempered by the freshness of the season. It was a perfect day for the outdoors. A perfect day in which to be in the country walking and boating and conversing with friends. It was a day to be enjoyed.

Rosamund ignored her tiredness. She had slept only in fits and starts the night before, and when she had dozed off she had had vivid and bizarre dreams. But she felt better this morning. She had adjusted her mind to the situation in which she found herself.

She had considered leaving Brookfield in order to return to Dennis's house or to go somewhere else—anywhere else. But she could not do so. Dennis had come all the way to Lincolnshire to fetch her home so that she would be able to be part of these celebrations. And if she avoided the awkwardness this time, it would have to be faced numerous times in the future. Besides, she could not afford to go somewhere like Bath or Tunbridge Wells.

She had to stay. And if she had to stay, then she would have to see Justin daily. And soon—in less than a week, in fact—she would have to listen to the announcement of his betrothal and probably the plans for his wedding. Those were simple, unchangeable facts. There was no point at all in fighting against them or in giving herself sleepless nights or in pining and remembering and indulging in what-ifs. No point at all.

And so that morning she had smiled at him and bidden him a good morning and taken a seat across from him at the breakfast table. She had looked directly into his eyes whenever she had spoken to him or he to her. She had conversed determinedly with everyone else and even flirted a little with Josh. And she had survived. The worst was over and she would continue to survive.

The Earl of Wetherby walked with Annabelle.

"Early spring," he said. "Is it not a lovely thought that winter is over at last?"

"Yes," she said.

"The trees are in bud," he said, "and the birds out in force."

"Yes," she said.

A one-sided conversation always lacked a great deal in profundity, he thought, looking down at her. He wondered if after a few days she would relax enough to smile at him. Strangely, he thought suddenly, he could not remember ever seeing the girl smile.

She looked up and met his eyes, seemed to realize that there was a conversation to sustain, and began to talk.

"Yes, I do love spring," she said. "Aunt Rosa and I found some snowdrops in the grass before we came to Grandpapa's. I love the roses later in the year. I wish it could always be summer and the roses blooming."

She was really very lovely, he thought, as they chattered on about nothing in particular. More classically beautiful than Rosamund, with a fuller figure. But then, of course, she did not have that intriguing upper lip that Rosamund had, the first feature that had attracted him to her. And she did not have Rosamund's dancing eyes and ready tongue and ever-present humor. She was far more dignified than her aunt— and far less fun.

But Lord Wetherby caught the direction of his thoughts and returned them to the girl on his arm and the conversation in which they were involved.

Annabelle tried to reorganize the way they were to divide themselves into two groups when they came to the boats, he noted with interest. When Josh mentioned that he and Rosamund would come with them, she spoke up.

"Perhaps Aunt Rosa and Valerie still wish to talk," she said.

Valerie laughed. "I think we are talked out for now," she said. "And we have been unsociable to everyone else for long enough."

"You will wish to be with your sister," Annabelle said, turning to the earl.

"We see quite enough of each other every day of the year in town," Lady Sitwell said, punching her brother playfully on the arm.

The arrangements remained the way Josh had organized them. He could have wished Annabelle had had her way, Lord Wetherby thought as he handed first her and then Rosamund into the boat—Josh was busy teasing Valerie about something. But what had been the girl's reason? Did she not like her aunt for some reason? Did she suspect the truth?

No, it could not be that. Neither of them had given the smallest sign except that conversation at the pianoforte the evening before. But then it would have seemed perfectly natural for him to talk with Rosamund for a few minutes. They were guests at the same house party.

It was decided that Lord Wetherby would row along the lake and Josh row back later. It was a very beautiful setting, the earl thought, looking about him at the long, narrow lake and the high wooded banks that almost surrounded it. The trees were in delicate bud. The water was a darker shade of blue than the sky.

"Why is it, I wonder," Lord Beresford said, "that for cows the grass is always greener on the other side of the fence and for humans the banks are always more picturesque on the other side of the lake? Shall we land and climb to the top?"

"Will you not tire your leg too much?" Rosamund asked.

He laughed. "Can't you tell that Rosamund has been a wife, Justin?" he said. "She is just like a mother hen."

"Pardon me for trying to be the voice of reason," she said. "By all means let us land. Perhaps you would care to climb the bank and run back around to where we started, Josh."

"A tempting idea," he said, "but it is my turn to row back." He turned to hail the other boat and point to the bank.

A few minutes later they were all stepping out onto dry land again.

Valerie and her betrothed decided not to climb, but to stroll along the bank beside the water. Lord and Lady Sitwell took a blanket from the bottom of their boat, spread it on the bank, and sat down to admire the view. Annabelle joined them.

"What?" Lord Beresford said. "Too aged to join us in a climb, are you, Annabelle? I never heard the like. Perhaps we should have a litter brought from the house to carry you back home from the other bank, should we?"

"The view is very lovely," she said. "I want to sit here and enjoy it."

"I shall stay with you," Lord Wetherby said with a smile. For some reason Annabelle was not enjoying herself. He wished that he had refused to join the boating trip and arranged to spend some time alone with her. "You are right about the view. It is quite magnificent."

"No," she said, "please don't stay on my account. I know you wish to climb, my lord. I shall be quite happy here, conversing with Lord and Lady Sitwell."

He looked down at her, considering. Was it his presence that made her uncomfortable? It was something he must find out within the next few days. Though what he was to do if it really were so he did not know. "Very well, then," he said. "We will not be long."

Lord Beresford had taken Rosamund's arm through his. "You know," he said, "the time was when I would have challenged you to a race to the top. I would have beaten you, too, but I would have had to run the whole distance to do it. Now of course, you are no longer a young hoyden but a dignified lady. I daresay you will have to be helped inch by inch to the top. Take her other arm, Justin, in case she drags me to the bottom with her."

"If it's a race you want, Josh," she said, drawing her arm away from his and gathering up her skirt, "you have it." And before he could realize her intention, she was on her way, running up the bank, dodging trees and concentrating on not losing her footing.

Lord Beresford passed her eventually, but only when they were almost at the top. They both collapsed onto the coarse grass there, laughing and panting and gazing down on the Earl of Wetherby, who was striding up toward them.

He was feeling like a staid old man, he thought, and like a jealous schoolboy who has been deliberately excluded from a game. He thought back to a certain snowball fight—only a month before. And he closed his mind to the memory again.

"Look at him," Lord Beresford said. "He is approaching his thirtieth birthday, I have heard, Rosamund. Poor gentleman. It shows, doesn't it?"

"But the lady did not challenge me to a race," the earl said, seating himself at Rosamund's other side. "For which I shall be eternally thankful. You missed seeing all the snowdrops and primroses among the trees."

"Oh, did we?" Rosamund said, looking at him wide-eyed and with genuine sorrow.

"We will view them on the way down," Lord Beresford said. "At the moment I am concerned with the painful necessity of trying to pump all the missing air back into my lungs."

"It was a good idea of yours to come up here," the earl said. "I'll wager that if we stood on that higher piece of ground over there we would be able to see the house."

"Do you know," Lord Beresford said, drawing up one knee and resting his forearm across it, "that girl ought not to have been allowed to get away with it—sitting on a blanket for all the world like a sedate and middle-aged matron. We should have insisted."

"I find it hard to justify insisting that someone else enjoy herself," the earl said. "Annabelle probably gets no joy from feeling hot and sticky and breathless."

"Well, she should," Lord Beresford said, rising resolutely to his feet. "I'm going back down for her. I'll pick her some primroses on the way back up." He grinned and was gone before either of his companions could protest.

"Oh, dear," Rosamond said, "Annabelle will not like this."

"Fortunately," the earl said, "my brother-in-law is down there to wrestle Josh to the ground or toss him into the lake if he tries to use coercion."

Despite the chorus of bird song, the silence around them suddenly seemed very oppressive. Damn Josh, Lord Wetherby thought. This was the very type of situation that he had most wished to avoid.

He looked at her tentatively, to find her looking back at him. They both smiled rather ruefully.

"Would you say it is a conspiracy?" he asked.

"It seems very like it, doesn't it?" she said.

There was a disturbing sense of familiarity, just as if there had been no intervening month since their last meeting. He looked down to the lake below them. "You found your brother quite quickly," he said. "You arrived home safely?"

"Yes," she said. "And you? How long did you stay?"

"I left the following day," he said.

"You had been intending to stay for a week," she said.

"Yes," he said. "I did not want to see the snowmen melt away or the snow angel disappear."

In fact, he had been very careful not even to glance their way except that once after her departure.

That was the worst aspect of the whole episode, he thought. If there had been only the lovemaking, it would have been easy to put it in the past—a memory to be set beside many such memories. But there had been so much more than the lovemaking.

There had been that silly snowball fight and the foolish competition with the snowmen. And her careful angel and his failed one, and her laughter. There had been a great deal of laughter.

"Let's go and see what can be seen from that higher point, shall we?" he asked, getting to his feet and reaching down a hand for hers.

Her hand was warm. Her fingers curled firmly about his. He had been wearing gloves when he had pulled her up from the snow after exerting the penalty of a three-minute kiss. He released her hand almost as an afterthought.

Oh no, he did not want this. He had come to Brookfield in all good faith to focus his mind and his attention and his affections on Annabelle. He had fought a hard and painful battle for a whole month to persuade himself that what had happened with Rosamund had been merely what they had intended it to mean. It had been a brief and pleasurable affair. And he had won that battle, or had been winning it. He neither needed nor wanted this.

They walked side by side along the top of the bank until they came to the higher point. He looked back across the lake, shading his eyes—and forgot again.

"Yes, I thought so," he said. "Look, Rosamund." He set one hand on her shoulder, his head close to hers and pointed across the lake and between two large clumps of trees to where the house was nestled in a hollow, surrounded by green grass. The formal gardens could not be identified from that distance.

"That means," she said, "that from the house we could see this exact spot."

Only Rosamund could even consider something so absurd. He grinned. "Something we would all wish to do," he said. "It is such a distinguished spot. A little piece of unmarked wilderness."

And a place where they had stood together, his hand on her shoulder, surrounded by spring and the singing of birds. He knew suddenly what she had meant.

"Actually," he said, the smile gone from his face, "it is a little piece of wilderness and I am glad I have not missed."

He wanted to turn her into his arms, to hold her against him. Not with passion. Just for the feeling of closeness again. The way he had held her on his lap that last evening when all her memories about her husband's final illness had come pouring out. He had felt closer to her on that occasion than he had ever felt to any human being. He wanted to hold her like that once more. Just for a few minutes.

He removed his hand from her shoulder and turned around.

And the next moment he had forgotten again. Both his hands came back to her shoulders and turned her.

"Look, Rosamund," he said.

He could feel her draw in a deep breath and let it out on an "Ooh." She leaned back against him. There was a grassy clearing among the trees on the downward slope behind them. The clearing was carpeted with blooming daffodils.

" 'I wandered lonely as a cloud,' " he said. " 'That floats on high o'er vales and hills.' "

She turned her head and looked into his face, smiling brightly. "Mr. Wordsworth," she said. "You know his poetry?"

He smiled back at her. " 'When all at once I saw a crowd,' " he said, "A host, of golden daffodils."

" 'Beside the lake, beneath the trees,' " she said, " 'Fluttering and dancing in the breeze.' "

"Except that they are not exactly beside the lake," he said, "and there is no breeze today. You like his poetry too?"

"Leonard bought me a volume," she said, "and then laughed at me because I loved the poems so much that I learned many of them by heart."

He released her shoulders and took her by the hand so that they could run down the slope together. She was laughing. When he let go of her hand, she stooped down to cup a bloom in her hands and to bury her nose against the golden trumpet.

"Oh, the smell of spring," she said, closing her eyes and lifting her face. "I have never seen so many daffodils all together, Justin. Have you?"

"No," he said. "But this must be nothing in comparison with Wordsworth's ten thousand."

"I think perhaps he exaggerated," she said. "I can imagine looking back on this and remembering that there were thousands of daffodils here." She held both arms out to the sides and twirled about, her face held up to the sun.

"Perhaps there are," he said. And he began to pick some of them and lay them in her arms. Gold against the blue of her pelisse and dress. Sun against the sky. He wanted to load her down with them until she collapsed beneath them. And he would follow her down and kiss her amongst all the blooms and all the smell of spring.

"Oh, glorious," she said, smelling them again and reaching out her free hand for more. And then she sobered, and her hand fell to her side. "These are for Annabelle, are they?"

He paused in the act of picking another bloom, his back to her. God! "Those are yours," he said. "The ones I am picking now are for Annabelle."

"Thank you," she said.

Where were Annabelle and Josh? It seemed that he and Rosamund had been alone for a long time, though he supposed that in reality not many minutes had passed.

Rosamund returned to the top of the rise and looked back along the bank. She raised her free arm.

"Over here," she called. "Come and see what we have found."

Suddenly, and quite beyond reason, the Earl of Wetherby almost hated her. Or himself. Yes, it was himself he hated.

Annabelle had asked Lady Sitwell about her two sons, both of whom were at school. She was listening carefully to the description of the two boys who were to be her nephews.

"Gracious!" Lady Sitwell said as there was a loud crackling of twigs and undergrowth from behind them. "Are they back already? It was hardly worth going."

But it was only Lord Beresford who came striding down to them. His hand was outstretched to Annabelle.

"Come along," he said. "We decided that no one below the age of thirty should be allowed to go without exercise. Up you get, Annabelle." He grinned at her.

"Thank you," she said, "but I am talking with Lady Sitwell."

"You can do that for the next two weeks," he said. "Besides," he winked at Lord Sitwell, "even couples who have been married forever occasionally like time to themselves."

Annabelle flushed slightly and allowed herself to be helped to her feet.

"Take my arm," Lord Beresford said with a mock bow. "I promise not to let you fall off any precipices."

"I am not afraid of falling," she said gravely. She ignored his arm and began to climb the slope.

Lord Beresford looked after her, shook his head, and followed.

"Annabelle," he said, "have you ever in your life smiled?"

"Of course I have," she said.

"Let me see, then." He caught her by the arm, stopping her progress, and turned her to face him. "Let me see you smile."

"Oh," she said, "one cannot smile for no reason at all."

"I can," he said, suiting action to words. "Let me see yours. Come on, Annabelle. There is only me to see."

"Please let go of my arm," she said, her eyes on his hand.

He sighed and let her go. "You are by far the prettiest of my cousins, you know," he said, "or second cousins, to be quite accurate. I have a feeling you could be a staggering beauty if you smiled.

"How absurd!" she said. "I do smile."

"When?" he asked. "When you see something pretty? There are some primroses, look. Justin said there were some. Rossamund and I were too busy racing each other up to notice. Shall I pick you some? Will you smile at me if I do?"

"Don't be silly, Joshua," she said. "I am not a child to be coaxed."

"When someone tells a joke?" he asked. "I have a storehouse of them. If I dredge up one suitable for a lady's ears, will you smile?"

"Are we going to stand here?" she asked. "I thought we were going to the top."

"When you are tickled?" he said. "Do you smile then?" He reached out for her.

But she jumped back and held out her hands in front of her. "Don't touch me!" she said.

He set his head to one side and regarded her closely.

"What is it, Annabelle?" he asked her quietly, serious for once. "Are you unhappy about something?"

"No," she said.

"Don't you like this marriage that has been arranged for you?" he asked. "You have had forever to get used to the idea, haven't you? How old were you when your grandmother matched you with Justin?"

"Nine years old," she said. "And of course I do not dislike the idea."

"Look," he said. "There are some snowdrops. Sit down for a minute and I'll pick you some."

She sat.

"I'm surprised she hasn't had her eye on me before now," he said. "Me being her husband's heir and all that. I have been in fear and dread for the last few years that she is going to notice that Christobel is growing up and in need of a husband."

"Don't you like Christobel?" she asked.

He shrugged. "I used to think it unfair that she was not the one to be matched with Justin," he said. "I wouldn't have minded you, Annabelle. However, as it has turned out your grandmother has not yet come to realize how splendid it would be to marry me off to one of her granddaughters. Perhaps her matchmaking urge came to an end with you."

Annabelle looked down at the fragile white flowers he had picked for her. "Yes," she said.

"Count your blessings," he said, sitting beside her and reclining on one elbow. "If it had not been Justin, Annabelle, you might have been landed with me. Then you would have had something to mope about. I teased you to death all through your childhood and girlhood, didn't I? You never could stand me."

She touched the petals of one of the flowers with one light fingertip. "I was so much younger than you," she said. "Does your leg still hurt?"

He laughed. "A diplomatic change of subject," he said. "Sometimes. In cold or damp weather. When I abuse it."

"Like today?" she asked.

"I will probably have to return to my room when we get back to the house to bite on a bullet," he said, grinning at her. He watched her touching the flowers for a few silent moments. "Why did you ask?"

She shrugged. "We were here at Grandpapa's when word came that you had been wounded," she said. "More than a month passed before there was further word."

"And you wept the month away in agonized solitude, did you?" he said.

"I was concerned about you," she said, "of course."

"Of course," he said, his eyes twinkling at her. "My injury was minor, Annabelle. Very minor."

"And yet you still limp," she said.

"To attract the sympathy of ladies like yourself," he said, getting to his feet. "Justin will think I have run off with you. And he will be planning to abscond with Rosamund just to spite us both."

"I don't think his lordship would think any such thing," she said, "or do any such thing."

He smiled down at her and helped her to her feet.

"One day," he said, "I am going to make you smile, Annabelle. I have just made it the goal and ambition of my life."

"How absurd you are," she said.

"How absurd you are," he mimicked, taking her by the chin and laughing down into her face. "I wouldn't mind having a guinea for every time you have said that to me during our lifetime, Annabelle."

They reached the top a short while later and were immediately hailed by Rosamund, who was standing on a higher rise a short distance away, her right arm loaded with daffodils.

Annabelle lost no time in hurrying toward her.

10

Annabelle was sitting at her grandfather's right hand at breakfast the next morning, Rosamund at his left.

"And what plans do you ladies have for today?" he asked. "All you young people made life very easy yesterday by entertaining yourselves."

"Lord Wetherby has asked me to go riding with him," Annabelle said.

The marquess looked toward the window. "It's cloudy and blowing," he said. "Not nearly as pleasant a day as yesterday. But fine for riding."

"Will you come as chaperon, Aunt Rosa?" Annabelle asked.

Rosamund looked up at her in surprise and dismay. And she glanced involuntarily down the table at Lord Wetherby, who had also heard Annabelle's request. She would do anything rather than have to spend another day with the two of them, Rosamund thought. She could not live through another day like the day before.

"Are you going to the abbey?" Christobel asked the earl eagerly.

"The abbey?" He looked at her inquiringly.

"Winwood Abbey," she said. "It is just a few miles away and a very picturesque spot. I'll come too, if I may. And Ferdie. Won't you, Ferdie?"

Rosamund breathed a little more easily.

"I will do myself the honor of escorting Lady Hunter," the Reverend Tobias Strangelove said. "Winwood Abbey is an admirable destination. I commend you on having thought of it, Christobel. It will be my pleasure to describe the ruins to you when we arrive, my lord.'' He inclined his head across the table to the earl.

"Splendid, splendid,'' the marquess said, rubbing his hands together. ''I shall have a talk with the other young people when they decide to get up from their beds.''

At least there was one consolation, Rosamund thought when she left the table a few minutes later in order to return to her room to change into riding clothes: at least there would be a crowd of them. For a moment it had seemed that there might be only her, Annabelle, and Justin.

When she reached her room, she bent to smell the daffodils, arranged in a large vase on the table beside her bed. She closed her eyes briefly. But, no, she would not think of it. She would not.

She glanced guiltily to the pile of four heavy books on the window ledge. She had carried them up from the library the evening be fore. One of the daffodils was being pressed between them.

Lord March was standing on the steps when Rosamund went outside, on her way to the stables. He smiled at her.

"A blustery day,'' he said, hunching his shoulders inside his greatcoat.

"You are not coming riding?'' she asked.

"I have promised to escort Lana and Claudette into the village to do some visiting and shopping,'' he said. ''I was pleased that you agreed to ride with Tobias, Rosa.''

She grimaced. "I did not have much choice,'' she said.

"He definitely has an eye for you,'' he said. ''You would do well to encourage him.''

"Dennis,'' she said, ''let's not start this.''

"I know he is rather pompous in manner,'' he said. ''But he could offer you a secure future, Rosa.''

"I refuse to quarrel with you this morning,'' she said. ''I am going riding. Everyone else must be in the stables already.''

"Just be careful of Joshua,'' he said.

Rosamund had turned away, pulling on her gloves as she did so. But she turned back, a half-smile on her face. "All right," she said, "I am taking the bait. Why must I be careful of Josh?"

"He has a shocking reputation," he said. "He might think that because you are a widow, Rosa, you are easy."

"Might he?" she said. "And you are afraid that perhaps I am?"

"Not for a moment," he said. "You don't have to flare up at the merest provocation, Rosa. I merely have your best interests at heart. I don't want to see you hurt. Men sometimes forget that widows can still be hurt."

"Do they?" she said, smoothing the gloves over her hands.

"He would not be allowed to marry you, you know," he said. "He is the heir to all this."

Rosamund smiled at him. "And I am merely your sister," she said, "and widow of a baronet who was not particularly wealthy. Well, Dennis, you have certainly succeeded in cutting me down to size."

"You know that was not my intention," he said. "Why must you always make me seem the villain, Rosa? You know I want nothing more than your happiness."

Her mouth was opened to make a stinging retort when the door opened behind him and the Earl of Wetherby stepped outside.

"Ah," he said, seeing Rosamund, "I thought I was late."

"You are," she said. "And so am I. I shall see you later, Dennis."

"Quarreling again?" the earl asked as the two of them strode toward the stables. "You looked as if you were about to swallow his head whole. I may just have saved his life."

"He will persist in treating me like a child who knows nothing of the world or the motives of men," she said.

"Perhaps," he said, "he loves you."

"Oh, undoubtedly," she said, "and would like to organize my life according to his own notions of happiness."

"I'm afraid it is a failing of relatives," he said. "Perhaps you should consider yourself fortunate to have only one brother. I have a mother and two sisters—a formidable army, I do assure you.''

She laughed. "Have they been pressing this marriage on you?" she asked.

"With increasing intensity as my thirtieth birthday has loomed," he said. "They already have the beginnings of my family planned, too. It is to be two sons first—one to be my heir and one to be the insurance—and a daughter third just so that some fortunate gentleman will have the privilege of marrying into my noble family at some time in the future. After that I believe I am to be allowed to please myself.''

Rosamund laughed.

"I am not to give my family a collective anxiety attack as my father did, you see," he said. "Two daughters two years apart, and one son all of seven years later.''

They had reached the stables to find that indeed they were the last to arrive. Lord Beresford and Robin Strangelove had joined the party, as well as Eva and Pamela Newton.

Had he talked deliberately to make sure that there were no awkward silences? Rosamund wondered. She was thankful that he had. He would not be able to marry to please himself, Dennis had said, talking about Josh. But the same would apply to Justin, too. Perhaps it was as well that he was already betrothed so that she would not be tempted to hope that he would marry her. Men tended to think that widows were easy, Dennis had said. They tended to forget that widows could be hurt.

Had Justin thought so? Had he made love to her only because he had expected that she would be willing? Had he made love to her with no regard to her feelings?

Stupid thoughts. She smiled more dazzlingly than she had intended at the Reverend Strangelove, who had approached to help her into the saddle, and set her foot in his cupped hands. She had been willing. And what did her feelings have to do with anything? He had told her quite openly even before they had adjourned to her bedchamber that he was about to be betrothed, that he did not wish to give her any wrong impression. And she had replied that all she wanted was a very brief affair.

This was no time to be feeling aggrieved. She had no grievance.

"Might I be permitted to say, Lady Hunter," the Reverend Strangelove said, drawing his horse close to hers, "that you look quite dazzling in that riding habit?"

"You may," she said gaily, touching him on the arm with her riding crop, "provided you call me Rosamund, Toby. The other sounds ridiculously formal."

"Rosamund," he said, bowing from his saddle. "I shall take this favor as a mark of personal regard. It is my sincerest wish, as I believe your brother may have prepared you to hear, that more than one happy announcement will be made during these two delightful weeks of my uncle's birthday celebrations."

"And it is my sincerest wish," she said lightly, smiling at him, "to take this horse to a gallop before we reach Winwood Abbey." She nudged her horse into motion.

He had asked Annabelle to go riding with him, Lord Wetherby was thinking rather ruefully, so that he might have some time alone with her, some time to get to know her better. He had not expected that on her grandfather's land and within a week of their betrothal they would have to worry about chaperones.

As it had turned out, they had eight chaperones. He could not suppress a smile of some amusement, despite his chagrin. House parties were designed to bring people together, he supposed.

He did succeed in keeping Annabelle and himself at the head of the group and in conversing with her the whole way to the abbey. She was neither silent nor mororse, he discovered. It was really quite easy to talk with her—except that at the end of the more than half an hour it took them to reach Winwood Abbey, he felt they knew each other no better than when they had started. Their conversation had been on quite impersonal matters.

The abbey was in ruins, though it was still possible to guess at its former splendor. Certainly it was situated in very picturesque surroundings, in a valley with a river flowing by and hills rising on either side.

"Grandmama and Grandpapa always organized picnics here in the summer," Annabelle said.

But their conversation was interrupted. The Reverend Tobias Strangelove was as good as his word and approached to give the earl a history of the abbey.

"It was sacked during the time of the dissolution of the monasteries," he explained. "A great blot on the history of our religion and civilization, my lord, one for which we must rightly feel deep shame and remorse, though it was our ancestors, of course, who were directly responsible. Ah, Joshua has a good idea, I see. Shall we dismount, too?"

Lord Wetherby resigned himself to the inevitable as he swung down from his saddle and lifted Annabelle down from hers. From one trial, though, he was to be released, he found almost immediately: Josh had come up behind Rosamund and set his hands at her waist.

"Toby is going to give Justin a history lesson?" he asked, winking at the latter. "Come exploring with me, then, Rosamund. I have been riding with Christobel and discover that I have heard quite enough giggles and shrieks to last me for one day."

"Exploring as in climbing walls and balancing along the tops of them?" Rosamund asked. "I beg to be excused, Josh. I will stroll sedately with you, though, if you wish."

"I wish," he said, grinning. "Come too, Annabelle?"

"Thank you," she said, "but I will stay with his lordship and Tobias."

More than once Lord Wetherby had asked her to call him by his given name. She had not yet done so. She took his arm now and listened attentively to the monologue that the Reverend Strangelove launched into. The earl covered her hand with his own and patted her fingers.

Lord Wetherby wondered over the following half-hour

what it would be like to sit through one of Strangelove's sermons. It was not an experience he craved. At least here there were other things to look at: Robin Strangelove sitting on a low wall, flanked by Pamela and Christobel; Josh clambering up on a higher wall, grinning down at Rosamund, and then stretching down a hand to draw her up after; Lord Carver standing in a stone doorway, gazing up at its Gothic arch and saying something to Eva that threw them both into fits of laughter; Josh limping along the top of the wall until he swayed and had to leap for the ground; and Rosamund, arms out to the sides, walking safely right along it and then laughing down at Josh.

"Yes, quite magnificent, indeed," he said to the Reverend Strangelove, not quite sure what he was appreciating.

Robin and the girls were standing at the head of what had been the nave of the church, looking along the line of broken pillars toward the grassy knoll where the altar had stood. Carver and Eva were strolling along to join them. Josh and Rosamund had diappeared behind the high wall into a copse of trees.

Annabelle drew her arm from the earl's and wandered off alone.

"Indeed, yes," he said. "Quite astounding."

"Of course," the Reverend Strangelove said, "there are not many young people today, my lord, who have your commendable interest in antiquity." He glanced at the main group—the girls were all sitting on different pillars while Lord Carver stood on another and Robin was stooping down on his haunches, talking to Christobel. "But then they have the high spirits of youth, and who are we to condemn?" He smiled indulgently at his relatives.

"I certainly would not do so," Lord Wetherby said.

Josh and Rosamund still had not come back into sight. Annabelle had disappeared too.

There was something quite fascinating about the altar of the old church, it seemed, something that the Reverend Strangelove had just that moment recalled and must confide to his lordship. His lordship meekly followed him to the grassy knoll. There Eva was unwise enough to approach and show interest in what was being said.

Lord Wetherby strolled along the nave. Where were they? Those trees were conveniently dense and secluded. He had probably taken her there deliberately. He fancied her, he had admitted quite openly just two evenings before. And they clearly got along together famously. They were probably out there somewhere, kissing and fondling.

And it was none of his business whatsoever, he reminded himself, unclenching his fists behind his back and strolling on. What he should do—and what he would do, in fact—was find Annabelle and occupy himself kissing and fondling her. It was about time he moved their relationship at least one step forward into something more personal than they had yet shared.

He stepped through the rubble of what had been a doorway onto the grass beyond and peered into the trees. There was neither sight nor sound of them. He strolled a little way into the trees.

"Josh," Rosamund had said, laughing. "You cannot climb up there. You are a grown man now."

"What you really mean," he said, grinning at her, "is that I am a man with a limp now and will fall off."

"And so you will too," she said, "and I will laugh at you."

"No, you won't," he said. "You will shriek and rush to tend my broken head."

And of course he had climbed up onto the wall that they and Valerie had climbed on as youngsters, and he had taunted her until she had climbed up there with him. And of course he had fallen off and she had grinned down at him and walked the whole length of the wall herself before jumping down.

They were just like a couple of children and should be ashamed of themselves, she told him. Heavens, she was a respectable widow of six-and-twenty.

"Oh, not quite like children, Rosamund," he said, taking

her by the hand and stepping over a pile of rubble where the wall had completely crumbled away to stroll with her along the outer side of the wall, where they were suddenly sheltered from both the wind and the sunlight by the trees.

"I know," she said, trying to withdraw her hand from his and failing. "This is where you start flirting with me, isn't it, Josh, and trying to steal a kiss?"

"It would not be theft if you gave it willingly," he said.

"I won't."

He turned toward her and let go of her hand. He set his own against the wall over her shoulder. "Won't you?" he said. 'Why not?"

"Because we are a couple of children when we are together, you and I," she said. "I would be mortally embarrassed if you kissed me. I would not know where to look."

"You are supposed to close your eyes," he said.

"No, Josh," she said. "I mean it."

He smiled at her. "Damn," he said. "Who else is there here to flirt with if not with you, Rosamund?"

"Try not flirting with anyone for two weeks," she said. "It will doubtless be good for your soul, Josh."

"You aren't sighing with love over Toby by any chance, are you?" he said. "He'll probably deliver a sermon every night before jumping into bed with you. And imagine all the little Tobys learning their lessons at his knee in years to come."

She laughed. "Don't," she said. "He is not a figure of fun, Josh. He is a very respectable citizen."

"Picture yourself in a front pew knowing that you have to remain awake and look interested through his Sunday sermons," he said. "Picture yourself having to keep all the little Tobys and their sisters from fidgeting."

"You are quite horrid and heartless," she said. "I am sorry to destroy your mental image, Josh, but I have no intention of marrying him, you know."

"Good," he said. "Let me kiss you, then. You may be surprised at how good I am at it."

"I don't doubt that you are an authority on the subject," she said. "Here comes Annabelle."

She was greatly relieved as he removed his hand and turned to smile at Annabelle. She liked him far too well to become involved in a real flirtation with him. She knew she could never have serious feelings for him, and she very much doubted that he could have any for her. There was not that spark that there was with . . .

It did not matter.

"All your aunt can do when I try to describe the bliss of her future life with Toby and all their offspring is laugh with a dreadful tone of levity," he said to the girl. "Perhaps you can talk some sense into her, Annabelle."

"Oh, Aunt Rosa," Annabelle said, looking at her in dismay, "you are not going to marry Tobias, are you?"

Lord Beresford chuckled. "Let's go and have a look at the hermit's cave down by the river," he said. "I haven't seen it for years." He extended an arm to each of them.

Annabelle took one of his arms.

"I am going to walk among the trees for a few minutes," Rosamund said. "You two go along."

"She is afraid I will pitch her into the river," he said to Annabelle.

Annabelle looked reproachfully back at Rosamund as she was led away.

Rosamund strolled among the trees, enjoying the brief period of solitude. She had not realized quite how tranquil and uneventful her life with her husband had been until the last few days. The activity she welcomed—she had always had a great deal of energy and a strong sense of adventure and fun. But the human entanglements were bewildering.

There was Toby hinting in his usual pompous, roundabout manner that he was about to make her an offer. She could not think why, since he had not seen her for ten years and must remember her as a spirited, mischievous girl who was most unsuitable for a parson's wife. And there was Josh inciting her to mischief just as if they really were still children. And trying to flirt with her. She had been flirting with him in the past two days, of course, but she had sensed that he was about to take the flirtation one step farther. And she had hesitated.

And then, of course, there was Justin. No, there was not Justin. She was just going to have to accustom herself to thinking of him as Annabelle's. Soon enough he would be. If she were wise, she would throw all her energies into a flirtation with Josh. He was handsome and attractive and experienced. She liked him a great deal.

She became aware of movement among the trees suddenly and flattened herself against a trunk. Not that there was reason to hide from anyone, she thought, closing her eyes and feeling her heart beating up into her throat. She did not even know who it was. But, yes, she did know. Of course she knew.

"Rosamund?" he said just when there had been a moment of silence and she hoped he had gone away. "Are you hiding?"

"Hiding?" she said. "Of course not. I am enjoying the shelter from the wind. Are you looking for Annabelle?"

"I was," he said.

"She has gone around to the river with Josh," she said, "to look for the hermit's cave. Actually I think it is a fox's den, but we always liked to think it was a hermit's cave."

He had come to stand in front of her. For some reason that she had not even begun to fathom, she remained pressed against the tree, her hands clasping it on either side of her body.

He nodded. "Perhaps we should go around there, too," he said.

"Yes," she said.

"Or are you afraid that the tree will fall down if you don't stand there holding it up?" His eyes were smiling at her in that way she had noticed before.

"Perhaps it will, too," she said. "You go and find them, Justin. I'll stay here."

He was looking very directly at her with those eyes. His hands were clasped behind his back.

"It's not as easy to be sensible as it seemed two evenings ago, is it?" he said.

"No." She sounded, she thought, as if she had just run a mile without stopping.

"I should have left you at the roadside," he said.

"I should have locked myself into that bedchamber," she said.

"I should have read aloud from my book of sermons until I put us both to sleep."

"I should have agreed meekly with Dennis' eagerness to match me with Toby."

"No, you shouldn't."

"I should have asserted myself, then," she said, "and said no and refused to say another word. I should not have set foot outside that carriage."

"I should not have left London," he said, "once I realized that I would have to travel alone."

"I might have frozen to a hedgerow if you had not," she said. "Dennis had lost a wheel."

"And you were trudging away in the opposite direction," he said, grinning suddenly. "You could well be a candidate for Bedlam one of these days, Rosamund."

"And you were loaded down with a trunk full of clothes for a mistress who was in London with a chill," she said. "Perhaps we will meet in Bedlam."

Only his eyes still smiled. "I wish we could," he said so softly that she had to read his lips.

"Go away, Justin," she said. "Please go away. Go and find Annabelle and Josh."

"Would it be different, I wonder," he said, "if we had had longer? A week perhaps? Two?"

"Two, yes," she said. "We would have used up all the snow making snowmen and had nothing else to do outdoors. We would have read all nine books from cover to cover. And I would have beaten you so many times at billiards that you would have had no self-confidence left."

"There would have still been cards to beat you at," he said.

"Perhaps," she said. "Perhaps. Yes, two weeks would surely have done it, Justin. We would have been mortally tired of each other."

"Yes," he said.

"Go away," she said. "Please go away."

But he lowered his head, his hands still behind his back, and found her mouth with his own. He slid his tongue inside and touched hers.

"I wish we had had those two weeks," he said, withdrawing only a couple of inches from her mouth. "I wish we were mortally tired of each other, Rosamund. I wish it more than I wish anything else in life."

She heard herself swallow.

"I'm going," he said. "But not to find Annabelle. The others must be ready to start back. It's a brisk day outside the shelter of the trees. You had better come with me."

"Justin," she said, "I wish I were the other side of the globe from you."

"I know," he said. "But you aren't. Come on. I won't offer you my arm or my hand. Will that help?"

"No," she said.

"Come with me anyway," he said. "What were you doing teetering along the top of a high wall earlier just like a twelve-year-old hoyden?"

"Taking a dare from Josh," she said. "And enjoying my triumph when he fell off and I did not. It was a dreadfully undignified thing to do, wasn't it?"

"Dreadfully," he said. "I was careful to keep the Reverend Strangelove's back to you all the time you were doing it."

They both laughed.

"And wishing I were up there with you," he said, "to show you that it could be done on one foot."

"Oh, nonsense," she said scornfully. "The surface is uneven. You would have fallen off and made a prize idiot of yourself."

He chuckled and she joined in his laughter again.

11

It's here somewhere," Lord Beresford said. "Do you remember exactly where, Annabelle?"

"I think we are going in the right direction," she said. "But I think we should be going back, Joshua. The others will be looking for us."

"After only five minutes?" he said. "I don't think so. Hold my hand—the slope is rather steep."

"But I am not a child," she said. "I don't need to hold your hand."

"There it is," he said, taking her hand anyway and drawing her laterally across the bank that led down from the ruined wall of the abbey to the river. "Can't you just imagine the hermit sitting here, Annabelle, in his sackcloth robe with long, matted hair and beard, and ashes on his head?"

"No," she said. "It is a silly idea. Why would any man crouch inside a cave he could not even stand up in and freeze in the winter when there was a perfectly serviceable abbey within a stone's throw?"

He grinned at her and released her hand in order to stoop down and peer inside the cave. "You have no imagination, Annabelle," he said, "and no sense of romance. Here we could be dreaming up the ghost of our very own holy man, and all you can think of is his getting a red nose in winter."

"He probably smelled too," she said. "He probably never bathed."

He straightened up and laughed at her. "What do you expect of the poor man?" he said. "That he would chip the ice in the river every morning just so he could have an invigorating bath?"

"No," she said. "I don't believe he even existed."

He set his head to one side and looked at her. "I have not set myself an easy task, have I?" he said. "Even the absurdity of this conversation cannot draw a smile from you."

"It's just silly talk," she said.

"Precisely." He rubbed at her chin with one knuckle. "But all of us are permitted some silliness some of the time. Some of us more than others, of course. You disapprove of me, don't you, Annabelle? I'm not serious enough for you."

"I would not presume either to approve or to disapprove of you," she said.

He threw back his head and laughed. "I sometimes forget that I am such a grand person that I am beyond reproach," he said. "Can Justin make you smile?"

"What a silly idea it is," she said, "that I never smile. Of course I do."

"Do you smile when he kisses you?" he asked.

"Joshua!" She flushed.

"Well, do you?" He took her chin in his hand, though she tried to pull away. "Do you like being kissed?"

"That is a very improper question," she said.

"Yes, isn't it?" He held to her chin and grinned at her. "Don't tell me he has not done it yet. What a slowtop." And he bent his head and kissed her firmly on the lips. "Smile at me now."

Annabelle drew back an arm and smacked him hard across one cheek. "How dare you," she cried. "I am a woman, Joshua. I am eighteen years old, if you had not noticed. I am not a child still, to be teased and humored and laughed at. Leave me alone."

Lord Beresford winced and held one palm against a reddening cheek. "Well," he said, "that certainly was no smile, was it?"

"I hate you," she cried. "You have always teased me as a little girl who cannot possibly have any feelings. You may be surprised to know that I have. And I don't feel happy when

I am close to you. That is why I don't smile, if you must know. I don't smile because I don't like you. I hate you." She turned sharply away.

But he caught her by the arm. "Annabelle," he said, "what is this? What have I done to hurt you so much? Have I always teased you? Yes, I suppose I have. But I tease almost everyone—everyone I like, that is. I have always felt an affection for you. Haven't you known that? Or is it something else about me that you dislike?"

She had her head turned away from him, staring at the ground. "I don't dislike you," she said. "I'm sorry I said I did. But you should not have done that. I belong to Lord Wetherby. I always have."

"I'm sorry too," he said gently. "I didn't mean any disrespect, Annabelle. We have known each other forever and I forgot that you are all grown up and not to be kissed teasingly like that. I didn't mean to hurt you. Forgive me?"

"Let's go back inside the walls," she said.

"You go," he said. "If I go back now, Justin will be challenging me to pistols at dawn when he sees the mark of your fingers on my cheek."

She looked up at the telltale marks and bit her lower lip.

He grinned. "I would hate to put a bullet between his eyes before he has even had a chance to kiss you," he said.

"Don't joke about such things," she said.

"I had better find the inside of the cave fascinating for the next five minutes," he said, turning away from her. "Here come Robin and Toby and Christobel."

The Earl of Wetherby rode beside Annabelle again on the way home. He wondered what she had seen or heard or imagined. There was a closed look about her face and a tightness about her jaw that had not been there before. Surely she had not seen anything.

The very last thing he felt like doing was conversing, deliberately setting himself to charm a young lady who looked as if she had no intention of being charmed. He wanted to bury himself in his own thoughts. He wanted to gallop away from the whole group, be alone for a few hours. The very worst thing about a house party was the lack of privacy.

"I'm glad the abbey was suggested," he said. "I would hate to have missed it."

"What?" she said. "Oh, yes, it is rather splendid, isn't it? I can't imagine how anyone would have wanted to destroy it."

Josh, fairly close behind them, was making Christobel giggle over something, Lord Wetherby could hear. Rosamund, he saw in one swift glance over his shoulder, was riding with Carver.

It was going to be hard to forgive himself for what had just happened. He had gone beyond the wall with the intention of finding Annabelle, of spending a few minutes alone with her, of kissing her even, if circumstances had been right. He had found Rosamund instead, ignored her request that he go away, and kissed her—not even in a chaste manner just for old times' sake.

Had he so little self-control? So little regard for Rosamund's feelings? So little regard for the girl who was to be his bride? The girl riding silently at his side?

"I had hoped to spend some time alone with you," he said. "I had hoped to become better acquainted with you, Annabelle."

She darted him a glance. Josh laughed merrily behind them and Christobel shrieked and giggled. "There is another way back," she said quickly, "over the hill. It is shorter but not as easy as this route."

"We will allow the others to pass us, then," he said, slowing his horse and drawing it to one side of the path so that within a minute they were at the back of the group.

"Annabelle is going to show me the difficult route home," he told Robin and Pamela.

And then they were riding off through widely spaced trees, the voices of their companions disappearing off to their left.

"This goes uphill?" he asked.

"Yes," she said. "There is a splendid view from the top."

They rode in near silence until they came to the crest of

the hill. As Annabelle had promised, there was a view down all four sides so that they could see the house and the lake off to one side of them, the river and Winwood Abbey to the other. Lord Wetherby directed his gaze to the lake and tried to pick out the little pieces of wilderness where he had stood with Rosamund the day before.

But, no, he would turn his mind from such thoughts.

"Shall we get down for a while?" he suggested. "The wind seems to have died down considerably."

He tethered their horses to a tree and they stood looking about them.

"What is it?" he asked, turning to her at last. The tension in her was almost a tangible thing. "Has something happened?"

"No," she said.

He smiled gently at her. "We both know that your father has approved my suit and that I will be making you a formal offer within the next few days," he said. "You probably know that your grandfather hopes to announce our betrothal on his birthday, at the ball. Does the thought disturb you? Would you rather it not be so soon? Or not at all?"

"It was first suggested when I was nine years old," she said. "It would be strange if I were not ready for it, my lord."

"Would you rather it had not been so arranged?" he asked.

"No," she said, "I am content."

"Content," he said with a smile. "Yet you will not even call me by my name."

"I will if you insist," she said. "But it is difficult. You were twenty years old when we first met. You seemed years and years beyond me, a very grand gentleman."

"Did I?" he said. "And doubtless I did nothing to make you feel more at ease. Twenty-year-olds do not always feel a great deal of respect for nine-year-olds. Is that the whole problem? Do I still seem like an elderly gentleman to you?"

"No, of course not," she said. "And there is no problem."

He set his hands on her shoulders and looked down into

her eyes. It was rather like looking at a stone wall, he thought. What was behind her eyes had been carefully shut off.

"It would be desirable for us to become comfortable with each other, wouldn't it?" he said. "We should try to be friends before I ask you to be my wife, don't you think?"

She did not look away from his eyes. He saw her swallow and knew that she did so quite painfully.

"Kiss me," she said suddenly. "Please kiss me . . . Justin."

He hesitated. The stone wall behind her eyes had become pain. He lowered his head and kissed her slowly, his lips gentle and closed. Her own were clamped together in a rigid line.

"You don't have to be afraid of me," he said. "I don't want to hurt you, Annabelle, and I will never demand more than you are prepared to give."

For answer she threw her arms up about his neck. "I am not afraid," she said. "I want to kiss you."

When he lowered his head again, she kissed him back with fierce passion, pressing closed lips against his own, thrusting her bosom against him, half-strangling him with her arms. He held her and gentled her, and rocked her against him afterward, her head against his shoulder.

Who was the man? he wondered. Someone she had met in London during the Season the year before? But he had not noticed or heard of anyone in particular. Someone at Brookfield? Unlikely. All the other house guests were her relatives, though some of them were of no very close relationship.

Most likely it was some poor ineligible soul from her own home. Though even an eligible gentleman would be beyond her grasp when she felt she had a nine-year-old "arrangement" to be honored.

God, what a coil! They were not even officially betrothed, yet they were both bound as tightly as if their nuptials had been celebrated and their marriage consummated—he because he had already spoken to her father, and she because she felt bound in duty to her parents' wishes, even though they had given her the freedom to make her own decision.

"Will you have a disgust of me?" she asked, her face hidden against his shoulder. "Will you think me quite lost to all conduct?" She lifted her head and looked up at him. "But it was not wrong, was it, my lord? We are almost betrothed."

"It was not wrong," he said, smiling down at her.

"I liked it," she said quickly. "I do have an affection for you already, Justin. I swear I do."

He kissed her lightly on the nose. "Then you must tell me more about yourself," he said. "Tell me who Annabelle Milford is. I want to know. We had better ride as we talk. I don't think your papa will be too happy with me if I keep you alone for much longer."

She talked quite freely as they rode down the hill and across the pasture to the park surrounding Brookfield. Perhaps, he thought, she was even trying to answer his request that she tell him who she was—though without much success. Who was this girl who had known at the age of nine that her future husband had been chosen for her, who had apparently put up no fight whatsoever against the arranged marriage, who was desperately trying to like him and want him? One thing was becoming increasingly clear to him: she was not a happy girl.

And he would swear that there was another man.

"No," she said in answer to one of his questions as they rode. "I had never been anywhere except here until we went to London last year for my come-out. Except to Lincolnshire, that is, when I was fourteen. Mama and I spent a month with Aunt Rosa and Uncle Leonard. I always wondered why she married him when he was so much older and she was so very lovely. But they were happy, you know. I think for him the sun rose and set on Aunt Rosa."

He smiled at her, willing her to continue.

"I cried and cried when news came that he had died," Annabelle said. "Papa had gone there when he was very low and sent word back. I knew Aunt Rosa would be quite grief-stricken. And now Papa is trying to marry her to Tobias. I do think it wrong of him.''

"I daresay he wants your aunt to be happy again," he said.

"Yes, of course," she said. "But Aunt Rosa chose for herself the first time and was happy. I am sure she can do the same again and perhaps chose someone younger, someone with whom she can spend the rest of her life. I do think people should be allowed to choose for themselves.''

There was a sudden and awkward silence between them.

"When they are older, like Aunt Rosa, and have had some experience of life, I mean," she said.

"And yet," he could not stop himself from saying, "she was only seventeen the first time.''

"Yes," she said. "Did I tell you that? That she was only seventeen, I mean?''

"I must have heard it somewhere," he said.

She began to tell him about her presentation to the queen.

She had been seventeen. Nine years ago—when he had met Annabelle for the first time and the match between them had first been suggested as a desirable possibility. Where had Rosamund been during that month? Had it been just after her marriage or just before?

If she had been at Brookfield with Annabelle, they would have met, she seventeen, he twenty. What would have happened? Would he have fallen in love with her then? And she with him? Would they have eight or nine years of marriage behind them by now? Perhaps several children?

But she had been afraid of younger men at that time. That was why she had married Sir Leonard Hunter. She certainly would not have fancied a young buck who had still expected every female to swoon at his feet if he merely favored her with an appreciative glance. And at that age he would not have fancied a female who could not immediately be tumbled into bed.

Though that was a strange thought, considering the speed with which he had bedded Rosamund at the age of nine-and-twenty. He had not changed so much, after all.

And was he in love with her? Was that a suitable

description of his feelings? Did he not merely want to make love to her again? Was it not a purely physical thing between them? Something that would wear off once he was married?

He hoped it was only that. He did not care to be "in love," whatever that expression meant. He was certainly hoping that it did not mean what he was beginning to think it might mean.

Annabelle was looking to him inquiringly, and he returned his attention to her. Obviously he had missed some cue.

The following day progressed far more to Rosamund's liking than any day at Brookfield so far. The marchioness decided to take her friend Lady Wetherby, Lana, and Annabelle about with her to visit various neighbors, and the Earl of Wetherby was enlisted to escort them.

"Everyone is dying of curiosity to see you, anyway, Justin," Lady Gilmore said, "with strange rumors about you beginning to circulate, and it would be too cruel to keep them waiting until the evening of the ball."

"You mean I am to have four ladies all to myself?" he said with a grin. "It sounds like my sort of day, ma'am."

"And if you think flattery is like to get you into my good graces, young man," she said, tapping him on the arm, "you are quite right. I have ordered the barouche. You will have to squeeze between your mama and Annabelle."

"And I can let my breath out," the marquess said, chuckling, "and start to think of billiards."

Rosamund had looked forward to spending the time with the other ladies indoors or walking in the formal gardens, where some spring flowers were already coming into bud. But she was not unduly disappointed when the Reverend Strangelove asked her to go riding with him.

"Robin and Christobel are to be of the party, too," he said, bowing to her, "so it will be quite unexceptionable for you to accept, my dear Rosamund. Indeed, Christobel will need your presence as chaperone. Of course, on my great-uncle's property there would be nothing improper anyway about a respectable widow riding alone with a man of the cloth. But even so, I would not wish to disturb your tender sensibilities or invite censure from any of my esteemed relatives or those of the Earl of Wetherby.''

"I shall be glad of the fresh air and exercise, Toby,'' Rosamund said before escaping to change into her riding habit. It was a beautiful day again.

The four of them rode together until they realized that they were close to the village and might as well ride the extra mile to enter it. Christobel remembered that she needed some new yellow ribbon to trim the ball gown she intended to wear for her grandfather's birthday ball. The Reverend Strangelove decided that the vicar would undoubtedly be hurt if he knew that a fellow member of the cloth had been in the village and had not called on him.

Robin escorted Christobel to the shops while Rosamund agreed to accompany the Reverend Strangelove to the vicarage.

They decided almost immediately not to stay long as the vicar was from home and the vicar's wife, who was within two months of a confinement, was clearly feeling unwell. Even so, by the time Toby had delivered several speeches in which he assured himself that Mrs. Crutchley would be far more comfortable left alone and then paused while she assured him that she was delighted to entertain visitors, almost an hour had passed. There was no sign of Robin and Christobel. They must have grown tired of waiting and returned home.

However, the marchioness's barouche was driving along the village street and stopped at their approach.

"Well met,'' Lady Gilmore said, smiling at them. "Are you coming from the vicarage? How is Mrs. Crutchley today?''

"Feeling rather tired, I'm afraid,'' Rosamund said.

"But very gratified by our visit, Aunt,'' the Reverend Strangelove added. "I do believe her spirits were lifted by a visit from a man of the cloth other than her good husband. And of course she was delighted at the condescension of the visit from Lady Hunter. Unfortunately, the Reverend Crutchley was from home.''

"And is just arriving back now, I believe," Lady March said, looking along the street toward the vicarage. "Perhaps we should postpone our call until another day, Mama."

"I should hate to disturb a poor lady who is close to a confinement," Lady Wetherby said.

"I am sure the good lady would be deeply hurt to know that you had been in the village and had not seen fit to wait upon her, Great-aunt," the Reverend Strangelove said.

"We will call for ten minutes," Lady Gilmore said, "and persuade Mrs. Crutchley to accept the services of a couple of maids for a while. They have only their cook."

"I shall take upon myself the privilege of returning with you, Aunt," the Reverend Strangelove said. "The Reverend Crutchley will be disappointed to have missed the chance of a conversation with another man of the cloth."

"I shall ride home," Rosamund said firmly.

"It would be very rag-mannered of all of us to allow you to do so alone, my dear," the marchioness said. "I have an idea that should be satisfactory to all of us. You must relinquish your horse to Justin, Tobias, and he will ride home with Rosamund. He has been extremely good in visiting all afternoon with us and charming all the ladies into collective sighs. It is time to reward him."

Rosamund sat tensely in her saddle while Lana and Lady Wetherby laughed and Toby dismounted, having commended the marchioness on her good sense and Justin on his kindness in being willing to accompany her home.

Justin looked at Annabelle.

"Aunt Rosa should not be alone," she told him gravely.

And so her day was to be ruined, after all. Just when she had thought she was to go through a whole day without the oppression of his closeness, she was being thrust into his presence for a long ride of at least half an hour. He swung himself up into the saddle of Toby's horse.

"Well," he said after they had ridden along the village street and out onto a country road, "there is really only one thing to be done about this, Rosamund." And he looked at her and chuckled until she joined in his laughter. "It is either this or cry, you know, and I hate crying. It seems such an unmanly occupation.''

"If Toby would only talk less and listen and observe more,'' she said, "he would have persuaded everyone to leave the poor lady alone to rest.''

"In other words,'' he said, "Toby is an ass. Do you promise faithfully not to marry him, Rosamund?''

"If you have a Bible on your person,'' she said, "I will cheerfully swear on it.''

"He is going to ask you, you know,'' he said. "Very soon, too. My guess is that he will want the announcement made at the birthday ball. And my second guess is that he will do the thing properly, on one knee. It might get sore, for I will wager that his proposal speech will last for at least fifteen minutes.''

"Don't,'' she said, laughing. "You are being unkind.''

"But quite truthful,'' he said, "as you very well know. I wonder what sort of a pompous speech he would deliver when bedding you.''

"Neither of us will ever know,'' she said, her laughter dying.

"I'm sorry,'' he said. "That was in bad taste. Must we take this road? Can we go across country?''

"Yes, easily,'' she said. "There is a gate into the pasture just a little farther along.''

They were soon riding across fields and past budding trees. They had lapsed into silence.

"How well do you know Annabelle?'' he asked her at last. "Does she confide in you?''

"Annabelle is a very private person,'' she said. "I don't believe she confides in anyone. Are you disturbed because she is always so very serious? That is just Annabelle, I'm afraid.''

"You don't know of any swain back in your brother's neighborhood who is sighing for her favors?'' he asked.

She looked at him sharply. "Has she said anything that makes you think there is such a person?'' she asked.

"Oh, no,'' he said. "There is no one more proper or more

accepting of the life others have arranged for her than
Annabelle. She is all good sense and duty and sweetness,
and she has shut the door to her inner self against all comers,
I believe. I thought perhaps she might have opened it to you.
She admires you a great deal.''

"She will be a good wife to you," she said.

"Oh, I don't doubt it," he said. "She will not give me
a moment's trouble. I will not hear a single sigh from her
over the mysterious swain.''

"What makes you think there is such a man?" she asked.

"She is trying to fall in love with me," he said. "There
seems to be little need to do so, unless she is trying to fall
out of love with someone else.''

Rosamund was silent, unable and unwilling to ask him if
he was trying to do the same thing. But then he did not believe
in love, as he had told her on an earlier occasion. Only in
satisfying his appetites—until now. And now in being faithful
and loyal to his chosen bride.

And it seemed very possible that there was someone else.
She had not really thought of it before, but it made perfect
sense. Certainly Annabelle had been crying the night before.
She had been puffy-eyed that morning when Rosamund had
called on her before breakfast, and she had claimed that the
birds singing outside her window had kept her awake and
given her a headache. But dawn did not come very early at
the beginning of March.

Rosamund had concluded that something had happened
between the girl and Justin, that somehow she was regretting
the betrothal she was about to make. And the thought had
made Rosamund feel quite ill. She still believed in her theory,
but it would make more sense if Annabelle were in love with
someone else. If she were not, then surely she would be
pleased, or at least accepting of the match that had been
arranged for her. After all, most eighteen-year old girls
would be over the moon at the prospect of marrying a young
and handsome and wealthy earl.

"Perhaps she is just overwhelmed by the occasion," she

said. "Next week, when the deed is accomplished, she will probably relax and be far more cheerful."

"Perhaps you are right," he said. "And will I be more relaxed? And will you?"

"I will not be here," she said. "I have fortunately remembered that Leonard has a distant cousin living just thirty miles from here. I shall visit her next week, after the ball. Dennis and Lana can take me up on their way home the following week. It will be better that way. I am relieved that I have thought of it."

"Yes," he said. "But how are you going to avoid me at my wedding and down through the years, Rosamund?"

"These feelings we have will wear off," she said. "It is just that it all happened little over a month ago. Eventually we will forget and find it easy to be in each other's company. But not yet. This time next week I will be gone. A few more days and then you will not have to be afraid that, try as we will, we will not be able keep out of each other's company."

"Meanwhile," he said, "there are still these few days. And I am still free, relatively speaking. And there is still what remains of this afternoon, when we did not scheme to be alone together but are alone, nevertheless. We are not far from the lake, are we? Let's ride that way. Let's enjoy this hour for what it's worth. Shall we?"

"You are asking me to go with you to make love with you?" she asked quietly.

He did not answer immediately. "I don't know," he said. "Am I? Yes, I suppose I am, and it would not do, would it? But let's have that hour together anyway, Rosamund. Let's ride to the lake and sit there quietly for a while. Let's see if we can find some peace that will take us through these difficult days. We were friends as well as lovers, weren't we?"

"Yes," she said reluctantly. He had noticed that, too, then. It had not been entirely physical for him. She was not sure she was glad he felt as she did. And it would be madness to go with him. Even if they did not end up making love, there was no peace to be found together. Only more torment.

"Will you come?" he asked.

"Yes," she said.

They turned their horses in the direction of the lake without another word.

12

The lake was calm and a deep blue as it had been two days before. A few fluffy clouds were floating in the sky. There was a suggestion of warmth in the air, early as the season was. For perhaps one hour he was going to forget everything but his surroundings and his companion, the Earl of Wetherby thought, reaching up his arms to lift her from her saddle.

He deliberately slid her down along the length of his body, feeling her warmth and her slimness. He kisses her briefly on the lips and watched her mouth curve into a slight smile. They had not exchanged a word since turning off to the lake, but he knew by a medium deeper than words that she had made the same decision as he about the next hour.

He tethered their horses and took her by the hand. They strolled to the water's edge—the bank was low at that point—and stood gazing across.

"Let's sit down," he said, breaking the silence between them at last. And he drew her down into the shade of an oak tree, setting his back against the trunk. She did not resist when he put one arm about her shoulders. She unpinned her riding hat from her hair, set it down on the grass beside her, and nestled her head against his shoulder.

"Spring has always been my favorite season," she said. "Everything is springing to new life and nothing seems impossible. Last year especially it was in the spring that I began to throw off my gloom. I filled the house with spring flowers and put crocuses and primroses on Leonard's grave."

He rubbed his cheek against the top of her head. "Are your daffodils still blooming?" he asked.

"Yes," she said. And after a small hesitation, "I have pressed one of them."

"Have you?" he said.

They lapsed into silence and he rested his cheek against her hair and stared out over the water, trying to impress the memory of the moment on his mind. He tried to draw comfort and peace from it and the strength to face life again after it.

"A flower can be pressed and kept forever," he said. "A snow angel can't."

She laughed softly. "You made more of a snow devil of yours, didn't you?" she said. "Did the head stay on my snowman?"

"It was off before you left," he said. "You took your prize under false pretenses."

"And you did not put it back?" she said. "How ungallant of you."

"I had not the heart for it," he said, and they were silent again.

"Justin," she said, reaching up a hand and tracing lightly the line of his jaw, "if you could go back and change everything—if you could have stayed in London or not insisted on taking me up or taken me farther along the road to find Dennis that first day. If you could change anything, would you?"

He took her hand in his and kissed the palm. "Yes," he said. "Yes, I would." He paused. "Would you?"

"Yes," she said quietly. "What would have happened if we had met as strangers this week? Anything?"

"No, nothing," he said. "I would have been merely your niece's betrothed. You would have been merely her aunt. It would have been far better so, Rosamund."

"Yes," she said.

But it could not have been so. He surely could not have met her this week and felt nothing at all for her. Surely even if they had been total strangers, he would have recognized her.

Recognized her? As what? As someone he could find

irresistibly attractive? As someone he felt drawn to as iron to a magnet? As someone he could fall in love with? As the love of his life? The missing part of his life?

And would he change the past if he could? In order to rid himself of the pain of the present and the awkwardness of the future, would he change the past? Would he be without those few days at Price's hunting box? Without those minutes in their little piece of wilderness two days before? Without this hour?

"No, it's not true," she said. "I would not change even one small detail, Justin. I wouldn't."

She fit so comfortably against his side, he thought, almost as if she had been made to be there. There were dozens of unseen birds singing around them, one repeating the same persistent call over and over again. There was a breeze fanning his right cheek. The air was fresh—not warm but not chill, either. It was a moment to be remembered and hoarded for a lifetime.

He hunched his shoulder so that he could see into her face. And yet he could find no words to express all he wanted to say to her. So many words were forbidden to him, and the others would not even form into coherent thoughts in his mind. He could only gaze into her eyes and tell her with his own all that words and thoughts could not express.

And she gazed back and her own eyes softened and smiled.

When he kissed her, he did so lightly, warmly, without passion, stroking the smooth skin beneath her chin with one knuckle. And she kissed him back, parting her lips beneath his, touching him with her tongue, sucking gently on his, drawing it into her mouth. He kissed her cheeks, her temples, her closed eyelids, her mouth again. And he smoothed back the hair at the side of her face, smiling at her once more.

"Do other men kiss like that?" she asked him, her fingers lightly stroking through his hair. "I had no idea until I met you."

"I don't know," he said, grinning at her. "I have never kissed another man."

She grimaced and laughed softly.

He undid the buttons of her velvet riding jacket and ran his hands over the warm silk blouse beneath. He cupped one breast in his hand, felt the soft tip with his thumb. And he began to undo the buttons of her blouse.

"Don't," she said when the job was half done.

"I just want to touch you," he said, his mouth against hers. "I want to touch your breasts, Rosamund."

"No," she said. "If you do that, Justin, we will both want a little more and a little more until we end up making love."

He swallowed. "And that would be so wrong?" he said.

"You know it would." She burrowed her head against his shoulder again, nudged his hand aside with her own, and began to do up the buttons again.

"And it was wrong a month ago?" he said. "Yet you just said that you would not change a moment of it."

"That was a little different," she said. "For both of us. We can't do it now, Justin. Not on the marquess's land when you are here to betroth yourself to Annabelle. We should not even be here."

He took her hand when it had finished buttoning the blouse, and squeezed it very tightly. "I'm sorry," he said. "You are quite right, of course. I'm sorry, Rosamund. Just don't leave me yet, please. Sit with me here for a while."

He set his head back against the trunk of the tree and closed his eyes. He could feel every heartbeat like a hammerblow against his chest. He breathed slowly and evenly and willed her not to move. Not like this. He did not want it to end like this when both of them were agitated. He had genuinely wanted to bring her here so that they could win some peace together.

What a mad hope that had been!

"Justin," she said, her voice light, almost teasing, "did your mistress recover from her cold?"

"Jude?" he said. "She was bubbling with high spirits when I got back to London. She could not resist showing me the emerald brooch my successor had already bought her, though she swore to me that she had remained faithful to me until my return."

"Did you give her the trunk?" she asked.

He hesitated. "The diamond bracelet, yes," he said. "She almost gobbled it up. I believe she even forgot the brooch for a few moments. Nothing else."

He did not tell her that he had found himself quite unable to give Jude the clothes that Rosamund had worn or touched or the perfumes with which she had enticed him.

"So you have said good-bye to her?" she said. "Were you sad?"

He had not even slept with Jude after his return, though she had clearly expected that such a service would be required of her in return for the bracelet and the large money settlement he had made on her. She had been wearing a red nightgown that hid nothing of her very generous curves, and the perfume that had used to drive him wild.

But he had still been feeling almost sick with longing for a certain snow angel who had melted out of his life apparently forever.

"No," he said. "Didn't your father or your brother or your husband teach you that you do not discuss a man's mistresses with him, Rosamund?"

"But Papa and Dennis and Leonard never had mistresses," she said. "I am as sure as I can be with Papa and Dennis, and I actually asked Leonard."

"I hope he blistered you with his tongue," he said.

"He laughed," she said. "Perhaps he would not have if there really had been a mistress, but there wasn't, you see."

"So I am the first depraved gentleman you have known," he said.

"Yes," she said. "It is rather funny that Dennis has been warning me against Josh, isn't it? He is supposed to be a rake. Are you? Have you had many mistresses, Justin?"

"That is too outrageous a question," he said. "I refuse to answer."

"On the grounds that the answer may incriminate you?

Or that I will think you are boasting if you mention the actual number? Or can you not count that high? I think you must have had many," she said. "You certainly have a large number of skills. Leonard did not know half as much."

"Are you doing this deliberately?" he asked, nudging her head away from him again and looking at her laughing face with sudden suspicion. "You are, aren't you? To lighten the atmosphere?"

"Well, you must admit," she said, "that it did need lightening."

Her eyes were dancing and her whole face was animated, the way he remembered from his first day with her. But how familiar and how very dear the sight of her had grown since then. He cupped her face with his hands.

"Yes, it did," he said. "I suppose we should be getting back now, shouldn't we? Are we worse off or better off for having come here? Was it very wrong of me to suggest it?"

"If it was," she said, "then it was equally wrong of me to agree. Don't let's add guilt to everything else. It has been an hour I would not wish to erase."

"Me, neither," he said, kissing her once more, warmly on the lips.

She turned her head sharply before he was finished, and they both looked over her shoulder to where Lord Beresford was standing thirty feet away, a startled look on his face . . .

Rosamund got to her feet unassisted and brushed at the grass that clung to her velvet skirt. She kept her eyes on what she was doing and resisted the urge to launch into a speech of self-defense. Lord Wetherby had got to his feet, too.

"If I could," Lord Beresford said, "I would have slunk away unseen. Unfortunately you took me by surprise."

His voice was rather grim, Rosamund thought. She had only ever heard it light and teasing.

The earl bent down to retrieve her hat and handed it to her.

"Under the circumstances," Lord Beresford said, "I suppose I should be thankful things were not a great deal more embarrassing than they were. This is not bad after a three-day acquaintance, Justin. You have got farther than I. And I thought my only competition was Strangelove."

"We have been acquainted for longer than three days," the earl said.

"I believe your next words are supposed to be something to the effect that this is not quite what it seems," Lord Beresford said.

Rosamund pinned her hat to her hair, keeping her eyes on the ground. She too had been expecting Justin to say those words and had been willing him not to.

"I don't believe either Rosamund or I owe you an explanation, Josh," the earl said. "I just hope you don't go blurting this out back at the house and causing a lot of pain."

"I am on foot," Lord Beresford said. "If I just had two sound legs, I would go tearing off to tell tales to Annabelle and then go rushing off to find Dennis and my great-uncle. It would be just the sort of thing to bring me amusement."

"Sorry," Lord Wetherby said. "My words were foolish."

Lord Beresford turned his eyes on Rosamund. "I expected better of you, Rosamund," he said. "This is not exactly in good taste, is it?"

She looked back into the good-humored, handsome face—now pale and tight-lipped—of her girlhood companion and saw herself through his eyes. It was not a pleasant image. She lowered her eyes and walked toward the tethered horses.

"Let her go alone," Lord Beresford said from behind her.

"I'll be all right," she said, turning. "I can find my own way back, Justin."

He followed her wordlessly and helped her into the saddle.

"I'm sorry," he whispered, his back to Lord Beresford, looking up at her with troubled eyes. "I'm so sorry, Rosamund."

She tried to smile back at him before turning her horse's head for the house a mile away. She had to concentrate on moving carefully through the trees so that she would not be struck across the face by a twig or branch. But she did so entirely by instinct. She saw nothing and heard nothing about her.

She saw only herself from the outside, as Josh would have seen her, sitting on the grass by the lake with Annabelle's suitor, kissing him.

It was a sordid image, indeed. The past hour had been all wrong, every self-indulgent moment of it. She had gone there to the lake with him and sat close beside him, her head on his shoulder. She had allowed him to kiss her and had returned his kisses. She had allowed him to touch her.

Oh, she had shown a good deal of sense and restraint by stopping him from unclothing her. It was quite unexceptionable to allow another woman's betrothed to fondle her through the silk of her blouse, she had seemed to be saying, though the depths of immorality to allow his hand on her naked breast. She could feel proud of herself for drawing such a firm line between what was right and what was wrong.

The truth was that she had indulged herself with a man who was forbidden to her. She might as well have allowed him to lift her skirts, as he undoubtedly would have done eventually if she had not stopped him when she had, and come right inside her. She was just as guilty as if she had allowed that ultimate intimacy. And perhaps a little more of a hypocrite.

One thing was sure: she was not going to change her mind about leaving Brookfield the morning after the ball. And she was going to find some way to avoid the wedding and all future meetings with Annabelle and her husband. In the meantime she was going to avoid him at all costs.

And she was going to throw away her pressed daffodil as soon as she had stabled her horse and gone to her room. It was over. It was a pleasant episode from her past, one to be held firmly there and forgotten about as soon as possible. No longer would she indulge herself by drawing out the memories for present enjoyment and nostalgia—not even at night.

It was over. As surely as her marriage was over. He was dead to her as effectively as Leonard was dead.

She dismounted from her horse in the stables while a groom was still hurrying toward her.

"Well," Lord Beresford said as the earl watched Rosamund ride out of sight, "do I plant you a facer now and be done with it, or is there some sort of explanation for this?"

Lord Wetherby turned to look at his friend. "I don't owe you any explanation, Josh," he said.

"I heard you had cast Jude off," the other said. "I was impressed, I must say. But I suppose there are limits even to your energy. Annabelle to get your heirs on, her aunt to play with. Who would need a mistress too?"

"I don't need this, Josh," the earl said wearily. "Not from you of all people."

"I of all people happen to be Annabelle's cousin," Lord Beresford said. "And I intend to see that she gets a fair deal."

"Her second cousin," Lord Wetherby corrected. "Since when have you been so interested in her?"

"Since always," the other said. "I might even have thought of marrying her myself if it hadn't been for you. But there was always you from the time she was a child. And the poor chit has been loyal to you ever since. I know the sort of life you have led, Justin, and I can't criticize because it is much the same as the life I am leading. But wives and mistresses don't mix in my vocabulary, especially when the wife happens to be Annabelle and the mistress Rosamund."

"Well." Lord Wetherby strolled toward his friend, who was standing with his feet apart, fists clenched at his sides. "Since you seem to have a genuine concern, Josh, I will say this: in a few days' time this betrothal will finally be official and there will be no other woman but Annabelle for the rest of my life. Does that satisfy you?"

"When did you meet Rosamund?" Lord Beresford asked. "She has been in Lincolnshire for years and only recently came back, so I have heard."

"We met recently," the earl said.

"Have you had her?" the other asked quietly.

"Oh, no." Lord Wetherby shook his head. "That is none of your concern, my friend. What are you doing out here alone, anyway?"

"Just be thankful that I am alone," Lord Beresford said. "My great-uncle beat me twice at billiards, Strangelove was not there to give me the benefit of his superior conversation, and Rosamund was not there to be flirted with. Besides, I had something on my mind. Annabelle, actually."

"Annabelle?"

"Did she tell you that I kissed her yesterday and she smacked my face?" Lord Beresford asked. "No, I can see she didn't. I didn't think she had, or you would doubtless have felt obliged to slap a glove in my face. I was teasing her, as I have done all my life, but she wasn't amused. You need to look to her, Justin. You need to find out why she doesn't ever smile. She doesn't know about you and Rosamund, does she?"

"No," Lord Wetherby said. He looked closely and consideringly at his friend. "And I'm not blind, either, Josh, or insensitive. I know she is unhappy. Have you always flirted with her?"

"Flirted?" His friend laughed. "She has been a child until very recently."

"Except that girls are not children as long as we are," the earl said.

"Well, anyway," Lord Beresford said, "I felt badly about it and came out here to think. And look what I found. I'm only thankful that you didn't have her mounted."

"Don't blame Rosamund," Lord Wetherby said. "I persuaded her to come out here with me after the marchioness and Strangelove between them forced us into each other's company. And she was the one who kept a cool head and saved you from major embarrassment."

"You would have had her, then," the other said, his jaw setting into a hard line, his hands in fists again. "You would have done that to Annabelle." He lifted one of his fists suddenly and hit Lord Wetherby a powerful hook to the jaw with it, the whole of his weight behind it. The earl fell heavily.

"Get up," Lord Beresford said, standing over him, "and fight like a man."

The earl got to his feet slowly, touching his jaw gingerly and working it from side to side, half-expecting that it was broken.

"No, I don't think I will, Josh," he said. "I have the feeling I rather deserved that."

The fight went out of his friend. "You love her, don't you?" he said. "Damn it, you love Rosamund and are going to marry Annabelle."

"I'll make her a good husband," Lord Wetherby said.

"Over my dead body!" Lord Beresford turned without another word and made his way back through the trees the way he had come. His limp, Lord Wetherby noticed, was more pronounced than usual.

And the earl was left to nurse his smarting jaw and bathe it with cold lake water and know that he had indeed deserved it, and more. It would have served him right if Josh had beaten him to a pulp. And he could probably have done it, too. He had been a soldier and even now spent far more time at Jackson's Boxing Saloon than the earl did, though he was by no means unfit. But if Josh had wanted to fight it out, Lord Wetherby was afraid that his heart would not have been in defeating him.

It was true. He had deliberately brought Rosamund out there, knowing full well that it was wrong to do so. And he had held her and kissed her and done nothing to struggle against his feelings for her. He would have made love to her if she had given him the smallest encouragement. It was pointless to deny that it was so.

What he had done was in the worst of bad taste, to say the very least. It would have been grossly unfair to Rosamund and he would have risked impregnating her. If the time had been wrong five weeks before, it was quite possibly right now. And it would have been unfair to Annabelle even if she had never known of it. If he could not control himself now, would he be able to do so for the rest of his life as her husband?

He stooped down beside the water, soaked his handkerchief, and pressed it against his jaw. He had not let her go at all, had he? Almost five weeks had passed since he had watched his carriage take her out of his life—as he had thought. But every day since, every night, he had clung to the memory of her. He had wanted her with every breath he drew. And now that she was back in his life, he did not seem to have the will to shake himself free of her.

He had never known anything like it, would never have thought it possible. Although for years he had kept mistresses for varying lengths of time and remained faithful to them for as long as they were in his keeping, he had always believed that changing his affections was something he could do at will.

He was not sure it was possible with Rosamund. Or rather he was sure. He was sure that it was impossible.

Josh must be right, he thought, getting to his feet and squeezing the moisture out of his handkerchief. He must love Rosamund.

And he noticed instantly how his thinking had undergone a subtle change. He had wondered before if he were in love with her, had even conceded that he probably was and would remain so until time wore off the feeling. Now he wondered no longer. He knew. And he was not in love with her.

He loved her.

His hands, he noticed as he folded his handkerchief and put it away in an outer pocket, were shaking.

13

Rosamund sank into a chair, laughing, and accepted a cup of tea from the hands of Lady Carver.

"It is really too bad that Eva has no imagination and Christobel could not stop giggling and Ferdie could not stop himself from talking out loud," Valerie Newton said. "You are quite splendid at charades, Rosamund. You deserved a better team."

"I believe you would have won anyway, Lady Hunter," Mr. Michael Weaver said, "if the other team had not had Lord Wetherby."

"No matter," Rosamund said. "It was just a game. And I am afraid I threw myself into it with all the dignity of a fifteen-year-old."

Indeed, the memory of the past two hours made her cheeks grow warm. Had she made a complete cake of herself? She had always loved charades, but she could not recall ever playing it with such dizzy abandon as she had that evening. And the same sort of madness had seemed to grip Justin, playing on the opposite team.

The marquess had even commented at one point that if the two of them were just teamed up together they would be invincible.

As it was, Justin's team had won handily. She looked up and caught his eye across the room—he was with Annabelle. And she held his gaze just a little too long. She could almost hear him ask what his prize was to be. And she could hear herself in the billiard room at Mr. Price's telling him that with Leonard and her it had always been a kiss. She looked away sharply.

"Rosamund." The Reverend Strangelove was bowing over her hand and even raising it to his lips and commending her on her condescension in playing with the young people and ensuring their happiness for the evening.

"Thank you, Toby," she said. "But it was entirely my own enjoyment I was securing."

He took a seat beside her while Valerie and Mr. Weaver moved away. Josh, she could see, was sitting on the window ledge, one foot up on the seat beside him, looking about him with a half-smile. He had not joined in the game of charades, to everyone's surprise.

She had avoided him in most cowardly fashion since the afternoon, staying far from him and making sure that she did not even look at him for fear their eyes would meet. What if he had arrived a few minutes earlier when Justin's hand had been inside her jacket? What if she had not stopped Justin at that point?

But even apart from the embarrassment at what he had seen, there was the guilt over what he must have thought. Or more important even than that, there was the guilt of having seen herself through his eyes. And she had always liked Josh. They had always been good friends. That was why she had not been able to contemplate a real flirtation with him.

"Excuse me, Toby," she said, waiting for him to pause to draw breath, "there is something I must talk to Josh about." She got resolutely to her feet.

Lord Beresford watched her as she crossed the room, that strange half-smile on his lips. He removed his foot from the seat so that she could sit beside him.

"One thing I always liked about you, Rosamund," he said, "was that you always scorned to avoid a potentially troublesome situation. I can remember that stubborn set to your jaw and that martial gleam in your eye—just the way you are looking now. You are not going to avoid me for the next week and a half, then?"

"No," she said. "If you have scorn to heap on my head, Josh, heap away."

"As Justin told me," he said, "what was happening out there between the two of you was none of my business."

"That is not good enough," she said. "Do you despise me?"

"Does it matter to you if I do?" he asked.

She looked at him and smiled ruefully. "Yes, I'm afraid it does," she said.

"I was shocked," he said. "I would not have guessed you to be the type to try to steal someone else's man, especially your own niece's."

"I was not doing that," she said. "Just giving in to a moment's weakness. It will not be repeated."

"A moment's weakness," he said. "I don't suppose you would care to satisfy my curiosity and tell me where you met him before this week?"

"A month ago," she said. "We were snowbound together for three days. I did not know who he was, Josh."

His mouth formed into a whistle. "Alone?" he said.

"Yes, I'm afraid so."

"Enough questions on that topic," he said. "The answer to the others that leap to mind are pretty glaringly obvious. You care for him, Rosamund?"

"He is to be Annabelle's husband," she said. "There will be no repetition of this afternoon. I would hate you to despise either Justin or me permanently."

"You care for him," he said, answering his own question.

"Thank you for not saying anything," she said. "You have not done so, have you?"

He laughed softly. "Did you really think I would bear tales?" he asked.

She shook her head. "But thank you, anyway."

"You should have decided to flirt with me this week," he said. "It would have been a way to divert your mind."

"That would have been using you for my own ends," she said. "I like you too well for that, Josh."

"But I would have been using you too," he said. "To avoid boredom and to ward off a little of something else, too, perhaps."

She looked at him inquiringly, but he merely smiled at her and flicked her jaw with one knuckle.

"Are we friends again?" she asked. "Or do I have to spend the next few days making very sure that we are at opposite ends of the room and that our eyes do not meet."

"Friends," he said. "And perhaps I'll prove a better friend to you than you think, Rosamund."

He did not explain his words. He got to his feet and strolled across to talk with Lord Wetherby and Annabelle. After a few minutes he and Annabelle left the room.

The earl looked across at her, hesitated, and came to occupy the seat Lord Beresford had just vacated.

"You made your peace with him?" he asked.

"Yes, I think so," she said.

"He has dragged Annabelle off to show him the portrait of his grandfather in the picture gallery," he said. "Late evening is not quite the time for viewing portraits, and Annabelle was clearly reluctant to go with him there, but he would not take no for an answer. I hope he is not going to upset her by saying anything about this afternoon."

"I don't think so," she said. "I don't think Josh would want to hurt her."

"Rosamund," he said, "I can't tell you how sorry I am about this afternoon."

"About going there or about getting caught?" she said, half-smiling. "I have been trying to sort out my feelings and have come to the sad conclusion that I would not be feeling nearly as guilty if Josh had not seen us together. But it was wrong, Justin. What we had in Northamptonshire was a purely physical thing and should be put behind us. We cannot renew that relationship and there can be no other except the aunt-nephew one. Stolen moments, stolen kisses are sordid."

"It did not seem sordid before Josh came," he said.

"No," she agreed. "Sometimes it is a shock to see ourselves through someone else's eyes, is it not?"

"Anyway," he said, "I wanted to say I was sorry." He smiled. "And sorry for beating you so badly at charades just now despite all your energetic efforts."

"You are not sorry at all," she said. "Doubtless you would be sulking if you had lost."

"Unfair," he said. "Did I sulk when you beat me at billiards? Or when you built a larger snowman than I—though that is arguable?"

"You sulked when you could not make as graceful an angel as I," she said.

"I punished you for making fun of me," he said. "That is not sulking. I greatly enjoyed administering the punishment, I must confess, but that is not sulking, either."

"I enjoyed being punished, too," she said, her eyes sparkling back into his. "But I ought not to confess as much, ought I? There is some perversion in enjoying punishment."

He laughed.

"Rosamund." The marquess was standing before them, one hand held out to her. "I know you have just finished a strenuous game of charades, my dear, but I really cannot have such a talented pianist sitting idle. Come and play for me."

She put a hand in his and smiled at him. "It would be my pleasure," she said.

"You will excuse us, Wetherby?" the marquess asked.

"I shall enjoy listening to the music," the earl said. "Lady Hunter has a great deal of talent."

"It would have been far better to come up here tomorrow morning when there would be daylight coming through the windows," Annabelle was saying to Lord Beresford as they stood in the gallery, holding up a branch of candles to the portrait of his grandfather, the Marquess of Gilford's brother.

"Not at all," he said. "Candlelight brings out the richness of a canvas."

"And you knew where the painting was," she said. "You did not need me to show it to you, Joshua."

"Ah," he said, "but if your brain is working, Annabelle, as I believe it is, you will know full well that visiting the gallery and gazing at the portrait were only excuses for getting you to myself for a while."

She stiffened. "I want to go back downstairs," she said.

"I have been doing you an injustice," he said. "For several years, perhaps. I have been thinking of you as a child when you have been a woman for some time. You made me aware of it yesterday with a stinging slap across the face that I can still feel."

"I know you meant nothing," she said. "Let's go back downstairs."

He set down the candles on a table and looked about him. "Let's sit in one of the windows and talk awhile, shall we?" he suggested.

Annabelle clasped her upper arms in a defensive gesture. "Talk about what?" she asked.

"About Annabelle," he said. "About Annabelle the woman. I only ever knew Annabelle the child, and I was always extremely fond of her."

"You were always horrid to me," she said.

"Yes, wasn't I?" He grinned. "But, you see, I have only ever been horrid to people I liked—if you exclude Bonaparte's troops, that is. I have always ignored those I don't. Come and sit down." He gestured toward one of the windows and the padded seat that formed its sill.

Annabelle looked at the seat for a few moments before moving toward it. "Mama will be wondering where I am," she said.

"Then Justin will be able to tell her you are with me," he said. "Safe with your second cousin."

She sat down, her back straight, her feet together, her hands clasped in her lap.

"Have you forgiven me?" he asked.

"Yes," she said.

"Well, that was easy, at least," he said. "What has it been like knowing for half your life who your future husband was to be?"

"I trust Grandmama's judgment," she said, "and Mama's and Papa's."

"Do you like Justin?" he asked.

"Yes," she said.

"Do you love him?"

"Love is something that grows," she said. "I shall do my best to show Lord Wetherby affection when we are married, and I believe he will do the same toward me."

"Yes," he said, "you are probably right. You are going to accept him, then, Annabelle? You have no doubts?"

"Of course not," she said.

"There has never been anyone else?"

She darted him a look before returning her gaze to her hands. "I am only eighteen," she said.

"But as someone recently reminded me," he said, "girls grow up far faster than boys. Has there ever been anyone?"

"I have always known what Mama and Papa want," she said. "I have never wavered in my duty."

He reached out and captured one of her hands in his. "That's not what I asked you," he said. "Have you ever felt a fondness for another man?"

"No," she said so quietly that he had to lean forward to catch her answer. She tried in vain to release her hand.

"Not said with conviction at all," he said. "I don't believe you."

"No," she said, rounding on him. "No, no, no! Now do you believe me? Let go of me, Joshua." She struggled against his hand again, but he merely raised hers and held it to his lips.

"There's no shame in it," he said. "You are not betrothed yet, Annabelle, and I have heard on good authority that your father has told you you are free to refuse Justin if you so choose. You don't have to accept his offer. You can go home free if you wish."

"How preposterous," she said. "Why are you saying these things?"

"Because I don't want you to make a mistake," he said. "And because I can see that you are unhappy."

"Because I won't smile for you?" she said. "What nonsense!"

"No," he said. "It's not just the lack of smiles. You are unhappy. Why don't you just simply say no to Justin?"

"I thought he was your friend," she said.

"Precisely." He smiled at her. "I would not want to see either of you unhappy."

"Why should you care about my happiness?" she asked. "You never have."

"I care," he said.

She looked at him warily.

"No one will bite your head off if you say no," he said. "Think, Annabelle. You could be free for almost the first time in your life."

She got abruptly to her feet, pulled her hand from his, and took two paces away from him.

"Why are you doing this?" she asked him. "Our betrothal is to be announced on Grandpapa's birthday. Everyone knows. And the announcement is just a formality. The betrothal is already as real as can be."

"No, it is not," he said. "One of the key players has not yet given her consent."

"I want to go back downstairs," she said.

He got to his feet and went to stand in front of her. He set a hand on each of her shoulders and lifted her chin with his thumbs.

"Don't be unhappy, Annabelle, when there is no need to be," he said. "You are eighteen years old. Suitors would come flocking to you if they knew you were free. You could choose someone you did not have to will yourself to care for." He drew her toward him suddenly and set his forehead against hers. "Don't cry. It's not by any means too late."

"Oh, it is, it is," she wailed, putting her hands up over her face.

"No," He drew her head against his shoulder and rocked her gently in his arms. "No, it isn't, Annabelle. It will just take a little courage and you can be free. Do you want me to talk to your father? Or your grandfather? Or Justin, perhaps?"

"No!" She recoiled in some horror and stared at him with two large tear-filled eyes.

"Not if you don't want," he said. "But do take advantage of the freedom your parents have given you because they love you, Annabelle. Say no. You cannot be expected to love a man just because your parents and grandparents like him. I'll wager you would have fought hard enough against them if they had chosen me, wouldn't you? And they might well have done so, considering the fact that I am your grandfather's heir."

She turned sharply away from him. "They would never have done so," she said. "They would have chosen Christobel, if anyone."

"Well," he said, "I would not have accepted Christobel. I would have insisted on you."

"You never liked me," she said. "You were always horrid to me."

"We seem to have talked ourselves full circle," he said, setting a hand on her shoulder from behind. "It was all just teasing because I was fond of you or occasionally, I suppose, because I was a horrid boy. And you haven't always hated me, have you? You said yourself that you were worried about me when I was wounded at Waterloo."

"We thought you were dead," she said. "We thought the fever would have taken you even if not the wound. I thought you were dead."

"There would have been one less person to torment you if I had been," he said.

She whirled around to face him, her face contorted by some deep emotion he could not interpret.

"Don't," she cried. "Don't make a mockery of all I—of all we went through at that time. We thought you were dead, don't you understand? *I* thought you were dead." She turned and hurried toward the doorway.

Lord Beresford picked up the branch of candles and went after her. He caught up to her at the top of the staircase and took her by the arm. "I sometimes find it hard to believe that anyone can really care for me," he said. "I tend to make a mock of claims like yours rather than take the risk of believing them."

They had reached the floor on which the bedchambers were situated.

"I spoke the truth, Joshua," she said before pulling her arm free of his grasp and whisking herself along to her room. "If you had died, I think I would have died too. So there!"

Lord Beresford was left alone at the head of the stairs leading down to the drawing room, his free hand stretched out to where she had stood. There was a still look on his face.

Rosamund was already in bed, the candles extinguished, when she heard the door of her bedchamber open. She sat up abruptly, her first mad thought that it must be Justin.

"Who is it?" she said, and found that she was whispering.

"Aunt Rosa?" a hesitant voice said. "Are you awake?"

Rosamund pushed back the bedclothes and got out of bed. "Come in, Annabelle," she said. "I'll light a candle. Is something wrong?"

The girl was in her nightgown and was barefoot. She was hugging herself and shivering.

"You had better climb into the bed," Rosamund said as the candle brought sudden light to the room, "and pull the blankets about you. This is not summer to be walking about like that." She pulled on a warm dressing gown and slipped her feet into a pair of slippers. Then she perched on the bed, where Annabelle was obediently sitting, the blankets pulled up about her. "Couldn't you sleep?"

The girl shook her head.

"You went to bed early too, didn't you?" Rosamund said. "A headache?"

"Aunt Rosa," Annabelle said, "when you married Uncle Leonard, Papa was opposed to the match, wasn't he?"

"He thought me too young to marry," Rosamund said, "and your uncle too old for me. I hope I convinced him over the years that I had done the right thing."

''How did you do it?'' Annabelle asked. ''How did you defy him?''

Rosamund laughed. ''It comes far more naturally for me to defy your father than to agree with him,'' she said. ''Indeed, it only now strikes me that we have not had a really good quarrel since our return from Lincolnshire.''

''But what did you say?'' the girl asked. ''What did you do?''

Rosamund looked closely at her. ''Is it about you we are talking?'' she asked. ''Has something happened, Annabelle? Something you cannot talk with your mother or father about? Did you come to confide in me? You may do so, you know. I will not run telling tales to either of them.''

''They want dreadfully for me to marry the Earl of Wetherby,'' Annabelle said.

''They consider it a good match,'' Rosamund said. ''It is.''

''They would be furious with me if I refused him,'' the girl said, clasping her knees beneath the blankets. ''Papa would be furious.''

''But both he and your mama have told you that the final choice is yours, have they not?'' Rosamund said.

''It is too late, though,'' Annabelle said. ''If I had said no last year when Lord Wetherby first asked, or some time over the winter or even last week or the week before, it would have been all right. Papa would have accepted it, perhaps, even if he had not liked it. But now? Everyone seems to know, Aunt Rosa. Everyone is taking for granted that there will be a betrothal and that it will be announced on Grandpapa's birthday. It is too late to change things now.''

''Has his lordship asked you yet?'' Rosamund asked.

''No.'' Annabelle rested her chin on her updrawn knees. ''But we have both referred to it. It is just a formality. We both know that he will ask and that I will accept.''

''Don't you want to?'' Rosamund asked quietly.

Annabelle lowered her face until her forehead rested on her knees. ''Yes, I do,'' she said. ''I had settled my mind to it. Mama and Papa and Grandmama and Grandpapa want it, and Lady Wetherby wants it. And he is a kind and an amiable gentleman, even though he is eleven years older than I. Yes, I want to accept. I have been feeling at peace with myself.''

"Have been feeling?" Rosamund said. "But are not now?"

Annabelle did not say anything for a long time. "Joshua says I am making a mistake," she said.

"Josh?" Rosamund frowned and felt her stomach turn over. What had Josh been saying to the girl?

"He says I do not have to say yes," Annabelle said. "He says all it would take is a little courage and I could be free for almost the first time in my life. I was only nine years old, you see, when I knew that the Earl of Wetherby would eventually be my husband."

"But do you feel unfree?" Rosamund asked. "Having a marriage arranged for you, falling in with the wishes of your parents and grandparents does not necessarily mean that you are oppressed. Sometimes parents do know best, Annabelle. Looking back now I can see that your father had good reason for opposing my marriage. I was seventeen and marrying a man of forty-nine. The chances were very strong that I would have been unhappy. It was a miracle, in fact, that I was not, especially as I scarcely knew your uncle when I married him."

Annabelle was looking at her. "Yes, that is true, isn't it?" she said. "I should not let Joshua discompose me at the very last moment like this."

Rosamund hesitated. Her niece was so young and impressionable. It was important to give her the wisest advice she was capable of giving. But before she could form her thoughts into words, the girl spoke again.

"Aunt Rosa," she said, "were you ever in love with someone, obsessed with someone, unable to let go of your feelings no matter how hard you tried?"

Rosamund swallowed. "Is that how things are with you?" she asked.

"Yes." Annabelle was looking at her with large, wary eyes.

"And does he love you?" Rosamund asked.

"Oh, no, of course not," the girl said. "I have been promised to Lord Wetherby since I was a child. No one would even think of falling in love with me. I will recover from it, won't I? When I am married and have a new home to run and children?"

Rosamund closed her eyes. Oh, poor Justin.

"I don't know," she said. "I don't know, Annabelle. But Josh is right, you know. However high everyone's expectations are, it is still possible for you to say no. Once you have said yes, you will be committed for all time. Do think carefully. Don't feel bound by a promise you have not yet made. But on the other hand, don't allow other people to undermine your confidence at a time when you must be feeling uncertain anyway."

Annabelle's forehead was on her knees again. "I don't know what to do," she said. "I must think first and foremost of his lordship. Will I be able to make him happy, Aunt Rosa? He is so much older and more experienced than I."

"Your Uncle Leonard was thirty-two years older than I," Rosamund said. "And he used to say I was the delight of his life."

"I don't think I could be the delight of anyone's life," Annabelle said.

"Oh, Annabelle," Rosamund said, "yes, you could. You are sweet and gentle and sensible. You think of other people, not just of yourself. I believe you are capable of deep love. And you are capable of making this decision for yourself."

There were tears in Annabelle's eyes when she looked up. "But there isn't any decision to make," she said. "Except that I cannot make Lord Wetherby happy unless I can forget . . . Aunt Rosa, why is there not always a right and a wrong answer to every question? Why can't we always know what is right?"

"It's called growing up, I'm afraid," Rosamund said.

"Being able to make one's own decisions. It is so much easier just to accept the decisions of our elders when we are children, and grumble about what tyrants they are, isn't it?"

Annabelle was frowning in thought. "If I say yes," she said, "that is just what I will be doing, isn't it? Accepting what Mama and Papa have always told me is right for me? But if I say no, it may just be a pointless act of rebellion against them. Oh, dear."

"Well," Rosamund said cheerfully, "if you didn't have a headache when you came in here, Annabelle, you must certainly have one now. I'm sorry Aunt Rosa could not simply take you in her arms and solve all your problems for you."

"But you have helped," Annabelle said. "You have helped me see that I am not a puppet on a string, though sometimes it is easier to be just that."

She threw the bedclothes aside and climbed out of the bed. She kissed Rosamund on the cheek, wished her a good night, and was gone.

And Rosamund was left sitting on the bed and staring at the candle and half-wishing that she had been unscrupulous enough to give the advice she had ached to give.

But she would not allow her mind even to begin to hope. For when all was said and done, she was only the almost impoverished widow of an almost obscure baronet and he a wealthy earl with more than one large and prosperous estate. And however briefly, she had been his mistress. Gentlemen did not marry their mistresses.

Her only hope—if she would allow herself to begin to hope—could be that he would invite her to a longer-term affair, one that would last until one of them grew tired of the other. That would be until he grew tired of her—perhaps six months, perhaps a year. Perhaps even longer. But not forever.

But for however long or short a time it might be—if a lot of ifs became certainties and if she would allow herself a glimmering of hope—it would not do. She might indulge in a very brief affair with a man if circumstances made him almost impossible to resist, but she would never deliberately become a man's mistress.

So . . .

Rosamund removed her dressing gown, kicked off her slippers, and blew out the candle. She climbed beneath the blankets and drew them up about her ears.

What a long day it had been. It had been a million years long. She cuddled her head against Justin's shoulder again, as she had done that afternoon, and felt the warmth of him and smelled his cologne. And when his hand moved over the silk of her blouse and his thumb found her nipple, she reached up and unbuttoned the blouse herself.

She wanted to feel his hand on her naked breast.

14

The Earl of Wetherby spent the following morning with the marquess, Viscount March, and some of the other gentlemen riding about the estate farms, in particular viewing the progress of the lambing season.

Lady March had mentioned at the breakfast table that Annabelle was still in bed with a headache. The earl hoped she would recover and be up by luncheon time. He had determined during a night of much thought and soul-searching to find some time alone with her that day and to spend that time talking to her about herself, about them. He intended to find out if there were any truth in the suspicions he had felt during their ride home from Winwood Abbey. He wanted to try to establish some closeness between them.

His plan succeeded more easily than he had expected. Annabelle was indeed up when the gentlemen returned to the house. She seated herself beside him quite voluntarily at luncheon and immediately launched into praises of the weather and expressed her longing to be outside and walking.

"It's chilly," he said to her with a smile, "but perfect for a walk. Shall we take a look at the lake?"

"Yes," she said, "that would be very pleasant."

He waited for her to announce their intentions and invite everyone else to join them, but she stayed quiet when Christobel and Eva declared that they would drive into the village for the afternoon if there were just someone willing to chaperon them. Rosamund set them to squealing by offering to accompany them. And the Reverend Strangelove sobered them again when he decided to do himself the honor of escorting three such lovely and vivacious young ladies.

Some of the younger people had spoken so enthusiastically about Winwood Abbey that the marquess and marchioness were to take Lady Wetherby, Lord and Lady Sitwell, and some of the older members of their family driving there.

At last, it seemed to Lord Wetherby, he would have Annabelle to himself for a couple of hours. And she seemed to be in an unusually cheerful mood.

"I hope your headache has quite disappeared," he said to her as they began their walk over rolling lawns and beneath widespread trees toward the lake.

"Oh, yes, thank you," she said. "I think it was just tiredness. These days have been unusually busy and exciting ones."

"Have they?" he asked, smiling. "You are used to a quiet life, then?"

"I like being at home in the country," she said, "with my horses and my dogs and my books and paints. I like being with people who are familiar to me. You live in town most of the time, my lord? Justin?"

"Yes," he said, "but it is the habit of a young man looking for some excitement to fill his life. I have always kept a close eye on the running of my estates. I believe that I would prefer to live mainly in the country when I am married and have a family."

Perhaps he was speaking too plainly, he thought. He expected to see the color rush to her cheeks and the stone wall to go up behind her eyes.

"Do you hope for that to be soon?" she asked. "I look forward to the time when I will marry and have my own home to run and my own children." She was staring brightly ahead, he saw in a downward glance. Her cheeks had more color than usual. "Look at the crocuses," she said. "There are so many of them."

"You were nine years old, I believe," he said, "when my mother and your grandmother conceived their now-famous idea. Were you brought up in the belief that some definite arrangement had been made at that time?"

"Yes." She glanced up at him.

"And last year," he said, "when you were taken to London to be presented and to enjoy the Season, was it in the knowledge that you would eventually marry me?"

Her cheeks were very pink. "But was I not right to think so?" he said. "You did ask Papa for me before we went home."

"Oh, yes," he said, covering her hand reassuringly with one of his. "And I did so quite freely. But you were very young, Annabelle—only seventeen at the time, only eighteen now. Have you missed not being able to encourage other suitors?"

"The gentlemen in London were kind," she said. "But there was no one I would have wished to encourage."

"And no one at home?" he said. "No one you grew up with that you have regretted not being able to grow more fond of?"

"No," she said.

"And no one here?" he asked. "None of the cousins or second cousins with whom you have grown up?"

"No, of course not."

Lord Wetherby found himself looking down at the crown and brim of her bonnet and being forced forward at a faster pace.

"Oh, look, we are at the lake," she said. "I am glad we are not to go boating today. It is too cold."

"Yes," he said, "it would be chilly on the water."

"Why do you ask?" she said, stopping on the bank a short distance from where he had sat with Rosamund the day before. "Am I too young for you? Were you forced into making Papa an offer for me? Is there another lady you would prefer to marry?"

"No." He set his hands on her shoulders and looked down into her eager, upturned face. "I offered freely because it is time I took a wife, Annabelle, and because when I met you last spring I found that I was content to make my mother's choice my own. But I am nine-and-twenty, you see.

I have had time to know something of life and to know what I want. I would not like to think that you are being rushed into something before you have had a similar chance."

"I'm not being rushed," she said, leaning a little toward him. "I want to marry you, Justin. I like you and admire you and I think I may even love you. I'm not being forced."

The stone wall was no longer behind her eyes. There was a fever there instead, a hot urgency.

"Well, then," he said, lifting one hand in order to cup her cheek with it. He wanted to sit down and draw her onto his lap and cradle her head on his shoulder. He wanted to comfort her and coax her to confide in him, just like a child in trouble. But she was not a child. She was the woman he was to marry.

She raised her own hand and covered his, holding it against her cheek. She looked at him with bright, expectant eyes.

"I believe I am supposed to wait another three days until your grandfather's birthday," he said, smiling at her.

"I don't want to wait," she said.

"Don't you?" He ran his thumb lightly over her lips. "Will you marry me, Annabelle?"

"Yes," she said, and she smiled radiantly at him, transforming herself into a remarkably pretty young girl. "Yes, I will, Justin."

He kissed her lightly on the lips and she threw her arms about his neck, as she had done two days before, and kissed him back with hot ardor.

"Now we have a definite problem," he said, holding her firmly by the waist a little way away from him and grinning at her. "How are we to keep secret for three days the fact that we have broken the rules?"

"I don't want to keep it a secret," she said, her eyes shining up into his, the fever raging behind them. "I want to go back and tell Mama and Papa and Grandmama. I want to have it announced today. Can we, Justin?"

"If it is what you wish," he said gently. "I don't think they will be unduly angry with us. But are you sure, Annabelle? Would you like to have those three days in which to discover if you are comfortable with your decision?''

"I will never regret it," she said. "And I will make sure that you never regret it, either, Justin. I will spend my life making you happy. It will be the sole purpose of my life to see to your contentment.''

"Well," he said, "what more could I ask of life?"

"When will we marry?" she asked.

He laughed. "I think we had better consult both our families on that," he said. "Weddings have very little to do with the bride and groom, I have heard, and everything to do with their families.''

"But it will be soon?" she asked, her hands smoothing the lapels of his coat. "This spring or this summer?"

"I don't think either side of our family will object to that," he said.

"And we will live in the country?" she said. "On your estate? I don't mind living in London if that is what you wish. Tell me about your homes.''

He drew her arm through his and began the return walk to the house. And he talked almost the whole distance, answering her eager questions about the life that was to be hers.

It was done, then, he was thinking. There were not after all to be three more days of certainty with that one tantalizing grain of uncertainty. It was done.

And he was glad. They would make their announcement as soon as the travelers returned from Winwood Abbey, and either Gilmore or March would doubtless make their betrothal known to the whole family. It would be irrevocable then. Even more irrevocable than it had been when his carriage had turned through the gates of Brookfield four days before.

It would be a relief.

It had been a trying afternoon. Rosamund would not have minded spending it with a pair of silly, giggly girls, whose heads seemed to be filled with nothing but bonnets and beaux. They made her feel positively aged, but they made her also more than ever thankful that she had been mad enough to marry at the age of seventeen a man who was almost old enough to be her grandfather. She was glad that she had learned the value of quietness and solitude and good sense.

She had been a foolish young girl, though never quite in Christobel's and Eva's way. And she still could be remarkably foolish—getting out of Dennis' carriage in a temper with a snowstorm approaching, giggling over a snowball fight with Justin, balancing on an abbey wall with Josh. But she was glad there had been Leonard and the knowledge that life could be calm and contented and rich with meaning that came from books and music and conversation.

She was fortified, she felt, against the intense pain that the next few days would bring. She had lain awake through much of the night and had forced herself to relinquish that faint glimmering of hope that Annabelle's words had brought her. And she was glad when at the luncheon table she heard the earl and her niece plan to walk to the lake together and saw Annabelle look so determinedly happy. She was glad that she had given up hope and prepared herself to face her future.

But it was a trying afternoon. There was her sick awareness that Justin was with Annabelle and that Annabelle was in a strange mood. And her awareness that they were walking to the lake, where she had been with him just the day before. And there was Toby maneuvering her into the churchyard, of all places, while the girls tried on bonnets at the milliner's, in order to ask her to marry him.

"I am greatly honored," she told him, "and I am fond of you, Toby, but I am not the right wife for you. I would be a great trial to you."

It took her all of ten minutes to persuade him that she was being neither coy or self-denying nor overly modest.

And then she looked at him, silent and hurt as he examined some of the older, mossy headstones, and wished that he could have been just a little different, just a little less pompous, just a little more sensitive to the feelings of others.

How good it would have been to be able to feel a fondness for him strong enough to take her into a marriage. She would not demand love, only a little fondness. She knew from experience that that could be enough. She had been only fond of Leonard when she married him. Yet she had grown to love him more dearly than she had loved even her father.

If only she could feel for Toby what she had felt for Leonard in Bath. They could have made an announcement that evening at dinner and she would have been safe. She would have had a definite life to plan and dream of while the main drama of the next few days unfolded around her.

But it was not to be. She could not marry Toby under any circumstances at all. And yet he was a person with feelings despite all the pomposity. She had hurt him.

The drive home was not a comfortable one. The girls talked and giggled and seemed to notice nothing strained about the atmosphere. But the Reverend Strangelove beside Rosamund sat very straight and very silent and very dignified.

She did not enter the house. She took herself off to walk alone, carefully avoiding the lake side of the house. Doubtless Justin and Annabelle had returned long before, but she did not wish to risk coming upon them. She walked for what seemed like hours, returning to the house only in time to hurry to get ready for dinner.

And she sat through dinner, between Lord Beresford on the one side and Sir Patrick Newton on the other, allowing them to carry most of the conversation, and she came to the conclusion that the situation was finally and totally intolerable. If she had to wait another four days until the ball was over before removing herself to Leonard's cousin's, she might well go into a nervous collapse. All her sensible thoughts of the night before really could not carry her through four more days.

Annabelle was sitting at her grandfather's right, Justin beside her. His mother and his sister and brother-in-law were at the marquess's left. The conversation seemed to be animated at that end of the table.

Rosamund waited impatiently for Lady Gilmore to rise and signal the ladies that they might leave the gentlemen. She was going to retire to her room, she decided, and if anyone came looking for her, well, then, she would have the headache that Annabelle had had that morning.

But it was the marquess who rose to his feet and signaled for silence. He smiled genially the length of the table at his wife.

"My birthday has been planned as the perfect day," he said. "Yet it seems that one of my relatives and one of my other guests have seen fit to spoil those plans."

He did not look by any means unhappy about it, Rosamund thought.

"My granddaughter Annabelle," he said, "and the Earl of Wetherby have shown a lamentable lack of patience today and have betrothed themselves three days early."

There was a buzz and a smattering of applause around the table.

The marquess held up one hand. "But being the old tyrant that seventy-year-old marquesses have every right to be," he said, "I hereby forbid anyone in this room to divulge the news to anyone outside this room. The public announcement will be made to our friends and neighbors at my birthday ball as planned. In the meantime, I think it is as well that we all adjourn to the drawing room together so that the ladies may kiss my soon-to-be grandson and the gentlemen my granddaughter." He beamed down at them and bent down to be the first to kiss Annabelle.

There were noise and laughter, the sound of chairs being pushed back. Only one sound penetrated Rosamund's consciousness before she forced a smile to her face and allowed Sir Patrick to pull back her chair.

"The devil," Lord Beresford muttered from beside her.

Well, Rosamund thought as Lady March turned to hug her

just inside the dining-room doors, tears in her eyes, there could be no headache and no convenient escape to her room now. She squared her shoulders and prepared to face the evening.

And if she had had any lingering hope of an early escape, it was dashed when she found her brother waiting for her outside the dining room.

"Well, Rosa," he said, "Anna is a naughty girl, isn't she, rushing things like this?"

But he looked pleased and proud enough to burst, she thought, reaching up impulsively and kissing him on the cheek.

"Gilmore had to be allowed to make the announcement," he said, "but I hoped perhaps to have one to make too." He smiled genially at her. "But that was being too greedy for one day, I suppose. Tobias is proving to be a slowtop, after all. I thought that was why he decided to accompany you into the village."

"It was," she said, looking suspiciously at him. "Did you set him up to it, Dennis? Oh, you are quite insufferable. What makes you think I could possibly endure Toby for a lifetime? I suppose he came asking you just as if you were Papa?"

"He asked me this morning, yes," he said, "as is only proper, Rosa. You refused him?"

"Of course I refused him," she said, "and hurt him into the bargain. You ought not to have encouraged him, Dennis. I am none of your concern. I am twenty-six years old and no longer your ward. You will kindly inform any other gentleman who comes to you of those facts. And once all this is over, I am going to return to Lincolnshire. Felix will let me live in the house and I can be free of meddling brothers."

She turned sharply away from him, but he caught at her arm. "What a spitfire you are, Rosa," he said. "I was about to say, if you had just waited, that I was glad. I mean, I would have been happy if you had accepted, and it would certainly have been a good match. And who was I to say no when

Tobias came and asked me? I told him he would have to put the question to you. But I'm not sorry you said no.''

"You aren't?" she said doubtfully.

"Quite honestly," he said, "if you promise not to repeat my words to anyone, I would have to say he is a pompous ass.''

She looked at him incredulously and then they both laughed guiltily.

"It's time you and I became brother and sister again, I think, Rosa, isn't it?" he said, opening his arms to her. "Come into the drawing room and share our joy over Anna.''

"Oh, gladly, Dennis," she said, going into his arms and hugging him wordlessly for several moments.

And so she entered the drawing room with her brother's arm about her shoulders and was led straight to Annabelle and the Earl of Wetherby.

Annabelle hugged first her father and then Rosamund, who kissed her cheek and hugged her in return.

"I did make my own decision, you see," the girl whispered to her, "and I am so very happy, Aunt Rosa." She smiled up at the earl, forcing Rosamund to do likewise.

"My congratulations, my lord," she said, extending her right hand to him.

But every other lady had kissed him. As he took her hand, she reached up to kiss him on the cheek at the same moment as he leaned down to kiss hers. But it was their lips that met in a brief aunt-nephew embrace that set every nerve ending in her body jangling.

"Thank you, Lady Hunter," he said, and released her hand.

"Soon enough you will be able to call her Aunt Rosa," Lord March said jovially, squeezing Rosamund's shoulder and laughing heartily at his own joke.

"I think not, Papa," Annabelle said. "Aunt Rosa is younger than Justin.''

Music and cards had been planned for that evening, but it was too festive an occasion for them to be so dull, the marchioness announced. They would have the carpet rolled up and there would be dancing. Lady Carver would play the pianoforte.

And so, Rosamund found, she was forced to dance and be gay. And when there was a waltz and she protested to Robin Strangelove that she did not know the steps and it turned out that he was not very proficient either, Annabelle, dancing alongside them with Lord Wetherby, suggested with uncharacteristic high spirits that they change partners.

"I learned the steps in London last year, Robin," she said, "and even danced them at Almack's. And Justin will be able to teach you in no time, Aunt Rosa."

Rosamund kept her eyes on her feet until she finally caught the rhythm. There was much laughter about them as several of the young people tried the dance for the first time.

She wished she had not learned so fast. She wished she could have spent the whole of the half-hour concentrating on the learning of new skills. But there were the warm touch of his hand at her waist and the long fingers of his other hand curled about hers. And there were his cologne and the distinctive masculine smell of him. And the strong muscles of his shoulder against her hand and beneath her wrist.

And there were his blue eyes when she looked up, eyes that had once watched her as he made love to her.

There was nothing whatsoever to say. And in such a public and confined setting she could not gaze into his eyes. She lowered her own to his neckcloth. And longed for the music to stop. And willed it to last forever.

He was as silent as she until the music finally drew to a close. He held her for just a moment before releasing her. His eyes were smiling at her in the way they had done when they were standing on the steps outside Mr. Price's house the morning she left.

"Good-bye, Rosamund," he said so quietly that she felt rather than heard the words.

She did not answer.

* * *

Lord Beresford took Rosamund by the hand when a set of country dances was forming.

"There is lemonade next door," he said. "Take me there before I die of thirst. Or are you one of those determined dancers who cannot bear to miss even one measure of a dance?"

"The lemonade by all means, Josh," she said.

It seemed that once they were outside the drawing room in the hallway, she could suddenly breathe more easily. She smiled at him.

"You, too?" he said. "A kindred spirit as you always were, Rosamund? To the devil with the lemonade. Go and fetch a cloak."

She did not argue but did as she was bidden. She did not even argue when he laced his fingers with hers as they stood outside the main doors, and took her in the direction of the formal gardens. All she knew was that she could finally breathe again.

"You were bracing yourself for it in three days' time, weren't you?" he said. "It was a shock to have it happen tonight."

"Nonsense," she said. "It was arranged nine years ago. What difference do three days make now?"

"I thought perhaps I had her persuaded," he said. "Little fool."

"It was wrong of you, Josh," she said, "what you did last night, that is. She has been brought up to expect this. It can only confuse her to put doubts in her mind at this late date."

"Or to force her to face the doubts in her own mind," he said.

"Any normal young girl would have some doubts before making such a momentous decision in her life, Josh," she said. "I'm not sure it means that she has serious doubts in reality."

"You have schooled yourself well not to hope, haven't you?" he said. "The time was, Rosamund, when you would have fought tooth and nail—literally—to get what you wanted.''

"I have grown up," she said.

"Hm," he said. "I'm not sure I have."

They were standing close to the marble fountain. He set his back to it and raised one foot to rest against it.

"Anyway," he said, taking her by the hand again, "to the devil with Justin and Annabelle and betrothals. Come here, Rosamund."

And before she realized his intention, she was against him and his mouth was over hers.

Her first instinct was to fight her way free. Her second was to seek comfort and forgetfulness in his arms. She stayed where she was, not participating in the embrace, but not impeding it, either.

Josh was every bit as experienced as Justin, she realized before much time had passed. She withdrew from him with some reluctance.

"Forget him," he said. "You've slept with him, haven't you? And you have fallen in love with him. There are other men who can give just as much pleasure, Rosamund, and love brings more pain than joy. It's better to enjoy the pleasure and forget about the rest."

"With you?" she said.

"Yes, with me." He flicked her chin with one knuckle. "I'll make you forget, Rosamund—for tonight, anyway, Perhaps for longer. Maybe we should join forces and marry. We like each other well enough. Come to bed with me. I'll prove to you that I know a thing or two about pleasuring a woman."

"I don't doubt for a moment that you do," she said. "But just for my sake? Just to help me forget? Why so selfless, Josh?"

"Perhaps I have some demons of my own to banish," he said. "I want you—now. Don't be coy, Rosamund. Please?"

"Josh." She set her hands on his chest, imposing a little distance between them. "I can't. Not because I don't want it. At the moment I do, shameful as it is to admit. But it would be totally divorced from all love or tender feelings. We cannot make love to each other just to banish demons.''

"Can't we?" he said. "Why not?"

She sighed. "Because it is an act of love," she said, "not of hatred."

"I don't hate you," he said.

"No," she said, "but you might in the morning. And I would hate myself."

He laughed softly. "The trouble with women," he said, "is that they are always thinking. They never simply do what they want to do. They stop to think. A pox on all women." He flicked her chin again.

"Josh," she said, "I am very fond of you."

"I don't need your fondness," he said, grinning at her. "I need your body, woman."

She smiled at him. "What brought this on?" she asked. "The betrothal? Why did you try to stop it last night?"

He put a finger over her lips. "I brought you out here to seduce you," he said, "not to have my soul stretched out and pinned for your inspection."

"Is Annabelle your demon?" she asked quietly.

"A pretty little demon, isn't she?" he said. "She was even smiling at him tonight, Rosamund. Are you feeling as blue as I am—in every imaginable way? We had better go inside. I don't suppose there are any seducible chambermaids in such a respectable house, are there?"

"I very much doubt it," she said.

He sighed. "Another night of celibacy, then," he said. "And don't tell me that it is good for my soul, Rosamund, or I'll throttle you."

"All right," she said, "but I'm sure it is."

They looked at each other and laughed a little ruefully.

15

There were times over the next two days when Rosamund regretted that she had not gone with Lord Beresford the night the betrothal was announced. Everyone about her seemed happy—Annabelle was positively bubbling with high spirits—and called upon her to share their joy.

Her brother was as good as his word, and was treating her as an equal instead of as a much younger sister for whose life and happiness he was responsible. He went riding with her one morning and confided his satisfaction in having secured such a dazzling future for Annabelle.

"And she seems so happy with her betrothal, doesn't she, Rosa?" he said. "That is what is important, after all. When I married Lana, I suppose there were those who saw it only as a very good match for me, but I think I would have married her if she had been a pauper."

Rosamund smiled and gazed fondly at him. Since the age of ten, she had seen him only as the elder brother who tried to play father to her. Now she could see him as a man of feeling, a man with a great deal of love for his family, including her. She regretted the lost years.

"And we have only Anna," he said. "It has saddened Lana that there were never any more. Anna's happiness has been the focus of all our hopes."

"Well," Rosamund said, "you will probably have half a dozen grandchildren to fuss over, Dennis."

He smiled at her while a pain knifed through her heart at the thought that the father of those grandchildren would be Justin.

And Lana was happy. She took Rosamund into her sitting

room one morning and talked about the wedding and the bride clothes while they both stitched at their embroidery.

"You must come to London with us, Rosa," she said, "to help Anna and me with the shopping. You have such a good sense of style."

"And yet," Rosamund said, "I have been shut away in Lincolnshire for nine years."

"But I am not talking about fashion," her sister-in-law said. "A sense of style and color is innate, and you have it, Rosa. Will you come?"

Rosamund smiled and agreed. Yes, she would help Justin's bride to dress in style. They were talking about a wedding trip to Italy.

Annabelle herself was like a coiled spring. She was almost constantly flushed and animated. She talked more in those two days than she had since Rosamund had returned home with Dennis. And always it was about Justin and what he had told her about his life and his home and what plans he had for them and where he was to take her.

"But finally we are going to settle on his estate," Annabelle said. "In the country, Aunt Rosa. Aren't I fortunate? My children will be born there. Oh, I hope I have a son first. I am so very happy."

Rosamund was a little afraid that the girl would work herself into a fever. There was something almost desperate about her happiness. Clearly she had made her decision during that night of doubts and was living out that decision with all her determination.

There had been a reply from Leonard's cousin, and Rosamund was very welcome to go there whenever she liked and stay as long as she liked. Her trunk was open in her room and many of her possessions packed away already. But the days before she could decently leave passed at a snail's pace and she seemed trapped inside everyone's happiness.

She smiled and tried not to draw attention to herself by behaving in any way different from what might be expected of the aunt of the newly betrothed girl.

But there were times when she regretted her rejection of Lord Beresford. A discreet affair would have distracted her mind. And she had no doubt that Josh would have made it a pleasant, even exciting, sexual experience. There was no reason why it should not have been as thoroughly satisfactory as her affair with Justin had been. Perhaps by the time she had left, she would have been in love with Josh.

After all, she told herself, there had been no more love or commitment when she had agreed to make love with Justin. Some of the reasons she had given Josh for not going with him were somewhat hypocritical.

But there was a difference. She had wanted Justin. Perhaps the wanting had been a purely physical thing, at least at first, but even so it had been he she had wanted. She did not want Josh. She merely wanted comfort, forgetfulness, distraction.

No, she decided every time she looked at Josh and wondered if it would be possible to get him to renew his offer, she could not do it. She could not make love with a man merely because she could not have the man she loved.

Fortunately, perhaps, for her fragile strength of will, Lord Beresford did not renew his advances or even speak with her privately.

When the marquess's birthday finally arrived, Rosamund felt almost cheerful. This was the final day of her ordeal—of this portion of it, at least. The next day she would be able to leave. And there was plenty of activity to keep her busy throughout the day. She helped with the gathering and arrangement of the flowers for the ballroom in the morning and part of the afternoon, and busied herself for the rest of the afternoon washing her hair and getting herself ready for the ball.

By the time dinner approached, she was counting the hours. She would have Dennis' carriage come for her immediately after luncheon. She had fewer than twenty-four hours left at Brookfield.

It was possible—yes, it would be possible after all to live through those hours.

* * *

Annabelle had tried to help with the flower arrangements rather than join in the actitivies of her other young cousins. But whereas she had been quite competent about the gathering of the flowers from the hothouses, she had never had an eye for arrangements. After either her mother or one of her aunts had rearranged several of the vases she had been satisfied with, she decided to wander off into the formal gardens and get some fresh air before going to her room to prepare for the evening.

Lord Beresford found her there.

"Have you been banished from the ballroom?" he asked. "Getting under everyone's feet, were you?"

"Just like a naughty child?" she said. "No, of course not, Joshua. I need some fresh air."

"Yes," he said, "and something to cool off those cheeks. They have been on fire for almost three days. Come walking with me." He held out a hand for hers.

"I must go inside soon," she said.

"Why?" he asked. "Does it take you five hours to get ready for a dinner and ball?"

"Joshua," she said, and looked helpless suddenly.

He took her hand and held it in a warm clasp. "Come walking with me," he said. "We'll stroll to the lake."

"That's a whole mile," she said. "I must not be long."

But she moved along at his side and glanced nervously at him a few times. He was strangely silent, strangely serious.

"I want to know," he said when they were some distance from the house and wandering among the trees, "what you meant when you said you would have died if I had died."

"Did I say that?" she asked brightly. "We were all very upset, Joshua. Grandmama scarce stopped crying for days. It was the not knowing, you see, the thinking that perhaps you had been dead for days or even weeks and we did not know it."

"You were not talking about everyone," he said. "You said that you would have died."

"It is a way of speaking," she said. "I meant I would have been upset."

"Would you?" he asked. "Why?"

"You are my cousin," she said.

"Second cousin."

"Second cousin," she said.

"Annabelle," he said, "tell me what you meant."

"Nothing," she said. "I did not mean anything, Joshua."

"Didn't you?" He turned her to face him suddenly and backed her two steps against a tree. "Your betrothal is to be publicly announced tonight, isn't it? And the notices sent to the London papers tomorrow? This is very definitely your last chance."

"My last chance for what?" she asked him.

He looked down at her in exasperation and set a hand against the tree trunk beside her head. "I've always been fond of you," he said, "fonder than of any of my other cousins. I have often thought that my great-aunt might have chosen me for you rather than Justin. But I suppose it's only this week that these feelings have crystallized—now, when it's too late, or almost too late, anyway."

"I've got to go back, Joshua," she said.

"I don't want you to make a mistake," he said. "I want you to be happy."

"I am happy," she said. "I have said that I will marry Justin, and I am happy."

"Are you?"

"Yes."

"Why are you so uncomfortable and so unhappy here with me, then?" he asked.

"I don't like to be so alone with you," she said. "I don't like you so close."

"Why not?" he asked.

She stared at him mutely.

"Because you are afraid I will do this?" he asked, closing the distance between their mouths and kissing her with parted lips.

She still said nothing when he lifted his head, but stared at him with wide gray eyes brimming with tears.

"Is this why you have disliked me?" he asked her. "Because I have threatened your world?"

"I haven't disliked you," she whispered.

"What, then?" he asked.

"I want to go back," she said, her voice shaking.

"What, Annabelle?" he said, lowering his head, his eyes on her lips. "Tell me."

"I worshiped you as a child," she said, closing her eyes, "because you were always so handsome and so carefree and full of laughter. And I haven't been able to stop. I have tried and tried. I used to listen to stories of your wild ways and your women, and I would try to despise you, to become indifferent to you."

"But you couldn't?" He brushed at her tears that had spilled over onto her cheeks.

She shook her head. "And I really thought I would die when we heard that you were hurt and then heard nothing and nothing for so long. And then when I heard that you limped and would never be able to walk without a limp ever again, I thought my heart would break."

He kissed her softly on the lips.

"Now laugh at me," she said. "Tell me what a child I am."

"I am awed," he said, "to know that I have been loved for so long."

"Tell me." She looked up at him suddenly with tormented eyes. "Tell me that you are not going to marry Aunt Rosa. I have seen you with her, both of you laughing and happy. And I saw you leave with her the night my betrothal was announced. But please, Joshua. Anyone else. Anyone else I will be able to bear, but please not Aunt Rosa."

"I'm going to marry you," he said.

She stared at him through her tears and laughed shakily. "Oh, yes," she said. "We will get Grandpapa to substitute your name for Justin's tonight. It's all very simple."

"There will be no announcement tonight," he said. "It would be in bad taste to have my betrothal announced when many people are expecting Justin's. We will let it be known some time next week."

"Joshua . . ." She reached into a pocket of her dress for a handkerchief and rubbed at her eyes with it. "Take me back to the house now. You have heard me make a perfect idiot of myself. Now you can feel satisfied."

"I love you," he said.

"Oh, don't," she said crossly. "I have bared my soul to you. It is cruel to mock me."

He took the handkerchief from her hand and put it into one of his pockets. And he drew her away from the tree and into his arms. And set about kissing her very thoroughly and with the expertise of years.

"I love you," he said at last, looking down into her dazed face. "And in a moment I am going to ask you to marry me. But before I do, I want you to know that I will look after everything—all the explanations, all the awkwardness. And after I have asked you and you have said yes, I will tell you something that will ease your guilt. Understood?"

"No," she said. "No, we can't be doing this, Joshua. This is madness. My promise is given."

He kissed her again, even more thoroughly than before.

"Understood?" he asked.

"Joshua . . ."

"Will you marry me, Annabelle?"

"Please, Joshua . . ."

"Will you?"

"You're mad. You're quite mad."

"Will you?"

"I'm already betrothed."

"Will you?"

"Will you let me go if I say yes?"

"No."

"Joshua!"

"Will you?"

"Oh, yes, then," she said. "For this moment of madness, yes, Joshua. But you know we must return to sanity when we get back to the house."

He was grinning at her and she reached up to place a finger against his dimple.

"Not very manly, is it?" he said.

"It has always turned me weak at the knees," she said. And she looked into his laughing face and smiled slowly at him. "Joshua, you know we can't do this."

"Anyone who fought with the Duke of Wellington doesn't know the meaning of can't," he said. "You wait and see. And before guilt starts to hit at you, do you want to hear something interesting?"

She looked at him dubiously.

"I'll wager our betrothal won't be the only one to be announced next week," he said. "I think Justin's will be, too."

She frowned at him in puzzlement.

"To Rosamund," he said.

She stared at him mutely.

"You wait and see," he said. He took her by the hand and turned her back toward the house.

"But Joshua," she said, "that is preposterous."

"Yes, isn't it?" he said, lacing his fingers with hers. "As preposterous as my proposing to you the day your betrothal to someone else is to be officially announced—and being accepted."

They walked on in silence for a few minutes.

"Joshua," she said at last, "you are serious about all this, aren't you?"

"Yes," he said, smiling down at her.

"My stomach is doing somersaults," she said, "and I don't think my legs will bear me up much longer. Is it true? Really true? You are not just doing it because you think I will be unhappy with Justin?"

"All hell is about to break loose," he said. "I would face that for only one reason, my dear girl: I love you."

''Well, then,'' she said, drawing a deep breath and letting it out rather raggedly, ''I am not going to hide in my room, Joshua. I am going to face hell with you.''

''Are you?'' he said, grinning.

''Yes,'' she said.

''Your grandparents? Your parents? Justin? All of them?''

''Yes.''

He squeezed her hand. ''Well,'' he said, ''I'm sure it is better to face hell together, Annabelle, than heaven separately. Does that help build your courage and strengthen your knees?''

''No,'' she said.

He laughed. ''It was always the knees that gave most trouble before a battle,'' he said.

''Are you comparing this to a battle?'' she asked.

''Not really.'' He grinned down at her and paused to kiss her swiftly on the lips before they stepped onto the cobbled courtyard before the doors of the house. ''This is worse.''

The Earl of Wetherby dismissed his valet and checked his appearance once more before the full-length mirror in his dressing room. He was wearing what he had planned to wear for the occasion: ice-blue knee breeches, silver-embroidered waistcoat, a slightly darker blue coat, all satin, white stockings and linen, a copious amount of lace at neck and wrists.

It was a very formal outfit for the country, but not too formal for a man whose betrothal was about to be announced to the world. And for a free man? He would wear the clothes anyway, he had decided. They were what Henri had prepared for him.

Did Rosamund know yet? he wondered for surely the dozenth time in the past hour. He could still hardly believe it himself.

Josh had summoned him from the billiard room to the library, and he had found Annabelle there, her face white and set. She had resisted Josh's attempt to take her hand and she had silenced him with one hand when he had begun to speak.

"No, Joshua," she had said. "I must say this."

Lord Wetherby had stood inside the door, noting every gesture, every expression, every exchange of glances, so that by the time Annabelle had turned to him, her eyes directly on his, and said what she had to say, he had been hardly surprised.

"Am I just being rejected, Annabelle?" he had asked her. "Or is Josh being accepted?"

She had flushed painfully and bitten her lower lip, and Josh had taken over the explanations.

It had all been over in five minutes. He had assured Annabelle that he honored her honesty and her courage in speaking to him herself, and he had hugged her and kissed her cheek and shaken Josh by the hand and wished them well. He had assured Annabelle that he would speak with his mother and his sister and that indeed they would not hate her for the rest of her life. And that of course he would attend the evening ball. Why should he not? He had been invited, as everyone else had, to attend the marquess's birthday celebrations, had he not?

It had all been over in five minutes. And then a stroll in the formal gardens with his mother on one arm and Marion on the other—a difficult half-hour, but one that had ended well enough. He was not feeling humiliated, he had assured them, or upset. Only a little relieved, perhaps, to have his freedom restored. And that had set his mother back to her normal self, reminding him of his age and his responsibility to his position, and applying her mind to the task of deciding which ladies of her acquaintance might be suitable matches for him.

There had, of course, been two more interviews, one with the marquess and marchioness, one with Lord and Lady March. Both couples had clearly been feeling mortified and distressed at having to face him, but again all had ended well enough. He had come on the understanding that Annabelle was to be free to accept or reject him, he had reminded them. And though she had accepted him three days before, it had been understood at the time that the betrothal was of a tentative and informal nature. He certainly did not feel as if he had been jilted.

"I am so sorry," Lady March had said, taking his hand. "I would have liked you as a son-in-law, my lord."

"We were looking forward to having you as a member of our family," Lord March had added, taking his hand in a strong clasp.

And so it was over, all of it, except for some embarrassment during the evening, he supposed. It was all over. He could scarcely believe it despite the turmoil of the past few hours.

And he wondered if Rosamund knew yet.

And if it would make any difference to her. She had told him just a few days before that what they had shared had been a purely physical thing.

Had it been, for her?

But he dared not think along such lines. Not yet.

Rosamund took one last look at herself in the full-length mirror in her room. Her dark-green silk gown flattered her figure, she thought, and was suitably plain and decorous for a twenty-six-year-old widow. Leonard had liked her to wear bright colors and to look youthful. But she was no longer youthful. It would no longer be appropriate to try to outshine the young girls—Eva and Pamela and Christobel and Annabelle.

For the same reason, her hair was dressed smooth and high with none of the stray curls or ringlets that the maid had wanted to add for the occasion.

Rosamund's mind flashed back to an occasion not long before when she had worn a bright-orange silk gown with an indecorously low neckline and slippers one size too large. She sighed and turned from the mirror.

It was almost over. She had to endure for only a few hours

longer. Perhaps, if the announcement was made early, she would even be able to slip away to bed before the ball was over without appearing ill-mannered. After all, she had the excuse of a journey to make the next day.

She wandered idly to the table beside her bed and picked up her Bible. It opened to the place where the pressed daffodil lay. She ran one finger lightly over it. She had still not thrown it away. She wondered if she ever would.

There was a knock on her door and Lord March answered her summons.

"How lovely," she said, smiling determinedly and snapping the Bible shut before returning it to the table. "Am I to have an escort down to the drawing room, Dennis? You do look fine."

"You haven't heard?" he said, coming inside the room and closing the door behind his back.

"Heard?" She looked at him with raised eyebrows.

"Anna has called off the engagement without even consulting Lana or me first," he said. "We thought you should know before you go down."

"Called off the engagement?" Rosamund said. "Impossible, Dennis. She has seemed so determined in the last few days."

"I could wring Joshua's neck," he said. "He has convinced Anna that he loves her and has got her to say she will marry him, and so a marriage planned nine years ago must go out the window."

Rosamund motioned him to a chair.

"And they went and talked to Wetherby before coming to Lana and me, the pair of them," he said. "This is a major embarrassment, Rosa. I don't know quite how to show my face tonight."

"But if it is true," Rosamund said, "then perhaps it is as well that the truth has come out before it is too late."

"Before it is too late?" He grimaced. "The family was told three nights ago, and doubtless all sorts of rumors have leaked into the countryside via the servants. The earl and his mother and sister are here. I wish a hole would open up in the ground and swallow me up. That's what I wish."

"How did his lordship take it?" Rosamund asked.

"Very decently, actually," he said. "He acted as if he had not just been treated as shabbily as a man can be treated."

"Perhaps he really feels that way," she said.

"He's just being the perfect gentleman," Lord March said. "For which we must be eternally thankful, I suppose. I have never raised my hand to Anna, Rosa, but I could cheerfully take her over my knee at this moment and spank her until my hand is too sore."

"No, you couldn't," she said, stepping behind the chair, setting her hands on his shoulders, and bending to kiss the side of his head. "You gave Anna her freedom, Dennis, just as you gave me mine, though I did not realize it at the time. And she has used that freedom, as I did, to do what you consider unwise. Let's hope that it turns out as well for her as it did for me."

He passed a hand over his face. "My mother-in-law has been weeping," he said. "She has had her heart set on this match for nine years. Gilmore is already reminding her that Joshua is his heir and that they should be over the moon with happiness at the way things are turning out. I suppose there is that way of looking at it."

"Yes, of course," she said. "Annabelle will be the Marchioness of Gilmore one day."

"He is a shocking rake," Lord March said.

"I have heard that rakes make the best of husbands," Rosamund said, wrapping her arms about him from behind and resting her cheek against his. "I don't think Josh would take marriage lightly, Dennis. And I have reason to believe that he really loves Annabelle."

"I hope you are right," he said. "You are going to ruin my neckcloth, Rosa. It took my valet all of ten minutes to get it just so."

"Did it?" she said, pecking him on the cheek before straightening up. "Escort me downstairs, then. I shall give you courage."

He sighed. "Sometimes," he said, "just sometimes, I feel glad there was just Anna. Imagine if there were half a dozen more."

"But you would have been quite an expert at the end of it all," she said gaily, patting his arm.

She would give him courage, she had said. He probably had no idea of the fact that she would have been quite unable to leave her room if he had chosen to leave without her.

The betrothal was at an end. Justin was free.

Not that it would make any difference to her, of course. In fact, it would have been better if things had remained the way they were. At least then she could have dreamed about the way things might have been but for circumstances.

No, it made no difference to her at all.

Justin was free!

16

It was immediately obvious to the Earl of Wetherby that all the house guests knew. As soon as he set foot in the drawing room before dinner, everyone treated him with almost exaggerated heartiness.

He was drawn into a group that included the marchioness, Lady Carver, and Sir Patrick Newton. Annabelle, he could see, was with her mother and Lady Newton, and Josh with Lord Carver and the Reverend Strangelove.

He had to be careful. He felt as if he were on display all evening. He had to make a special effort to converse at table as if nothing momentous had just happened in his life, and when the ball began, he had to dance with as many ladies as possible and smile and converse.

He even danced once with Annabelle, who kept her eyes lowered through much of the set. But there was a strain of courage in the girl, as he had found that afternoon. She looked determinedly up at him before the dance came to an end.

"Have I caused you terrible embarrassment tonight?" she asked him. "Are you very angry with me?"

"No on both counts," he said smiling at her and feeling other eyes on them. "I would have been angry had I discovered much later that you had left Josh unhappy and made yourself miserable by doing what you thought proper. I sincerely wish you well, Annabelle. Josh is a friend of mine, you know."

"You are very kind," she said. "And I am so very sorry."

She did not dance with Josh. But, then, of course, Josh never did dance a great deal because of his leg. Not that he allowed his handicap to curtail many activities.

He had to be careful, the earl felt. So many people were watching, even the neighbors who had come from miles around. Clearly word had leaked out about the announcement that was to have been made. Whether those people were still waiting for the announcement or had already heard that it was not after all to be made, he did not know. But he had that very uncomfortable feeling of being on display.

He would not dance with Rosamund or even stand beside her between sets to talk with her. He would not even look at her deliberately. He would not open his feelings for her to the interested scrutiny of half a county.

And he was afraid to dance with her or talk with her. For as long as she had been forbidden to him he could dream of what might have been if only he had been free. He could dream that her feelings matched his own. Now he was free, and he was afraid to put those dreams to the test of reality.

And so suppertime came and he led Christobel in and seated them with Michael Weaver and Valerie Newton and with Lord Carver and a local beauty. And he participated quite as much as anyone else in the conversation that developed and was aware with some amusement of the blushing glances darted his way by Carver's beauty.

And every moment he was aware of Rosamund at quite the other side of the room with Strangelove and Marion and David and an unknown couple. She was to leave the next day. Should he let her go without a word? Find her out at a later date, perhaps, when the present family embarrassment had dimmed in memory? Should he try to find the opportunity of a private word with her the next morning before she left? Or should he let her go and forget about her, preserve the memory of his snow angel and their brief affair and not risk having the sweetness of that memory melt before his eyes?

He smiled as everyone else in his group laughed at one of Lord Carver's anecdotes.

And then he became aware out of the corner of his eye of Rosamund's getting to her feet with Strangelove, who made her a bow and raised her hand to his lips. David and the other gentleman also rose, and Rosamund turned away and left the room alone.

"Excuse me," Lord Wetherby said. "Carver, will you escort your sister to the ballroom when supper is over?" He got to his feet and made for the door. He did not particularly care whether people watched him or not.

Rosamund knew as soon as she entered the drawing room on her brother's arm. She could not have expected him to rush across the room to take her into his arms, of course. She could not even have expected a special look or smile. But there would have been something, something umistakable if there had been any hope.

As it was, there was nothing. She doubted he even noticed her entrance. And all through dinner, though they were seated at no great distance from each other, there was not so much as a glance. In the ballroom later, though she was frequently free until the music was about to begin, he did not once ask her to dance. He did not once speak with her or look at her.

It was as if she were not there at all. For days she had felt his awareness of her as if it were a tangible thing. And yet now, when that awareness was no longer a forbidden thing, there was nothing.

The lure of the forbidden—that was all she had been to him. She had known it deep down, of course, but hope is sometimes a stubborn beast.

It was lowering. She felt humiliated. She supposed that when she was finally alone, she would feel far more painful things than humiliation, but that was quite bad enough.

He was probably feeling some anxiety, she thought, wondering if she were about to make claims on him that he now had no excuse to avoid. But, no, the Earl of Wetherby was doubtless quite adept at warding off hopeful females— of which number she had become one for a brief and unwilling moment a few hours before. It was humiliating.

She danced and smiled and talked. She smiled so dazzlingly and talked with such animation to the Reverend Strangelove that she feared perhaps he felt encouraged to renew his addresses. Certainly he assured her, as he led her into a vigorous country dance, that he did not feel it at all inconsistent with his calling to kick up his heels on occasion in order to dance with a lovely lady.

Somehow, she thought, smiling at him, one could not quite imagine Toby kicking up his heels.

But she need not have feared that she had raised his hopes again. Whenever the pattern of the dance brought them together, he told her about a lovely and modest young cousin of his patron, a lady whose character quite made up for the fact that she was impoverished. The patron, it seemed, had hinted at his willingness to arrange a match between his cousin and his pastor. Toby was in the process of persuading himself that he would be doing both the young lady and himself a favor by agreeing.

It was the supper dance. Rosamund sat at supper with the Reverend Strangelove and two other couples and felt that the evening must surely have been three nights long already. The noise level was high—all the guests seemed to be enjoying themselves and everyone drank a toast to the marquess with great heartiness.

Annabelle, who had not danced with Lord Beresford all evening, was now sitting beside him. They were holding hands beneath the cover of the tablecloth, Rosamund saw with a fleeting smile.

And Justin was sitting across the room, smiling charmingly and talking as he had all evening. Looking breathtakingly handsome in his formal evening clothes. Looking so achingly familiar that she found it hard to swallow the food she had put on her plate. And as unaware of her as if they had never been so much as introduced.

"I am afraid I must retire," she said suddenly. "I am so very tired, and I have a long journey to make tomorrow."

"But of course, my dear Rosamund," the Reverend Strangelove said, scraping back his chair to rise with her, and bowing and raising her hand to his lips. "I shall do myself the honor of escorting you to your door."

"Please don't," she said. "I shall just slip away unnoticed.

Good night." She included all the occupants of the table in her greeting and smile.

Lord Sitwell and Mr. Cathcart also got to their feet to make her a bow and she turned and fled from the room, willing herself to walk, not to break into a panicked run.

There was air in the hallway, air that would blessedly fill her lungs. She paused briefly, closed her eyes, and drew in a deep breath of it. And then she hurried to the stairs and up them. But she was only halfway up when there was a buzz of noise as the dining-room doors were opened again, and quietness as they were closed.

"Rosamund?" a voice said.

She closed her eyes and stood where she was.

"Where are you going?" He stood looking up at her.

"To bed," she said. "I am tired and I have a journey to make tomorrow."

But instead of continuing on her way up the stairs, she looked down into his blue eyes. He could not have had his hair cut since they were in Northamptonshire, she thought irrelevantly. It was now decidedly longer than was fashionable. Her knees felt rather as if they were made of jelly.

She had no idea how long the silence between them lasted. But finally he moved. He rounded the bottom of the staircase and vaulted up the stairs two at a time until he was level with her.

"Let's get out of here," he said. "Dress warmly and come out with me."

"Justin . . ." she said.

"I'll knock on your door in ten minutes' time," he said. He stood beside her, one foot on the stair above, looking very directly into her eyes.

She felt enormously weary. He had but to crook a beckoning finger and she would come running. It had been that way from the start. "I want to make love to you, Rosamund," he had said, and she had taken him into her bed. And now he wanted to take her out into the darkness to tumble her once more before sending her on her way.

Had she no pride?

No conception of the pain she was inviting all over again when she left him again the next day?

"Please, Rosamund?" He touched the back of one of her hands with his fingertips.

"Ten minutes?" she said.

"Yes."

She nodded and continued on her way up the stairs and along the corridor to her room without looking at him again.

And she stood inside her room, her hands behind her on the knob of the closed door, her eyes tightly closed for a whole minute before crossing to the wardrobe and pulling out a long-sleeved woolen dress and her warmest cloak and hood.

It had been a warm day for early March. The night was cool, but not cold. The Earl of Wetherby took Rosamund's hand in his as the doors of the house closed behind them, and turned her in the direction of the lake.

They had not spoken a word since he had tapped on the door of her bedchamber and she had stepped outside, wearing the same cloak as she had worn when he first saw her trudging along a snowy highway with red cheeks and nose and chattering teeth.

And they continued to say nothing, though the silence between them was not uncomfortable.

He had acted impulsively. It had been bad-mannered to leave the young lady he had led in to supper, and reckless to leave a ball at which he had been unwillingly the focus of much curious attention. It had been unwise to invite Rosamund out of doors. It might have been better, under the circumstances, to invite her into the library or some other room not in use that evening.

What was he proving by bringing her outside and taking her to the lake—was that where he was taking her? She had known and he had known that he was asking her just as badly as he had asked her at Price's hunting box to come and make love with him. It was a purely physical relationship, she had said a few days before. It had certainly been that at the start. Was it to end that way, too?

Was there to be nothing else between them? Could they express their mutual attraction only through their bodies? He was afraid to hope for more. It was a foolish fear, he supposed. Without undue conceit he could still say that over the past eight or nine years he might have had almost any bride he had cared to offer for. He had his land and his title and his fortune. Rosamund, he was well aware, was on the fringes of poverty, only her position as daughter of a viscount and widow of a baronet making her eligible.

But he was afraid. Afraid to take anything for granted and therefore afraid to hope at all.

He should have taken her into the library and made her a formal offer and been done with it.

Rosamund, walking silently at his side, assumed they were on their way to the lake, probably to the very spot where Josh had surprised them together a few days before. There they would do what they had both wanted to do on that occasion.

And then, what? Would one encounter satisfy his appetite for her? Would he want her to go away with him for a few weeks? And would she go?

She would not! She could not so demean herself. Tonight was different. Tonight was the end of an affair, a final good-bye. But not the beginning of anything. Not the beginning of a sordid affair. And certainly not the beginning of anything else. He had ignored her all evening.

"Cold?" he asked her.

She shook her head and smiled at him, but he set an arm about her shoulders anyway and drew her against his side. She rested her head on his shoulder as they walked on.

"Ah," he said.

And he needed to say no more. The moon was shining across the water of the lake. They stood still on the bank just a few feet from the oak tree beneath which they had sat.

"It's lovely," she said. "I'll remember it this way all my life."

"Will you?" He looked down at her and laid a cheek against the top of her head for a brief moment. "And that I was with you here?"

"Yes," she said.

She waited to be taken to the tree. She waited for him to make love to her. And she yearned for the moment and regretted that it had come so soon and would soon be over. So much living to be done in the next few minutes. So many memories to be stored.

She was going to be happy. She was going to allow herself to be fully and finally happy. For happiness, she had learned in her twenty-six years, was never eternal—at least not in this life—but came in brief and glorious moments.

It was not right, he thought. There would be something almost sordid in coupling with her beneath the tree where they had been caught together. He was not sure he was going to be able to make love to her at all. It was not quite what he wanted. He did not want a brief moment of sensual satisfaction with her. He wanted a lifetime of total satisfaction.

And yet he could not speak to her. He was afraid to speak. He was afraid of ending something before he was ready to let it go.

He looked along the bank to the boathouse, where the two boats were kept. And he knew at last. There was a little piece of wilderness that would mean nothing at all to anyone else except the two of them. It was their piece of wilderness, visible from the house, but quite unremarkable except to two people who had stood there together and had wanted to remain there together forever, forgotten by the world and forgetful of it.

"I'll get one of the boats," he said, and he knew by the way she turned with him toward the boathouse and by the fact that she did not protest being taken boating in the middle of a March night that she understood.

And he knew finally his own foolishness. He knew that she could not be the other half of his soul unless he were the other half of hers. And he knew that such a feeling would be impossible unless she shared it. For the first time that night he relaxed and was happy. He kissed her briefly on the lips before going alone to launch one of the boats.

Rosamund sat idle in the boat a few minutes later, trailing one hand in the water until its coldness threatened to turn her fingers numb. And she glanced in wonder at the man who rowed the boat, the capes of his greatcoat making him look even more broad-shouldered than usual, his eyes smiling at her.

What had changed? Was it the calm water and the moonlight? When had peace taken the place of anxiety? When had she known beyond any doubt that their minds, their very souls, were in as great a harmony as their bodies?

Was she deluding herself? Was she being foolish in the extreme, not fortifying herself against pain to come?

But, no. She knew where they were going. And there was only one possible reason why he would take her there.

"It's beautiful," she said, gazing out across the lake, aware that she was repeating herself.

"Yes, you are," he said softly, and they smiled at each other.

"The daffodils are still in bloom," she said in some wonder. They were standing hand in hand at the top of the rise from which they had looked to the house on a previous occasion.

"Of course they are," he said. "It has been less than a week."

"Has it?" she said. "It seems like forever ago."

"But most of them are closed up for the night," he said. "And their color is not so apparent in the moonlight. I wonder if Wordsworth ever saw his ten thousand daffodils at night."

"Daylight, moonlight, it doesn't matter," she said. "It is an enchanted place."

"Our own little piece of wilderness," he said.

"Yes."

"Have you ever made love among daffodils?" he asked. She shook her head. "No."

"Me neither," he said. "It will be a new experience for both of us."

"Justin . . ." she said.

But he hushed her and stooped down to lift her into his arms, her knees resting on the blanket he carried. And he took her down into the clearing and twirled once about with her before setting her down on her feet.

"You see? There is no breeze down here. It is almost warm." And when she smiled, he said, "Well, we can pretend it is almost warm."

"Justin . . ." she said.

"My snow angel was far more talkative than this," he said.

"Your snow angel?"

"She chattered and played and laughed—and cried," he said.

"She was happy," she said. "For two days and two nights she was utterly happy."

"Was she?" He turned from her to spread the blanket on the grass smong the flowers and drew her down to lie beside him, her head on the crook of his arm. "Can it be recaptured, that happiness?"

"It already has been," she said. "Now, at this moment, I am happy, Justin. And I don't care about anything else but this moment. Nothing else exists. All we ever have is the moment."

"And the hope of many more beyond it," he said, his hand parting her cloak to touch her beneath it. "As many moments as there are, Rosamund. I want them all. I never said I was not greedy, did I?"

"Justin . . . " She turned her face in to his neck as his hand found one breast and fondled it and then moved behind her back to undo the buttons of her dress. Her own hands began to open the buttons of his greatcoat.

"I want you," he said against her mouth. "You understand me, don't you? I don't mean just this and now. I want you, all of you for all time."

"Yes," she said. "Yes." And she waited for his hands to slide her dress from her shoulders and down her arms before opening his coat and putting herself inside it.

"Tell me you want me too," he said, his hand raising her skirt, smoothing over her warm thighs.

"I want you," she said.

"But not just in this way, Rosamund?"

"No," she said, "not only in this way, Justin."

And she was inside his coat and his waistcoat and his shirt, her hands and her breasts against the firm muscles and rough hairs of his chest, and his mouth was wide over hers and his tongue moist and seeking against her own, and his hand found her beneath the warm bunching of her skirt.

"Make love to me," she said. "Please make love to me, Justin."

Smiling eyes looked down into hers. "That's what I am doing, love," he said. "Haven't we had this conversation before? Where do you want me to love you? Here?"

"Yes, there," she said. "There. Please, Justin."

He had intended to take longer. He had wanted to touch her, to play with her all night if possible before the final consummation. But she was right. This was not play. This was love. And he needed union with her as much as she needed it with him.

The moon was bright in a clear sky, the air crisp. They were surrounded by long grass and daffodils and the scents of spring. And the woman beneath him was hot and welcoming and moaned for him when he came into her.

All the glory of a spring night was above her. Her face was bathed in moonlight and starlight. The night air was cool on her bare legs. But the man above her and in her, his hands beneath her cushioning her as his body thrust her against the hard ground, was warm and heavy and wonderful.

They cried out together and clung to each other as the moonlight streamed down and the daffodils at the upper edges of the clearing waved in the breeze.

"I should have asked," he said, his voice husky, feathering kisses over her face as he held her warmly against him many minutes later, his greatcoat and her cloak wrapped about them both. "Is there any chance that I have got you with child?"

"Yes," she said.

"Ah." He kissed her mouth. "It will have to be by special license, then, and not by banns and betrothal parties and the gathering of trousseaux and St. George's and all that. Will you mind?"

"What will have to be by special license?" she asked, running a finger along his jaw. "Have I missed something?"

"No," he said. "That was not only your body you just gave me, Rosamund. It was yourself. Do you think I did not feel that? Do you want me to ask you formally?"

"Yes," she said.

"Not on one knee, I hope," he said. "You will get cold if I have to get up."

"We will dispense with the bended knee, then," she said.

"Will you marry me, Rosamund?"

"Yes," she said.

"Will you mind it being by special license?"

She shook her head.

"Will you mind too much if I have got you with child?"

She shook her head.

"Mute again?" he said, nudging her head away from his shoulder so that he could look down into her face. "What are you thinking?"

"Of what Leonard used to say," she said. "That one day I would know what real love is. That the second time I must marry for love."

"You think he would approve of me, then?" he asked.

"Yes." She smiled at him.

"That is important to you, isn't it?" he said. "I do not have an easy act to follow, do I?"

"I loved him," she said. "I always will, Justin, just as I will always love Papa. But Leonard was right. There was another kind of love, a greater love. It's what I feel for you."

"And I for you," he said. He smiled. "I seem to remember telling you not so long ago that there was no such thing as love, only a physical craving. They seem very foolish words now. It seems that your Leonard knew a thing or two.''

"He was wise and wonderful," she said.

"I had to leave Northamptonshire before your snow angel disappeared," he said. "It would have been too painful to watch all trace of you melt away. But I know now that it was right for it to melt. You and all that you were to me were not meant to be frozen into memory. We were meant to move on here to find that there was after all a way for us to have a living, breathing love. I can still hardly believe that it was possible, that it has happened.''

She was lying with closed eyes, a smile on her face, he saw when he looked down at her again.

"What are you thinking now?" he asked her, touching her upper lip, which had always intrigued him.

"That you did a great deal of rowing to get us here," she said. "And that I have not thanked you.''

"You think I need thanking?" he said, grinning at her as she looked up at him. "Rewarding, maybe?"

"Definitely," she said.

"Ah," he said, "this sounds promising. What is my reward to be?"

"The usual," she said.

"You will pour my next cup of tea?"

She put an arm about his neck and drew his head down to hers. "No," she whispered to him, laughing against his mouth, "the other usual.''

"Ah," he said, drawing her more closely to him. "And this is my reward, to be taken in my own way?"

"What exactly did you have in mind?" she asked.

"Oh, I'll be sure to show you," he said. "It may take a while because I can be a dreadful slowtop when making love, but I'll certainly show you."

"Mm," she said, the sound almost a purr of pleasure.

And he began to claim his reward in thorough and leisurely fashion.